PRAISE FOR

Whispers Beyond the Veil

"Exciting and engrossing, this book captures you from the first page and doesn't let go until the end. Jessica Estevao has given us a great read with a delightful heroine and a wonderful setting."

—Emily Brightwell, *New York Times* bestselling author of the Victorian Mysteries

"You'll love the not-so-innocent heroine of this delightful new series where no one and nothing is quite what it seems. Intriguing Ruby Proulx pretends to be a medium, but is she really pretending? And whom can she trust among the many new people she meets? Jessica Estevao will keep you guessing until the very last page!"

—Victoria Thompson, national bestselling author of *Murder in the Bowery*

"Old Orchard, Maine, at the turn of the twentieth century provides the setting for Estevao's excellent series launch. The richness of the character backstories allows Estevao to strike a perfect balance, neither relying on a deus ex machina ending nor telegraphing the solution too early."

—*Publishers Weekly*

BERKLEY PRIME CRIME TITLES BY JESSICA ESTEVAO

Whispers Beyond the Veil
Whispers of Warning

WHISPERS OF WARNING

JESSICA ESTEVAO

BERKLEY PRIME CRIME
NEW YORK

BERKLEY PRIME CRIME
Published by Berkley
An imprint of Penguin Random House LLC
375 Hudson Street, New York, New York 10014

Copyright © 2017 by Jessie Crockett
Penguin Random House supports copyright. Copyright fuels creativity, encourages
diverse voices, promotes free speech, and creates a vibrant culture. Thank you for
buying an authorized edition of this book and for complying with copyright laws by not
reproducing, scanning, or distributing any part of it in any form without permission. You
are supporting writers and allowing Penguin Random House to continue to publish books
for every reader.

BERKLEY is a registered trademark and BERKLEY PRIME CRIME and the B colophon
are trademarks of Penguin Random House LLC.

Library of Congress Cataloging-in-Publication Data

Names: Estevao, Jessica, author.
Title: Whispers of warning / Jessica Estevao.
Description: New York : Berkley Prime Crime, 2017.
| Series: A change of fortune mystery ; 2
Identifiers: LCCN 2017009984 (print) | LCCN 2017013329 (ebook) |
ISBN 9780698197176 (eBook) | ISBN 9780425281611 (paperback)
Subjects: LCSH: Women psychics—Fiction. | Old Orchard Beach (Me.)—Fiction.
| Maine—History—19th century—Fiction. | BISAC: FICTION / Mystery &
Detective / Historical. | FICTION / Mystery & Detective / Women Sleuths. |
GSAFD: Mystery fiction.
Classification: LCC PS3603.R63535 (ebook) | LCC PS3603.R63535 W49 2017
(print) | DDC 813/.6—dc23
LC record available at https://lccn.loc.gov/2017009984

First Edition: September 2017

Printed in the United States of America
1   3   5   7   9   10   8   6   4   2

Cover photos: *Woman* © Miquel Sobreira/Arcangel Images; *Railing*
© Brian Dennett/Eyeem/Getty Images
Cover design by Katie Anderson
Book design by Kristin del Rosario

ACKNOWLEDGMENTS

Every time I start to write a book I wonder if I'm going to be able to complete it. In those dark moments, when I'm quite certain that I won't, there are people in my life who support me, encourage me, and cheer me on. This is the place where I have the privilege of thanking them.

As always, I appreciate my blog mates the Wicked Cozy Authors: Sherry Harris, Julie Hennrikus, Edith Maxwell, Liz Mugavero, and Barb Ross. Thanks for always knowing why it's hard and also why it's worth it.

I also wish to thank my agent, John Talbot, and my editor, Michelle Vega, for their continued support. Without them this book would still be a figment of my imagination.

I wish to especially thank my dear friend Kathleen Kimball for suggesting a research road trip to the extraordinary village of Lily Dale, New York. Without her making the arrangements and providing such delightful companionship, I very much doubt I ever would have gotten there. This book was much improved by that experience, and memories of our time there, and of our friendship, are amongst my most cherished.

No list of thanks is complete without mentioning my family. My children: Will, Max, Theo, and Ari were endlessly patient and constantly encouraging.

And thanks also to my husband, Elias, who brings his own sort of magic to my life.

Chapter One

The atmosphere of the suffrage rally had far more in common with a medicine show performance than the attendants would likely have enjoyed hearing. In my experience, crowds of people composed of some filled with hope and others with skepticism create the same impression, no matter the subject of the gathering. Even the setting was similar. A steady breeze flapped canvas tents that ringed the border of the campground's natural amphitheater. I felt oddly at home and deeply uncomfortable all at the same time.

As I headed for the seat my aunt Honoria had reserved for me near the front, I met Officer Lewis from the Old Orchard Police Department.

"I am pleased to see you support a woman's right to vote, Officer," I said, giving him a bright smile. "Not everyone is so enlightened."

"I'm not sure if I support it or not. I'm on duty this evening."

"On duty?" I wondered if something had occurred to warrant police attention. "Surely there's no cause for concern when a group of politically minded women gather together to promote equality?"

"Rallies like these can easily get out of hand. Emotions tend to run high on the matter of suffrage." Officer Lewis bent toward me. "Sometimes it's the ladies who are the most unruly."

"What is it that they do to get into so much trouble?" I asked. "Do they speak their minds? Wear bloomers? Smoke cigars?" Officer Lewis blushed to the roots of his hair. He shook his head and stammered.

"They chain themselves to fences and use language I haven't even heard the local fishermen use," Officer Lewis said.

"Some of them even have been known to hit men over the head with their parasols," said a deep voice in back of me. I turned around to see Officer Warren Yancey standing directly behind me.

"I understand the urge," I said. "Although I think it rather ungentlemanly for you to remind me of past sufferings." Officer Yancey and I had met a few weeks earlier when a passing pickpocket had targeted me as soon as I had alighted from the train in Old Orchard. Since my purse had contained all my worldly goods, save the clothes on my back and my trusty parasol, I had used the latter to drive him off. In the course of doing so I had managed to fall and strike my head on the pavement. Officer Yancey considered himself to be my rescuer. I was convinced the credit for that stayed with me.

"Have you a place to sit?" he asked me. "They are already stopping people at the gate and asking them to listen as best they can from the outside." Officer Yancey was right. Every bench was filled and people stood along the back.

"My aunt is holding a seat for me near the front. I'd better join her." I gestured to a spot near the stage where Honoria had turned around and was beckoning me.

"Just be sure to mind your fetching hat when the rotted fruit starts flying." He tipped his own cap at me as he took his leave. I hurried to where Honoria awaited me, all the while sneaking peeks at the other attendees for signs of produce. I settled myself just as a hush descended over the crowd and Sophronia Foster Eldridge took the stage. A cheer of welcome went up from the crowd and then the amphitheater quieted again as she motioned with her hands for the noise to stop.

Sophronia was one of the country's most renowned suffragist leaders, one who used her abilities as a psychic medium to channel messages of equality from beyond the veil. Which is precisely why she reserved rooms at the Belden for her visit to Old Orchard. My aunt had realized some time ago that her modest hotel could not compete with the grandeur offered by the neighboring competition in our seaside community.

Like the savvy businesswoman she was, my aunt decided the only way to remain solvent was to create a niche for herself in the market. Honoria, who was a dedicated Spiritualist, decided to staff her establishment with paranormal practitioners and offer readings and development opportunities to spiritually inclined guests.

So far the venture was proving profitable and the arrival of Sophronia was expected to help make it even more so. In fact, Sophronia's choice of the Belden as her base in Old Orchard was a magnificent peacock plume in Honoria's straw bonnet. We found ourselves completely booked for the rest of the summer as a result of her stay.

Even though she was a guest at Honoria's hotel I had yet to lay eyes on her. A delay in her train's arrival had necessitated her heading straight from the station to the amphitheater. Honoria and I had had to content ourselves with welcoming her steamer trunks and valises. I could tell from her upright posture Honoria was even more eager than I for her first glance of our famous guest. She had nearly exhausted herself, not to mention the hotel staff, over the last few days ensuring every detail was in readiness for Sophronia's arrival.

Sophronia stepped into the center of the stage. Her severe black gown highlighted the pallor of her cheeks and gave her an otherworldly appearance. Despite her ephemeral appearance her voice projected across the natural amphitheater with ease. Honoria leaned forward like an eager child. I felt a thrill of anticipation run across my stomach as I awaited her message.

"I am gratified to see that so many of you have turned out today in support of enfranchisement for women." Sophronia's cheeks pinked as she warmed to her subject. "I am here this day to encourage you to imagine a world where women not only have the right to vote in elections but are, in fact, a great force which shines their uniquely moral outlook on those in public office." All around me voices began to murmur in agreement.

"No longer shall those in power abuse their positions without exposure, without consequence. Men have used the argument that we women are too noble, too pure, to sully ourselves by becoming involved in the moral morass that is politics." The murmurs grew and Miss Foster Eldridge raised her hands for quiet once more. "I say the world of politics is shockingly in need of a dose of purity, or nobility. The very traits men fear are too delicate to survive the rough-and-tumble shenanigans of the world beyond the hearth and home are the ones most needed to guide our nation."

She paused and looked out across the crowd. Her compelling

gaze landed on several different points. My heart gave a little lurch and I found I was glad that gaze had not fixed on me. There was something about her that made me feel like she could see straight into the subject of her attention.

"For too many years such reasons to keep us at arm's length have been offered. The quest for the vote has been slow and by no means steady. Year after year we gather and rally and ask for our due. And what have we accomplished of late? Very little, if you ask me." Sophronia swept an accusing finger across the crowd. "Men of corrupt character freely and routinely hold positions of power in every branch of industry as well as government. For some time now I have received visions and messages from my spirit guide concerning secret dealings and corruption of all sorts and I have been urged by that same spirit to bring those dark deeds before the public. I have nearly finished compiling these messages into a manuscript. When it is finished I fully intend to offer it to the publisher who offered the highest bid. Not only will the world be forced to consider the consequences of men and their misuse of power but I will be in possession of a tidy sum to be used to fund further suffrage efforts."

The murmurs swelled to a roar. All around me the amphitheater buzzed with noise and rustling as people turned in excitement to those around them. The din pressed against my head like the sound of an oncoming train. There was an uneasy feeling in the atmosphere and I felt the sudden urge to flee. I looked back over my shoulder at the exit, which seemed much farther away than it had when I entered.

Honoria seemed to sense my concern and she placed a reassuring hand on my forearm. I felt my shoulders unclench. Honoria was a dedicated suffragist with a great deal of experience at such rallies. If she noticed no cause for alarm I would trust there was nothing of concern about to transpire.

"You can't possibly expect anyone will give credence to rumors you say you've received from a disembodied spirit?" A man stood in the row and shouted at Sophronia. "The notion is entirely ludicrous, even for a woman. If you have any sense of decorum you will quit the stage at once and save us all from more of these outrageous remarks." Beside him a small woman in a white summer dress sat gazing up at him with what I interpreted to be a look of adoration upon her face. The man looked familiar but I could not say I had ever before seen him in person. I wondered if I had seen a photograph of him in the newspapers. He had the unchecked self-assurance of a man used to effortlessly getting his own way.

As if on cue Sophronia's head lolled forward. The noise of the crowd cut off as if their voices had been snatched from their throats by an unseen force. She raised her head again and a voice entirely unlike her own rattled up from her chest and out from between her lips. Her eyes remained closed and she swayed slightly back and forth. Her hand lifted and she stretched a slim finger in the direction of her heckler.

"Your confidence is misplaced. Repent or you will be harried and castigated. You will be thwarted at home and afield." Sophronia's voice cackled and she raised her other hand and pointed it at him as well. "You will be brought low by your past and cut off from your future. Change your ways before it is too late." Sophronia's voice tapered off at the end and her arms dropped to her sides. A woman from the wings rushed to her and supported her by wrapping a capable arm around her waist.

Before Sophronia's eyes opened the man began once more to shout. "How dare you threaten me? You are nothing more than a charlatan and a harlot." Another roar went up from the crowd and all around me people surged to their feet. I was about to stand myself when I felt Honoria's restraining hand on my arm.

"Best to stay put. When Nelson Plaisted begins a tirade there will likely be projectiles." She inclined her head in the direction of the man who had raised his voice to Sophronia. "I suggest we take cover before the onslaught begins." With that, Honoria reached below the bench in front of us and retrieved an umbrella, which she deftly popped open above our heads. I pressed myself under its sheltering canopy just in time to hear something land on the waxed canvas above me.

"You know his name?" I said.

"Of course I do," Honoria shook her head and exhaled deeply. "That odious fellow is Congressman Nelson Plaisted. I rather suspect he's here running for reelection."

Chapter Two

THERE WERE FEW THINGS YANCEY DISLIKED MORE THAN DIS-
banding unruly crowds. Especially those comprised mostly
of women. Even more especially when the crowd contained his
sister. His mood was not improved by the inclusion in the fray of
Miss Honoria Belden and her niece, the irrepressible Miss Proulx.

Fruit had, as he had predicted, been flung, but he was relieved to note as he caught sight of Miss Proulx that none of it
clung to her hat or any part of her costume. As she passed nearby,
her hair tumbling out of its pins and framing her face in damp
curls, Yancey's heart gave a tight tug at the sight of her. That was
until she approached and began to speak.

"There was no cause for you to insist on dispersing the crowd.
If I wasn't inclined to give you the benefit of the doubt I'd be
forced to think you did not want women to have a public forum
for progress." Miss Proulx's hands had crept onto her hips and her
words pelted out of her like rock salt from a shotgun. Yancey felt
like a crow in a cornfield.

"Protecting the citizenry is part of my job. I will rely on my
own judgment as to how best to perform that duty," Yancey said.

He was irritated to note he felt the unwelcome familiar heat at the back of his neck he generally experienced when interacting with Miss Proulx.

"But that's exactly why we are here. Without the right to vote we cannot truly be considered citizens."

"Citizens or not, I doubt those pelted with spoilt produce were unhappy with my decision to clear the amphitheater."

"No one was hurt."

"But they would have been if we hadn't insisted on disassembly. Rocks would have been flying through the air next. The meeting had become passionately overheated." Yancey felt he could be speaking for himself as much as for those involved more directly in the meeting. There was just something about Miss Proulx that set his nerves jangling. Not for the first time, he wished her far from his presence so he could better concentrate on the matters at hand. Before he could extract himself from her absorbing company she spoke again.

"I would have thought an experienced police officer such as yourself would not have been so easily rattled. It was just a handful of wizened apples and an onion or two," Miss Proulx said. Yancey could hardly believe what he was hearing. Of all the unreasonable attitudes.

"Have you ever witnessed the unbridled power of a mob?" Yancey asked.

"Would it surprise you to hear I have been in the very thick of riots on more than one occasion?" Miss Proulx tipped her head back to better look him in the eye. Upon a closer inspection of her face he spotted a streak of what looked like strawberry pulp marring the smooth complexion of her right cheek.

"Miss Proulx, it would not surprise me in the least to hear

that not only were you in the very heart of many a mob but that you were, in fact, the cause of every one of them."

"I see we understand each other completely." With that, Miss Proulx turned her back and flounced away.

"Miss Proulx is a remarkable young woman." Yancey turned to see Thomas Lydale standing nearby. "And while I am in accord with her opinions concerning the vote for women, I can't agree with her about breaking up the assembly." Thomas patted the front of his jacket and leaned in, lowering his voice. "From what I caught on film, things were getting ugly, fast."

"Trying out a new detective camera?" Warren asked. Thomas owned a photographic studio on Old Orchard Street, across from the police station, where he spent most days paying the bills by taking souvenir photographs of rich socialites and their families. But his real passion was candid shots of ordinary people going about their normal lives. He claimed people behaved differently as soon as they knew they were being photographed, or even if they knew a camera was in the area. He used a variety of hidden cameras to get the most natural results.

"I am indeed. I ordered this one from a Sears and Roebuck catalogue. It came in the post a couple of days ago."

"And you thought this rally was a good place to test it out?" Yancey looked around at the overturned benches and a cluster of flies settling on a bruised pear.

"Someday, when women have finally gotten the right to vote events like this rally will be historically significant. I may be the only one capturing these exciting moments the way they really unfolded."

"*Exciting* is one way to describe it. I know a lot of men feel angered by the mere suggestion of women voting, but that man in the front row sounded more like it was personal."

"That's because it was." Thomas nodded for emphasis. "He was engaged to be married to Sophronia at one time."

"That would explain the vehemence. Do you happen to know who was responsible for ending the engagement?"

"My understanding is that he did but I believe he would say that she forced him to do so," Thomas said. "Sophronia became a supporter of suffrage after he had proposed marriage. Nelson Plaisted had political aspirations even then and a wife with suffrage leanings would have proved too much of a liability." Thomas shook his head. "It's one of life's cruelties that a man like that captured the favor of two lovely ladies while neither you nor I have a sweetheart between us."

"Speak for yourself, man. I have a great deal more female society than I prefer at present." Yancey's glance moved toward the exit, where Miss Proulx was engaging in a lively conversation with his younger sister, Lucy. Miss Proulx's dark head leaned toward Lucy's fairer one and both women were gesturing animatedly in his direction. He hardly dared to think what sort of mischief the two of them were concocting. He dragged his thoughts back to the matter at hand. "How do you know so much about Miss Foster Eldridge's private life?"

"Quite a number of years ago, I worked up in Portland for her at a newspaper that she and a partner founded."

Yancey was intrigued. He didn't know Thomas all that well but every new piece of information he shared about his past revealed another interesting facet to his life. He couldn't help but feel a bit of a pang when he considered how impressed his sister and Miss Proulx would be by a man who so forthrightly admitted to working for a woman. "Was it a suffrage newspaper?" he asked.

"No. It was temperance rag."

"I wouldn't have taken you for a temperance man." Yancey had mixed feelings about the subject of alcohol. He'd been to enough domestic disturbances to know overindulgence in strong drink caused a lot of misery. But no good came of driving the liquor trade underground, either. Those poor saps who wanted it would find a way to get it no matter what the hurdles in their path. It likely would just drive their already poor families to the brink of destitution while lining the pockets of the suppliers.

Yancey hadn't any use for the laws himself and usually turned a blind eye on any harmless tippling. In his opinion enforcement of prohibition laws were a waste of police time and public resources. The community was best served by dealing with violent men and hardened criminals. He would have guessed Thomas would have agreed.

"I didn't say I supported the idea, just that I worked for the paper. I was just seventeen at the time and I had a far-fetched notion of the nobility of journalism." Thomas hoisted both of his bony shoulders in an apologetic shrug. "It seems foolish now but back then I would have done anything to work for a newspaper and, in fact, I basically did."

"What sort of anything?"

"I took the photographs, wrote some of the articles under a female pen name, and served as a general dogsbody."

"When was this?"

"About a dozen years ago, more or less." Thomas's usually sunny face clouded over. "It was a real nice job while it lasted. But then the paper folded and I was out of a job. It wasn't a good time to look for a new one, either." Thomas was right about that. The Long Depression had sent people from all walks of life onto the breadlines. A man who had worked for a suffrage newspaper would not have had an easy time competing for what little work could be found.

"Did the paper go under because of money troubles?" Yancey asked.

"No, it was because of the broken engagement between Sophronia and Nelson Plaisted." Thomas fiddled with his vest as though the memories were hard to revisit. "Nelson saw a greater political advantage in marrying a girl with better social connections. Especially one whose father owned a newspaper," Thomas said. "Nelson proposed to Sophronia's business partner and before they even set a date they shut down the paper."

"Was that his wife that was with him? Was she the former business partner?"

"That's her—Caroline Plaisted."

"It's a wonder Miss Foster Eldridge wasn't the one doing the shouting."

Thomas patted his vest again. "You were wise to clear the amphitheater. Given their history, it will be a wonder if matters don't escalate to violence despite your best efforts."

Chapter Three

GENERALLY, WE DID NOT SERVE REFRESHMENTS IN THE LA-
dies' writing room but Honoria had decided an exception
could be made. When I offered to collect the tray from the kitchen
myself, my aunt gave me an indulgent smile and said she'd be
waiting to introduce me. The tray held a pot of tea and an assort-
ment of Mrs. Doyle's very best baked goods as well as a pot of
strawberry jam and another of salted butter.

Everything looked as delicious as ever but strangely, I found I
had no appetite. I had never met anyone famous before, and all
Lucy's talk of how important Miss Foster Eldridge was caused
me to lose my nerve. I crept to the side of the door and was just
about to peek my head around the doorjamb when the floorboard
below my foot let out a groan. I pulled back and held my breath.

"Do show yourself, whoever you are," a rich voice warmed by
a trace of good humor called out. Embarrassed, I took myself in
hand and stepped through the doorway.

The ladies' writing room was one of my favorite rooms in the
hotel. Sunlight streamed in through the tall windows and bathed
the dusty rose carpet and polished walnut furniture. Cut glass

shades on the lamps provided a bit of sparkle, and every comfort for attending to one's correspondence sat easily at hand. A matched brass set of blotter and inkwell perched on the writing desk tucked into the turret window at the end of the room.

I didn't need to look into the room to remember the details of the space. They had delighted me so much I could recall them all in my sleep. Even after residing at the hotel for some weeks the pleasure of the place and the luxury of the furnishings had not worn off. I crossed to the settee at the far end of the room and placed the heavy tray on the low table in front of it. Honoria sat next to a slight, fair woman dressed all in black.

"Sophronia, allow me to present my niece, Ruby Proulx." Honoria raised a plump hand toward me and smiled reassuringly.

"Hello, Ruby." She glanced up and down at me as I stood there like a private under the scrutiny of a commanding officer. "Your aunt told me you were a lovely young woman and she did not exaggerate."

I never knew how to take a compliment on my appearance. For one thing, I was not used to them. My life had not provided me with many opportunities to fuss over my looks. Traveling with my father in a medicine show was hardly the sort of environment needed to school oneself in the finer art of hairdressing or fashionable clothing. I hadn't even had a mirror large enough to see my entire figure until I arrived at the hotel. My knowledge of my appearance came from a sliver of shaving mirror my father had kept amongst his meager possessions.

According to Millie, a maid at the hotel who had helped me to pick out appropriate clothing and to dress my hair, my head of thick, brown curls was worthy of a bit of pride. She fussed over it and arranged it and tucked combs into it in just the right places to keep it piled upon my head. I would not have managed the first week or so at the hotel without her. She had provided guidance at every turn. But even with her encouragement I still found comments like Sophronia's disconcerting. I found it easiest to change the subject before I became flustered.

"Shall I pour some tea?" I asked, gesturing to the teapot. I glanced at Honoria, and she nodded. "For you, Miss Foster Eldridge?"

"Only if you consent to join us," she said. "And please do call me Sophronia. I dislike formality in all its guises."

"It would be my pleasure." I lifted the pot and poured out three steaming cups. Sophronia seated herself on the settee and patted the place next to her. "Sit. Tell me about yourself."

"There isn't a great deal to tell, I'm afraid." I lowered myself into a delicate armchair and offered her the sugar bowl.

"It has been my experience that every woman has a story to tell." Sophronia dropped four lumps of sugar into her teacup and stirred gently. "I have no reason to believe you should be the exception to the rule."

"What sorts of things do you want to know?"

"Honoria tells me you are a gifted medium whose talents are the backbone of the hotel's success this season," Sophronia said, smiling at my aunt.

"Honoria is more kind to me than I deserve," I said. It wasn't just a polite bit of conversational deflection. It was the truth.

Honoria had welcomed me with open arms and an open heart when I appeared without warning and with nowhere else to turn. She had saved a space for me in what I felt was the loveliest room in the hotel ever since she had received a message in a dream that my mother would never have need of an earthly home again.

Honoria encouraged my interests, solicited my opinion, and defended my reputation at the risk of her own. I had done little but use a lifetime of experience conning true believers to earn my keep or her esteem.

The only real claim I could make of a metaphysical gift was my connection to a voice I heard in my left ear advising me from time to time. It had aided me all my life with whispered suggestions and warnings. Before arriving in Old Orchard the voice spoke to me sporadically and unbidden but now it came frequently and I was able to ask its advice. Still, even with that gift to offer, I felt unworthy of Honoria's generosity and was determined to do all I could to live up to her expectations of me.

"She also mentions that you are quite a modern sort of young lady."

"I like to think I am," I said, looking to Honoria for a clue as to how best to answer. Honoria gave me a tiny nod I took to be encouragement to speak my mind. "I believe a modern woman's obligation is to pursue whichever interests her own heart indicates. I have no particular interest in the attentions of men or the dictates of fashion but I do believe in the right of others to enjoy them if they so choose," I said, sitting as tall as I could manage, a bright smile fixed on my face.

I had learned over the years almost anything could be uttered aloud so long as it was said with a smile. I hoped this would be the case with Sophronia. It wouldn't do to offend the guest most responsible for our current financial state.

"So you aren't the sort of girl who chases after young men and thinks of nothing besides the latest fashions?" Sophronia asked.

"I am far more interested in whizzing about Old Orchard on my bicycle with my friend Lucy," I said. "She's spoken of nothing but your arrival for weeks." Lucy's enthusiasm for Sophronia's impending arrival had been the only thing on her mind for at least two weeks. While I felt disloyal even thinking it, truth be told, conversations with her had become ever so slightly tedious.

"Is your friend Lucy a suffrage supporter, too?"

"Lucy is a committed suffragist. She was at the rally today and was terribly disappointed not to make your acquaintance." Lucy had hoped to meet her after the rally but with the unwarranted haste with which her brother had cleared the amphitheater she had not had the opportunity.

"Is that so?" Sophronia turned to Honoria. "Do you know this Lucy, too?"

"I do. She's the daughter of my oldest friend," Honoria said. "And at the risk of sounding biased I would say she is a passionate and capable young woman with a tremendous zest for life."

"Lucy sounds like exactly the sort of young woman I've been hoping to meet," Sophronia said. "Ruby, if you will be in contact with her soon, would you make an offer to her on my behalf?"

"I have a picnic planned with Lucy this afternoon. Would that be soon enough?"

"Absolutely."

"What is the message?"

"Please tell Lucy I am in need of a secretary of sorts. I always find an energetic local woman to take under my wing in every town I visit. That way each town I visit has at least one person experienced at organizing for the cause after I leave. It sounds like Lucy is just the person to fill that role in Old Orchard." Sophronia looked at Honoria and then back at me. "Unless one of you would rather fill the position?" Honoria and I looked at each other.

"I am flattered that you would extend such an invitation to us but as for myself my obligations here at the hotel must be my first priority. Ruby may, however, feel differently." Both women turned their attention on me.

"I would be happy to show support in whichever way that I can. But my first obligation is to my aunt and to my duties as the hotel medium. Lucy has the time to devote to the cause and she has the passion. Besides, if you are looking for someone with secretarial skills Lucy knows how to use a typewriter." The clock on the mantelpiece chimed noon and I placed my cup on the table before me. If I hurried I'd have just enough time to prepare for my outing.

"She sounds like the perfect choice. I look forward to meeting her."

"Why don't you invite her for dinner here this evening and the two of them could get acquainted? I am sure Lucy will be delighted to accept your proposal. Wouldn't you agree, Ruby?"

"I believe there is nothing in the world Lucy would like more." I stood to take my leave. "Except the vote."

Chapter Four

I STARED WITH MISGIVINGS INTO THE GLASS OF MY VANITY TABLE. While I had reproached Officer Yancey for overreacting to the outburst at the rally, it appeared Honoria's umbrella had not been as protective as I had believed. I was mortified by the truth the mirror revealed and felt my cheeks flush as I realized how I must have looked to him when I questioned his motives for dispersing the assembly. Remnants of some sort of juice clung to my cheek, and my hair had mostly eluded the pins struggling to hold it in place. I could not possibly leave the hotel in such a state, especially not considering the plans Lucy and I had made.

A quiet knock landed on the door. I opened it to find Millie framed in the doorway, holding a steaming pitcher of water. As I stepped aside for her to enter I detected the faint smell of lavender billowing from the vessel.

"Millie, you needn't have bothered with me. I'm sure you are run off your feet with all the guests."

"Mrs. Doyle sent me. She heard about the troubles at the rally and was sure you would have been right in the center of whatever mischief was going on." Millie poured the hot water into the bowl on the washstand. "It appears she was right." Millie handed me a washcloth and pointed at my cheek. She motioned for me to turn around and then busied herself with the hooks of my dress. If it hadn't been for the willing ministrations of Millie, the Belden's best housemaid, I would not have made it through my first appearance in the hotel's dining room anywhere near properly attired, let alone all those in the weeks that followed. I was happier than I could express to have her help as I worked up the courage to don the outfit I promised Lucy I would wear for our outing.

"I can hardly be faulted for Honoria's decision to reserve seats near the stage," I said, slipping the plum-colored gown from my shoulders. "At least she advised me to wear this rather than the white ensemble I had planned. I doubt it would have survived the fray."

"Was it as bad as people are saying?" Millie asked as I stepped behind the dressing screen and gave myself a thorough scrubbing. "All the guests are talking about it."

"I suppose that depends on what they are saying." I rose up on tiptoe to look at Millie over the top of the silk screen.

"I heard the police dragged off dozens of women who were using language that would blister a pirate's throat." Millie's eyes glowed with excitement. "The man delivering ice told me he heard some of them were foaming at the mouth."

I stepped out from behind the screen, all traces of the fray removed. "All reports are exaggerated. No one was arrested. Things were just a bit heated, that's all."

"My parents will be glad to hear that," Millie said. "My father is none too happy about me working here with Miss Foster Eldridge as a guest. He's threatening to send me back to the mills instead."

The idea of Millie leaving the Belden for the mills in Biddeford was unthinkable. Not only because we had become friends, but she had left the mills to go into service because of her respiratory troubles. Her breathing had improved a bit since then but it was still common to find her gasping and wheezing when the weather got too hot or the air was filled with pollen. I hated to think guests lodged at the Belden might have anything to do with her health being placed at risk.

"Do you think he really will do that?"

"I can't rightly say. He won't allow any talk of suffrage in the house and I do my best to make my job sound like I have very little to do with the guests. Especially outspoken women like Miss Foster Eldridge. Millie glanced at the wardrobe and then back at me. "Speaking of outspoken women, let me retrieve the outfit you promised Miss Yancey you would wear today." I suddenly worried what her father would say to her if he knew about the getup Millie was about to help me into.

It had been only a few weeks since I had convinced myself to try wearing a modern bathing costume. It had been a difficult thing to leave the changing room at the bathhouse in a garment that had so completely exposed the shape of my calves. Somehow, I had managed to make my way out from behind the curtain and down onto the beach. I had even found it possible to enjoy myself. In truth, I had gone back to the beach so often Honoria determined it would be more cost efficient if I purchased a bathing costume of my own rather than renting one from the bathhouse. I told myself that a cycling outfit was not so different than that bathing suit. After all, it was too late to change my mind.

"I hung it in the wardrobe yesterday as soon as I picked it up from her mother." Millie skipped to the tall, carved wardrobe and turned the handle. She slid silk, satin, and fine lawn gowns out of the way until she arrived at the item she sought. With a small gasp she lifted a brass hanger from the far side of the clothes bar and pulled the outfit close for a thorough look.

"I've never seen anything like it up so close," she said as she laid the ensemble, piece by piece, upon the high bed. "You're sure you are going to put it on?"

"Of course I'm sure," I said with considerably more confidence than I actually felt. "I promised Lucy and I certainly wouldn't have wasted Orazelia's time in making it if I thought I would lose my courage." Millie silently handed me a black-and-white-striped shirtwaist. I pulled it on and fastened the row of gleaming pearl buttons. Next came the truly worrisome part of the ensemble. Millie bit her lip as she passed me the knickerbockers. I had argued for a more traditional-looking divided skirt with a front flap to hide the split. Lucy, however, had insisted the flap was not only unnecessary but that it was cowardly as well, and thus unworthy of us and women everywhere. I gave in to her insistent enthusiasm and now I was about to face the world in a garment many would view as scandalous.

"You'd better hurry, then or you will be late," Millie said. I glanced at the clock, and spurred on by urgency I stepped into the legs of the short trousers and pulled them up over my hips. I looked down, then over at Millie for encouragement. "I think they button at the side to keep them up." She stepped to my side and gave me a hand. I tried to convince myself I was at my ease as I pulled on the matching jacket. I reached for the buttonhook on my vanity and used it to fasten my boots. Gathering my courage in both hands I stepped in front of the wardrobe mirror and tried to decide what I thought of what I was seeing.

"It isn't so very different than a skirt and shirtwaist ensemble. Is it?" I asked. Millie cocked her head to one side and looked me up and down. My calves, covered only in thin stockings, felt mortifyingly exposed. The knickerbockers looked so much like a young boy's pair of short pants that I felt like I couldn't possibly be seeing myself in the mirror.

"Put these on and then I'll decide," she said. I took the cloth bicycle leggings from her hands and bent to tug them on. They slid over my boot and stockings and met the bottom of the knickerbockers just below my knees. I fastened the legging strap across the underside of my boot, then stood and gave a little twirl. How strange it was to not to feel a heavy skirt swishing around me as I spun. I felt strangely unfettered. I took a wide step forward and startled myself with the view of my own leg. I stopped and looked at Millie.

"It is very daring. I don't think I am brave enough to wear it," she said.

"Are you brave enough to be the one who helped me add the hat?" I asked.

"Sit yourself down and I'll see what I can do." Millie pointed at the vanity stool and we settled into the routine I had come to value over the last weeks. Before I arrived at the Belden I had never had anyone to help me to dress and Millie had never before been a helper. Well, except for assisting her older sisters in preparing for dances and such. Between the two of us we managed to navigate the bewildering world of proper ladies' attire with remarkably few rent seams or lost buttons.

But where Millie really added value was as a hairdresser. I had managed my own wavy locks as best I could while traveling with the medicine show. Father had coerced a string of different ladies to help keep my easily tangled mane smooth and presentable when I was too small to do so myself. Most of the ladies were far more interested in finishing the job quickly than with doing it well or even doing it gently. Every so often, one of the women had taken a shine to my father and proceeded to take her time with my hair in an effort to show him her maternal instincts. They soon learned my father's interest in women had nothing whatsoever to do with how they treated me.

As soon as I could, I convinced Father I was capable of managing on my own. He was more than happy to allow it as every penny he needn't have spent on me he could use on dubious business ventures or even less wholesome libations.

Millie's ministrations with a brush were an entirely different experience. Somehow she managed to stroke a shine into my unruly hair and to do so without inflicting pain. She patiently and artistically coaxed braids and ringlets into masterpieces I could never have imagined.

What had once been the bane of my existence had become a crowning glory. I felt a shiver of expectant excitement as I pondered what she might do with the small cycling cap. She placed it upon my head for a moment before whisking it away and concentrating her attention on the hairstyle that would support it.

She rolled and tucked the long strands into a tight, sleek foundation for the cap to sit upon. By the time she slid the last hairpin in place the hat felt like a part of my head.

"There. That ought to stay on no matter how much swooping around you get up to." Millie gave the back of my head a final pat and I got to my feet.

"It feels very stable. Thank you so much." I tried to smile but then I remembered the picnic hamper. "Would you be willing to do me another small favor?"

"What do you need?" Millie laid the brush down on the vanity next to the matching nail buffer and hand mirror.

"Would you collect the lunch basket from the kitchen? I don't think I can face Mrs. Doyle."

CHAPTER FIVE

NO MATTER HOW MANY TIMES I HAD RIDDEN, THE FEELING OF freedom I had whilst on a bicycle was equally exhilarating every time. Lucy had spent the last few weeks introducing me to the delights of cycling and I was overjoyed to realize I had become a confident rider. There was an independence and a power to riding that was quite unlike anything I had ever before experienced. But today, clad in my new cycling outfit, I found I was enjoying the experience even more.

Despite my initial qualms and the curious looks I had attracted from more than a few passersby I was quickly becoming enamored of the freedom knickerbockers provided. I had never realized how many of my thoughts turned to modesty and the unfortunate effects a stiff breeze could have upon a gown until I no longer needed to consider such problems.

Something about my costume filled me with an unfamiliar recklessness and I surprised myself as I applied the brakes with more confidence than usual. I hopped down from my seat with no fear of entanglements then lifted the picnic hamper from the rack on the back of my bicycle. Lucy spread a colorful blanket in the shade beneath a grove of towering pines. Fern Park provided a cool and shady respite from our exertions and I was grateful to be out of the fray of Old Orchard for a few peaceful hours.

Even as far as we were from the seaside I could still make out joyful shouts from merrymakers down on the beach. I had every reason to believe Lucy would be just as loud when I relayed Sophronia's request to meet her. I decided to enjoy lunch in peace before sharing the news. If I told her straightaway she might insist on heading back to the hotel immediately. The idea of returning Mrs. Doyle's lunch untouched didn't bear considering. Besides, I had worked up a powerful appetite during my exertions.

"So what do you think of the cycling suit now that you've tried it?" Lucy sat on the blanket and, in a totally unladylike show of independence, folded up her legs like a meditating guru from the Far East. Only an hour before I might have balked at doing the same. But having experienced the joy of unrestricted movement I was eager to try it myself. I plunked myself down unceremoniously on the blanket beside her and crossed my own legs. "I'll take that as approval." She pointed at my lap.

"Unreserved approval. Although I think Millie may not recover from the shock of a woman wearing any sort of trousers."

"Things won't change until all women embrace this type of freedom," Lucy said. "I wish she had been able to attend the suffrage rally with us. I think she would have been inspired by what took place." I sometimes thought Lucy forgot there are many women who must work for a wage. Lucy's family was not wealthy but there had never been any mention in my presence of either her mother or herself earning a living.

"I am not sure the fracas at the rally would have convinced her to support suffrage," I said. "Even if she hadn't been needed at the hotel I understand her father would not have allowed it."

"But that is exactly the point." Lucy's eyes shone with passion as she warmed to her subject. "Millie should be allowed to make her own decisions rather than quivering under the burden of her father's rules." It was all well and good for Lucy to preach about how fathers should be handled but, as she did not have to deal with one of her own, I did not believe her in a position to instruct those girls who did. Perhaps Mrs. Doyle's tempting treats could be relied upon to smooth things over.

I pulled a waxed paper packet of sandwiches from the hamper and offered one to her. I rooted around for tin tumblers and a flask of lemonade and poured us each a glass. Further investigation of the hamper revealed a brown paper–wrapped parcel of fried chicken, two wedges of strawberry pie, and a box of peanut butter cookies. I spread all the comestibles out on the blanket and was pleased to see Lucy unable to resist Mrs. Doyle's magic. I took advantage of her chewing to introduce a new topic.

"Has your brother been staying busy with his duties now that the pier is almost ready?" I asked. Lucy made a moaning noise as she inhaled the aroma of a crispy chicken thigh before answering.

For years town elders in Old Orchard had dreamt of opening a pleasure pier to attract even more of the lucrative tourist trade. After all, with seven miles of sugar-fine sand, a flat beach for strolling, and a train station only a block from the shore there was no reason Old Orchard could not be developed in such a way as to rival any other summer resort town.

At long last it seemed it would. The Old Orchard Pier Company had pledged the money and within a few days the world's longest steel pleasure pier would open to the public. Investors had taken to calling the town the Coney Island of New England. But growth came at a cost and much of that was in the form of increasing crime.

"Warren has been rather out of sorts lately. He's been working double shifts since his chief still refuses to add more officers to the force despite the increase in thefts and other crimes."

"I thought the arrests he made recently would have helped to quiet things down amongst the criminal element." Lucy's brother had been a police officer with the Old Orchard Police Department for only about a year. Just a few weeks earlier we had worked together to solve a murder and to break up a pickpocketing ring. While I was sorry to hear that had not provided a solution to the crime rate in town, I felt a stir of excitement as I wondered if Officer Yancey might benefit from my assistance again soon. I had rarely felt a satisfaction that equaled that of helping to bring a criminal to justice. If my father could see me siding with the enemy, I doubted very much he would approve. The idea that he would be thoroughly displeased made the notion all the more appealing.

"It seems there is a never-ending supply of opportunists and sneak thieves. And now with Miss Foster Eldridge's visit he is even more crotchety than ever." Lucy bit into a pickle and shook her head. "He has had nothing but complaints about her coming."

I was surprised to hear it. Officer Yancey and I had not seen eye to eye on a number of topics but he had seemed like someone who supported the underdog. In my opinion no one was more worthy of that distinction than the female population of the United States.

"Does he not believe women should have the right to vote?"

"It isn't that." Lucy looked down at the blanket, her cheeks pinking up despite the cool breeze rippling through the ferns surrounding us. "You know how he feels about mediums."

Indeed I did know. Although I did not consider myself to be a genuine medium, when Honoria's psychic had failed to uphold her obligation of employment I had thrown myself into the breach. Since I was raised by my father, a snake oil salesman on a variety of medicine shows, I was very good at telling people what they wanted to hear.

From a very early age my father had offered my services as a miracle medical healer and tarot card reader. There was little I needed to do to apply those same skills to the sitters at a séance. The voice I heard, *clairaudience* Mrs. Doyle called it, proved very handy as well. Not that Officer Yancey was inclined to believe in the voice any more than he credited astrological predictions or tea leaf readings.

Officer Yancey had made no secret of his disdain for psychic practitioners of every ilk but he entertained a special dislike for mediums. His mother, and Lucy, too, had consulted many of them over the years looking for answers to a family tragedy. Officer Yancey warned me off from his family as soon as he discovered I had conducted a reading for them. I, of course, ignored his high-handedness. Our relationship had improved a little since I helped with a murder investigation but the peace was a tentative one.

"I am well acquainted with your brother's attitude toward mediums and psychics of all sorts. But surely he isn't expecting a crime wave to spread across the town just because he doesn't like mediums." I tore the wrapping from my sandwich and took a bite.

With my mouth full I would be far less likely to say something regrettable about her brother.

"He's worried that any plans on the part of suffragists may tarnish the festivities planned for the pier opening. Suffragists are almost always a lightning rod for controversy. Trouble follows Miss Foster Eldridge like ants follow a trail of sugar water." Lucy took a sip of her lemonade. "The chief of police has orders from the selectmen that if the pier opening isn't the most newsworthy event to come out of Old Orchard this season everyone on the police force will be out of a job."

"No wonder he's worried," I said, reaching for a cookie. "Jobs are still difficult to come by." Despite the explosion of growth in Old Orchard on account of the pier, the economy was in no way robust. Anyone with steady employment would be loath to lose it.

"I'm sure Chief Hurley is just saying that to get away with working the officers extra hours with no pay. After all, what could possibly overshadow something as exciting as the opening of the world's longest pleasure pier?" Lucy reached for another sandwich and took a bite.

Now seemed the perfect moment to share Sophronia's invitation. "I'm thinking of something that might overshadow the pier as far as you're concerned. At least for today," I said. Lucy stopped chewing "Do you have any plans for dinner this evening?"

She swallowed slowly. "No, not this evening. Why do you ask?"

"Sophronia has expressed a desire to meet you." Lucy dropped what remained of the sandwich right into her lap.

"It isn't kind to tease so," she said, a spot of color coming to each of her smooth cheeks. "You know how much her visit means to me."

"I would not think of making up such a thing. She really does want to meet you. She has a proposition she would like to discuss with you over dinner."

Lucy's jaw flapped open and a strangled little gargle slipped out. But she recovered quickly and looked to me with her eyebrow raised before speaking. "Did she say what kind of proposition?"

"She did indeed. What would you say if I told you she wants you to act as her personal secretary while she is here in Old Orchard?"

"I would say I never would have expected such an opportunity as that." Lucy's eyes shone bright with suppressed excitement. "Do you really think I am the one for the job? There must be many women who would be overjoyed to have the chance to work with Miss Foster Eldridge."

"Well, they aren't going to get the chance. I already told her you were sure to accept her offer." Lucy sat stock-still, her face frozen in surprise.

"What if when she meets me she doesn't like me?" Lucy asked. "What if I'm so nervous I say entirely the wrong thing or spill my dinner all over myself?"

"That won't happen. I've never seen you put a foot wrong."

"But why would she think I was qualified for the role?"

"Honoria and I both recommended you. We said you were the most passionate and energetic suffragist in town and that there was nothing you would like more than the vote for women," I said, bringing an even deeper blush to Lucy's cheeks. "I also said you already possessed some useful secretarial skills."

"Well, I can take notes, and for Christmas two years ago Warren bought me a typewriting machine. I've become quite adept at using it."

"I told her you could type. She seemed very pleased that you have practical skills to bring to the arrangement."

"A letter of reference from Sophronia might come in quite handy if I decide I would like to try my hand at being the sort of modern woman who goes out to a job. I could even move to Portland and work in an office one day."

"I didn't know you were considering such a thing." I had the disloyal thought that I regretted helping Lucy to have the means to leave Old Orchard. I valued her friendship too much to consider the possibility she might leave town. Lucy and Millie were my first real friends and I was enjoying the experience of having other women my age to count as such. Adults had staffed the medicine show almost entirely and I had spent my early years mostly devoid of the companionship of other children. My father and I moved far too frequently to establish relationships with the people in the towns we visited.

Besides, if the business you conduct requires you to take advantage of others, the situation does not foster amiable sentiments. Those few times we had not snuck out of town under the cover of the stars we were run off by angry mobs demanding their money back. Should I have had the great fortune to strike up a friendship with another girl it would have been impossible to maintain.

"I shouldn't have said it was a goal but it may be what things come to if I don't want to marry. After all, Mother won't live forever and I would hate to impose on whichever woman could put up with my brother when he finally decides to settle down." I fought down an urge to defend Officer Yancey. Lucy had the right to her opinion but I could not say I agreed with her estimation of her brother's charms. While he could be exasperating he was also a good man with a steady character. Many women likely found him quite appealing. Still, I could understand her reluctance to depend on the welcome of such an unknown quantity as a future sister-in-law. "Now, if I already knew and liked the lady in question it would be another matter entirely." She gave me an exaggerated and disconcerting wink. I decided it was time to head back to the Belden before she could expand on any matchmaking notions.

"If you are to have time to return home and to prepare yourself for dinner we best pack up." Lucy nodded and drained her tin cup before replacing it in the hamper. I brushed a few stray breadcrumbs from my knickerbockers and began gathering up the remains of the lunch.

Chapter Six

I PARTED COMPANY WITH LUCY NEAR HER HOUSE AND THEN CON-
tinued on my own toward home. I cycled slowly to a stop in
front of the Hotel Belden. As brave as I felt moving forward on
two wheels, I had to admit, if only in the privacy of my own mind,
that stopping was an entirely different matter. Not long after I
had learned to balance, Amanda Howell had informed me that
there was a real risk of being thrown over the handlebars and being left in a vegetative state if one braked too quickly.

I had not wanted to believe her but after confirming her story
with several knowledgeable cyclists I could never brake without
feeling a tightening in my stomach and a nagging suspicion that
I might be experiencing my last conscious moment. Unfortunately, Amanda was walking to the front of the hotel at exactly
the same moment I arrived. If there was one person in the world
I would not enjoy seeing me disgrace myself on my bicycle, it
would be her.

Amanda had done little to endear herself to me since my arrival at the Belden. She had made every effort to make me feel

unwelcome from the moment we met and little had changed in the intervening weeks.

It was obvious that the source of her loathing was twofold. Firstly, I believe she had cherished hope that Honoria would take her under her wing as a protégée when Amanda realized Honoria had no children of her own. My arrival could be seen as the thing that dashed those hopes.

Perhaps even more important, I was the only other young and unattached woman at the hotel. Well, that is if you did not count the maids or serving girls whom I was certain Amanda would never consider. Amanda appeared to be constantly searching the environment for eligible gentlemen with whom to make a permanent match and she viewed me as the competition.

Her object of greatest attention was Ned, the hotel numerologist. Ned was a likable young man who appeared oblivious to Amanda's advances. Either that or he was doing a bang-up job of appearing to not notice them every time I was in the same room with the pair. No matter how I tried to avoid inflaming her jealously, it was impossible to avoid in a hotel so small.

I stretched my toe toward the ground and dismounted as gracefully as I knew how. My new cycling costume had made such a maneuver ever so much more possible. I was sorely tempted to take to wearing it day in and day out. I felt exhilaratingly liberated by the freedom my legs had to move about athletically. I felt quite sorry for Amanda as I noticed her working to hold her gown up off the dirt of the street. But my generosity of spirit evaporated as soon as she spoke, as was generally the case during our interactions.

"Really, Miss Proulx, how could you allow yourself to be seen

out in public in such an outrageously unladylike thing as that?"
She slowly moved her gaze down my frame, lingering at my ankles in their neat leather boots before sliding back up to scowl in
my face. "Does Honoria have any idea of the damage you are doing to the reputation of the hotel?"

"I think it hardly needs mentioning that we have vastly differ-
ing opinions about what constitutes ladylike behavior," I said. "I
was raised to understand a lady would keep such unsolicited opinions to herself."

"That just goes to show your upbringing is decidedly against
you in this regard. And likely most others." Amanda rolled her
eyes at me.

"After spending the day in this ensemble I predict that intel-
ligent and stylish women from all walks of life will one day wear
trousers more often than not." I wasn't just trying to get a rise out
of her. I truly believed once more women tried outfits like my
own they would not be content to be hobbled by gowns for the
rest of their lives.

"I cannot imagine how you could possibly make such a preposterous prediction."

"I expect it has something to do with my tarot card reading
and mediumship. Predictions are my specialty." That remark had
been beneath me, and as soon as I said it I regretted doing so.
Amanda's psychic discipline involved psychometry, reading the
energy of objects. She truly seemed able to pick up a personal
belonging and to know surprisingly accurate details about the
owner. Not just physical descriptions, either. She could reveal the
state of mind or the overall character of the person.

As impressive as her gift was it had proven far less popular

with the guests than had disciplines involving the future or contacting those who had passed into spirit. Day after day, sessions
with Nell, the palm reader, Cecelia, the astrologer, and even with
me were completely booked. Amanda had days with only a client
or two scheduled for appointments. I wasn't at all sure that Honoria would engage her for the following summer.

I leaned my bicycle against the front porch railing and mounted
the steps with Amanda close on my heels. I shoved open the door
with a bit more gusto than strictly necessary, considering the hinges
were always kept faultlessly well oiled.

"I predict I would never be seen in such a vulgar thing as you
are wearing. Nor will I choose to associate with the sort of woman
who would." Amanda wrinkled her nose as though she smelled a
dead mouse in the walls.

The porch door of the Hotel Belden opens directly onto the
lobby. Ben, Honoria's faithful man of all work, stood as silently as
ever behind the gleaming walnut reception desk attending to a
lady who appeared to be checking in, if the small trunk on the
floor by her feet was any indication. The woman turned and looked
at us as we entered. She was athletically built, and of above average height. I was surprised and gratified to see she was clad in a
bicycling costume even more daringly cut than my own.

"Hello," I said. "I'm Ruby Proulx, the proprietress's niece. You
must be one of our new arrivals?"

"I am Miss Theda Rice. I wrote some weeks ago requesting
a reservation." The woman used a tone of voice that suggested
she habitually expected to encounter problems. I wished Honoria
were there to greet her instead of me. She was gifted at pleasing
guests no matter how determined they were to be unsatisfied.

Maybe in time I would possess some of her skill but for now I fell back on my medicine show experience and relied on a bright smile.

"We have been eagerly awaiting you," I said, hoping I sounded genuinely like I had heard of her before that very moment. "We hope that you will enjoy all the services and opportunities the Belden has to offer."

"Perhaps I will do so," Miss Rice said, peering down through her wired spectacles at me. Behind me Amanda cleared her throat. She never missed an opportunity to advertise her services.

"May I present the hotel psychometrist, Miss Howell." I turned to Amanda, who wore an even showier smile than my own. She took a step forward and angled herself just enough in front of me for the movement to be taken for the slight I guessed she meant it to be.

"You needn't bother with introductions. I overheard your conversation. As I am so vulgarly dressed, surely that one will not wish to make my acquaintance." Miss Rice gave Amanda a crushing scowl and waved her away with the flick of her hand. Amanda had the good grace to blush before she scurried off down the hall.

I wish I could say I had such fine character as to not have enjoyed seeing her get her comeuppance but in truth, I enjoyed it immensely. "That girl is exactly what is wrong with this country," Miss Rice said, shaking her head as she watched Amanda's retreat. "I see I have my work cut out for me here."

"Are you engaged in some sort of work that brings you to Old Orchard?" I asked, hoping to distract Miss Rice from Amanda's gaffe.

"I am a suffragist and I intend to take advantage of the masses who will be assembling here for the opening of your new pier and pass out leaflets to the crowds."

"What a coincidence," I said. "Do you perhaps know Miss Foster Eldridge? She is staying here as well."

"It is my privilege to call her my dearest friend," Miss Rice said. "She's the reason I've come to Old Orchard. My intuition told me she would be in need of my support." Miss Rice's pasty cheeks dotted with red and she pressed the corner of her eye with a plain white handkerchief. Her words were similar to those of many of the guests at the Belden.

I had learned almost upon their arrival that this was a group led by impressions and intuitions more than any other I had ever encountered. As I was still learning to acknowledge my own metaphysical abilities, sometimes I was uncomfortable with the enthusiastic professions of others. I wished again that Honoria had been the one to greet Miss Rice. I asked for guidance but even the voice was silent. I decided to fall back on a stock welcome.

"Then you will feel quite at home here. I am sure that you will find the hotel to your liking and hope that your stay will be a long one," I said.

"You can rest assured that as long as Sophronia is here representing the cause of women's suffrage I will be here, too, to support her." Miss Rice turned toward the door. "Clearly there is much work to do if we are to overcome the attitudes of people like that young woman you came in with." I did not feel I was successfully smoothing Miss Rice's feathers. Perhaps an apology might be the right approach.

"I am so very sorry for you to have had such a poor welcome. I can only imagine what you must think of us." I looked to Ben for some sign of encouragement but he stood silent as ever behind the desk.

"When one works tirelessly for a cause as reviled as suffrage one becomes accustomed to feeling unwelcome." She gestured to my outfit. "Still, now and again one has cause to be hopeful for the future." With that, she strode out of the room.

Chapter Seven

As soon as Miss Rice was out of sight I raced up the back stairs and thumped on Honoria's bedroom door. I was certain she would wish to know Miss Rice had arrived. As I stood in front of her door awaiting an answer I considered how odd it was for her not to have been in the lobby to greet Miss Rice personally. It was her habit to be on hand to meet guests herself when they checked in to the hotel. One of the ways the Belden distinguished itself in a resort town was by providing just that sort of attentive, personal service.

When she did not immediately answer I knocked again. After a long moment I heard shuffling in her room and when she opened the door I could see her hair was mussed and her eyes clouded with sleep.

"Please tell me nothing has gone terribly wrong?" she asked, pulling me into her room and shutting the door firmly behind me.

"Not at all. I've just come to let you know Miss Theda Rice has arrived and Ben has ensconced her safely in her room," I said.

"What a relief." Honoria looked around the room as if she were looking at it for the first time. "I am so pleased I can count on you to assist with the guests." Honoria passed a hand over her hair to smooth it into place. It proved a futile effort. She looked so out of sorts I thought it best to sound reassuring. I also decided not to apprise her of the unpleasantness between Miss Rice and Amanda.

Honoria let out an enormous yawn. I looked past her to the high, four-poster bed at the far end of the room. The coverlet was rumpled and the pillow showed a head-size dent. Millie would never have left a room in such a state. I was dumbfounded. Honoria was such a whirlwind of energy it was difficult to imagine her sleeping at night, let alone in the day.

"Did I wake you?" I asked, hoping she was not becoming ill. The thought of an illness sweeping through the hotel was not something I wished to consider. I had seen the effects of sickness in close quarters too many times on the medicine shows not to experience a horror at the mere thought of it.

"I'm afraid you did. But not because I was tired. Rather, I was completely overcome by a dream."

When I first arrived at the Belden, Honoria had mentioned her unusual dreams to me. She claimed she had known about my mother's death through a dream as well as a myriad of other events that had come to pass. But she had not had one since I had been living at the hotel. I wasn't sure how to react or whether or not to show enthusiasm.

I was still not sure how much to credit my own psychic experiences. It was even more difficult to understand those of another. I wasn't sure what to say, as I had no desire to offend her.

Honoria was a true believer and she had never expressed the doubts that assailed me. She appeared to have complete faith in the metaphysical, no matter which form it took.

When I had worked the medicine shows with my father we had built a business on the true believers. They were amongst the quickest to part with their pennies and also the most faithful in their attendance at any given show. They were also the most notional as to how the spirit world and the manifestation of miracles were supposed to occur.

As a result they were hard to please. I had learned, to my peril, that you needed to discover their expectations for a spiritual experience before you attempted to provide them with one. Since I had no background in psychic dreams I decided the best course would be to simply ask questions.

"You experienced one of your prophetic dreams?"

"I was deep in the midst of receiving a message that felt urgent when you knocked. But I awoke before I got to the end of it." Honoria twisted her rings on her plump fingers. The lines between her eyebrows deepened into a trough you could slot a penny into. Clearly the dream had not been a pleasant one.

"Do you want to tell me about it?"

Honoria nodded and led me to the settee in the center of her private sanctuary.

"I was sitting on the edge of the bed thinking about the busy week ahead when I was completely overcome by a sense of lightheadedness as I always am when a prophetic dream is about to take place." She waved in the direction of the rumpled bedclothes. "Before I realized it had happened I had fallen deeply asleep."

"Do you remember the dream itself?"

"I remember only vague pieces and disjointed images. I do remember hordes of trampling feet and screaming." Honoria placed her hand upon her chest and closed her eyes as if she sought to conjure the dream images anew. "I believe there was a man who was in danger but then at second glance it became clear a woman was the one who really was harmed. I can't stop thinking of my father telling me to be careful of catching a chill and that I should follow his example and wrap myself up warmly." Honoria shook her head as though she wished to jostle the dream either into or out of it, I had no idea which. "Sadly, most of it fled from my memory as I regained consciousness, as is so often the case when one awakens abruptly."

"I'm very sorry to have disturbed you."

"You could not have known what was happening in here. I didn't even know myself until I awakened. Please don't give it another thought." Honoria pushed a stray strand of silver-streaked dark hair from her face and tucked it behind her ear. "The one thing I am certain of is that there is danger coming to someone here in the hotel."

"Do you know to whom?"

"I have suspicions but no real certainty." Honoria paused and I had the unusual experience of suspecting that she was keeping something from me. "I am sure of nothing. I just know I am very much afraid."

"Afraid of what?" I wasn't sure I truly wanted to know.

"Ruby, I wish I knew. I just have a sense of disquiet that I cannot escape."

"Have you no sense of the source of the concern or the form it will take?"

"I am certain this was a dream that warned of peril."

"Danger can come in many degrees. Perhaps it will be something of little consequence."

"I have never found that to be the case. In fact, the dreams have always preceded an event of serious import." I felt all the excitement and anticipation for the upcoming week's festivities drain from me. "Spirit does not make itself known for paper cuts or missed trains."

"Is there nothing you can do to comfort yourself when you have a dream such as this one?" I asked.

"I shall do what I always have done. I will bring the dream before the Divination Circle and ask for their help in interpreting what little I know," Honoria said, drumming her plump fingers on the arm of the settee. Honoria, her lifelong friend Orazelia Yancey, and Honoria's devoted suitor, George, met twice a week to develop their psychic gifts.

In fact, the day I first arrived at the Belden I interrupted one of their sessions. It was one in which they were working on contacting spirits of those who had passed beyond the veil. Honoria had misinterpreted my presence and had mistaken me for my dead mother. Fortunately for me she was at least as happy with my appearance as she would have been with her sister's.

Over time the group had turned its efforts to developing a wide variety of spiritual disciplines. Honoria's vast collection of metaphysical books housed in the library reflected the interests of the Divination Circle members. Tasseomancy, rune casting, astrology, all tickled their fancies and engaged their attention at one time or another. If anyone could provide her either the sort of comforting counsel that would take her mind off the dream or make sense of it, it would be they.

"Do you plan to meet soon?" I asked.

"As the fates would have it, they are due here within the quarter hour." Honoria stood and smoothed her wrinkled skirt into place. She looked so uncharacteristically somber I felt a cold wave of worry wash over me. "I would very much appreciate it if you would join us. I have a troubling feeling the dream involves you."

CHAPTER EIGHT

GEORGE AND ORAZELIA ARRIVED BEFORE I HAD TIME TO change out of my cycling costume. Honoria apprised them of her upsetting dream as soon as they entered the séance room. Her face still held the same befuddled look she had worn when I first awakened her.

I found myself relieved to have avoided being exposed to the strenuous effects of her prophetic dreams before now. It was difficult to see how it had turned my confident, exuberant aunt into a fidgeting mound of uncertainty. I was relieved beyond telling for Orazelia and George to share the burden of consoling her.

Sadly, George looked at least as off his game as my aunt. His usually waxed and luxuriant mustache drooped. If I was not mistaken a bit of his lunch remained tucked into its bristles. George's waistline was habitually a source of concern for him but his waistcoats were invariably a thing of beauty. I had never before seen him dressed without attention to his appearance. Today his shirt sported stains down the button placket and his seersucker jacket was rumpled at the elbows, the back, and even along the lapels. It would be less than kind to mention the state of his trousers.

Orazelia gave both Honoria and George a quick once-over and then turned her usually dreamy blue eyes on me. If I hadn't been looking for it I doubt I would have noticed the pursing of her lips and the quick dip of her head letting me know she would take matters in hand and that I should follow her lead. Frankly, I had not thought she possessed such a manner of thinking. She always appeared fluffy and easily led by her strong-willed daughter, Lucy. There were hidden depths to Orazelia that I would be remiss to ignore. I could not have been more pleased.

"The rest of us will sit in a circle whilst George allows the spirits to come through him and he will transcribe their messages." We all took seats at the séance table in the center of the room except for George who took up his post at the writing desk at the end of the room.

While George was as devoted to the Divination Circle as Honoria and Orazelia, his own talent seemed to me to be the least authentic. Although he was dedicated to the practice of automatic writing, the messages that flowed from his pen in one of his self-proclaimed trances most often concerned those things preying on his own peace of mind in the physical realm. I had no real confidence his skills would actually serve to soothe Honoria. But Orazelia had taken the lead and I had no desire to question her judgment aloud.

Honoria's hand trembled in mine as Orazelia began to speak. I wondered once again if she had seen more in her dream than she had shared with me.

"Spirits, we beseech thee to attend our call and to advise us on the law of your world. Do we bear responsibility to act on the fragments of Honoria's dream?"

The room grew silent except for the occasional sound of merrymakers on the beach or the screech of a gull. Then the sound of a pen scratching began to fill the air. Honoria squeezed my hand and one of her many rings dug into my palm. The sound of George's pen grew faster and I heard a page of paper flutter through the air as if he had flung it from the desk with abandon. Over and over the sounds of writing and flinging repeated until they slowed to a stop and Orazelia spoke once more.

"We thank you, spirits, for gifting us with your wisdom from beyond. We are complete." Orazelia released my hand and stood to open the plush velvet drapes blocking out the light. How George had managed to write so much without the aid of his eyes was a mystery to me. Scattered over the carpet were sheet upon sheet of foolscap covered with words. I pulled my sore hand from Honoria's grasp and bent over to collect the papers.

Much of it appeared to be gibberish. Some pages didn't even look to be composed of a language sharing our alphabet. Scratchings and scrawlings, tipping and turning every which way, careened over the surface of the papers. But every now and again I could make out a word or two that appeared to be written in English. The phrases *beleaguered knight* and *unexpected interloper* appeared more than once. I handed the stack to Orazelia to see what she would make of it all.

She spread the papers out over the midnight blue tablecloth covering the séance table and considered each carefully, running her finger this way and that following the maze of George's scribblings. Honoria simply leaned back in her chair awaiting a verdict. I had never seen her acting as a bystander. My stomach fluttered uncomfortably. I told myself I was probably hungry but I knew I was lying to myself. Orazelia gave me a deliberate look once more and cleared her throat.

"Based on the symbols I see here, it is clear we are beset by difficulties either at present or in the very near future. The source of concern is unclear but comes to us from outside our usual circle. My sense from the spirits is that while we have been warned to be on our guard against danger and to gird ourselves for its inevitable arrival, there is nothing we can do to turn the course of events. Nor should we try."

"Are you quite certain?" Honoria asked. "Is there nothing we can do but sit idly by?"

"Spirits assure us it is not our path to turn others from their journeys. It is our privilege to have early notice of troubles. Such privilege does not confer the burden of turning the tide of another's destiny." From the corner of my eye I watched as Honoria's hands stilled in her lap. Her posture straightened and a long sigh escaped her lips. She drew herself to her feet and she reached out to touch her friend on the arm.

"Thank you for your interpretation, Orazelia. I am much reassured." She turned her attention to George. "Still, I feel the need of some fresh air to revive me sufficiently to attend properly to my guests. George, I would be most grateful if you would accompany me on a walk along the beach." She crooked her arm, which he took wordlessly. Honoria called over her shoulder to me. "I trust I can rely on you to keep the hotel running for half an hour or so, Ruby?" I nodded, and they were gone without another word.

Chapter Nine

As soon as they were out of earshot I turned to Orazelia. "I am very grateful for your visit. I have never seen Honoria like I found her after her dream."

"I can only imagine how it must have startled you. Her dreams always take a toll. It is not an easy gift. I am glad you were spared her distress when she dreamt of your mother's passing into spirit." Honoria had told me when I first arrived that she had known before my father's letter had arrived that my mother had died. I had clearly understood the news had grieved her terribly but I had not comprehended the scope until today. "She will be back to her usual self by the time they return. The one I am really worried about is George."

"He didn't seem to be himself, did he?"

"No, he did not. And after what little I got out of him during the carriage ride and his easily interpreted worries"—Orazelia pointed to the papers spread between us—"I am certain he'll have no peace until his brother concludes his visit."

"George has a brother?" This was news to me. I had never

heard him mention family other than his recently deceased mother, whom he frequently mentioned with affection and regard.

"Osmond. An odious man who thinks far more of himself than is justified, considering he's done nothing in his life to crow about other than to marry a wealthy woman." Orazelia smacked her hand against the table smartly. "He decided at the last minute to attend the opening of the pier and all the hotel rooms in town were already booked. George received a letter by the morning post announcing Osmond and his wife will be arriving just before suppertime this evening."

"That sounds most unfortunate."

"It certainly was. Osmond has spent all his life letting his older brother know how much more successful he thinks he is and how right their mother was to favor him over George."

"But George always speaks so highly of his mother."

"George is a remarkably loyal person. Despite the fact that his mother was a thoroughly poisonous woman, he never had a cross word to say about her. In fact, I believe his attitude toward her was one of the reasons Honoria never consented to marry him."

That was enlightening. George's regard for Honoria was unmistakable and her affection for him seemed constant and genuine. I had wondered from time to time why they had never married. I had chalked it up to Honoria learning from my own parent's disastrous marriage but this information shed a different light on the situation.

"I can't see Honoria holding her tongue where she saw injustice."

"Exactly. She knew if she shared a household with George his mother would be part of the bargain. And she also understood that either she would drive a wedge between them or he would come to resent her for her opinion of the old wretch." Orazelia's cheeks pinked. I had never seen her look cross before. "Every time George spends any time with Osmond he is thoroughly miserable."

"There was no way George could refuse to host them?"

Orazelia shook her head. "George is ill equipped for any form of confrontation. Osmond and his wife will just plow right over his feeble attempts to put them off."

"No wonder he looks a little peaked. How long does Osmond plan to stay?"

"George seemed to have no idea. But he did mention that they planned to be here at least until the opening festivities for the pier had taken place. His wife insisted she mustn't be left out of the social event of the season, and knowing her they will arrive lock, stock, and barrel."

"I'll check to see if we've had any cancellations. Perhaps we could offer them rooms here at the Belden if it would help George."

"I'm sure he would appreciate it no end, Ruby dear." Orazelia said. "I just hope inviting them isn't at the bottom of Honoria's dream."

Chapter Ten

Dinner at the Belden was always an elaborate affair. Mrs. Doyle, the formidable cook and housekeeper, justifiably prided herself on the meals she provided and I'd never yet heard a guest complain. The dining room was the largest room in the hotel and to my way of thinking one of the most beautiful. During the previous winter Honoria had redecorated and renovated most of the hotel and the dining room had received a large share of the budget and the attention.

Round mahogany tables of varying sizes dotted the room. Heavy velvet draperies hung alongside the long, mullioned windows. The wallpaper provided diners with a sense that they were seated in a fairy-tale aviary. Images of bright birds and colorful flowering branches patterned the walls. Crystal glasses sparkled under the new electrified chandeliers, and the singey, starchy smell of freshly pressed table linen gently wafted toward my nose. Although I would not say so to Honoria, my favorite part of the decor was the profusion of floral displays Mrs. Doyle somehow managed to find time to lovingly and expertly arrange. Tonight's creations featured an abundance of late peonies and sprigs of fragrant lavender.

Mrs. Doyle was not the only one who made dinners at the Belden such a success, however. Honoria supervised the seating arrangements herself every morning. One of the strengths of her plans was the way she seated a faculty member at each of the tables to provide the guests an opportunity to spend unstructured social time with one of the Belden's paranormal practitioners. She also usually had an uncanny knack for sensing the rippling undercurrent between hotel residents and almost unfailingly avoided seating people together who disliked each other's company.

Honoria did not know of Amanda's earlier encounter with Miss Rice and unfortunately proceeded to direct the newcomer to her table. I should have regretted not telling Honoria about the unpleasantness on the subject of my cycling ensemble. In truth, I must admit I felt a small amount of satisfaction when I noticed Amanda's flushed face as Miss Rice took the seat next to her. I could only hope that Amanda would have enough sense not to provoke Miss Rice further.

I watched with untainted pleasure as Lucy and Sophronia entered the dining room arm in arm and sat at Honoria's own table. It appeared they were going to get along just as splendidly as I had hoped they would. As I reached my own table I saw that a Mr. Dewitt Fredericks had been seated to my right and a couple by the name of Clemens were to be on my left. I watched the door to await their arrival.

Before long a solitary man entered the dining room and approached Honoria's table. He nodded a greeting to all the ladies at the table, and appeared to speak to Sophronia and to nod at Miss

Rice, before Honoria pointed in my direction discreetly with an elegant inclination of her head. The slim man followed the tilt of her head and after giving Honoria a slight bow, headed in my direction. The light shining down from the chandelier bounced off the heavily pomaded curl pressed against his high forehead. His lips were as full as a catfish's and his pale skin did little to hide his veins.

Nevertheless, I smiled as he approached. I learned early on in the medicine show that one's own preferences concerning the company one kept were of little consequence when compared to the preferences of one's rumbling stomach. Although it did me no credit now that I had vowed to go straight, I could still fake sincerity to a shocking degree.

"Good evening. You must be Mr. Fredericks. Welcome to the Belden," I said, giving him a bright showman smile. "I'm Ruby Proulx, the hotel medium. I hope you will enjoy your stay with us." I watched with surprised fascination as he pulled a handkerchief from his waistcoat pocket and spread it out on his chair before gingerly taking a seat.

"I am certain I shall. My exhaustive research has indicated that this location will be highly conducive to my work." Mr. Fredericks sniffed loudly. My heart lurched and I wondered what the nature of his business might be. I had no desire to host anyone committed to debunking Spiritualism or to proving fraud was being perpetrated within our walls. But, if he were here to investigate us it would be better to know sooner rather than later. As much as I was dreading the answer, duty demanded that the question had to be asked.

"Many people have found the atmosphere at the Belden to be very supportive of spiritual pursuits. May I presume to ask the nature of your business?"

"I flatter myself that I am an author." My dinner companion's face contorted and he dug quickly into his waistcoat pocket for a second handkerchief before releasing a chandelier-rattling sneeze.

"You are an author, Mr. Fredericks?" I hoped I had hidden my astonishment. Reading was one of my greatest passions. On the road it had been impossible to attend school but Father felt he would be best served as someone purporting to be a man of medicine if his daughter appeared educated. He decided in our situation the only recourse was to teach me to read at an early age and then to keep me well supplied with a wide variety of books. I had taken to reading with a zeal I had never felt for anything else. Meeting an author was something I had always dreamt of doing.

Although, I must confess, I had not imagined anyone at all like Mr. Fredericks. Still, if one is not to judge a book by its cover, perhaps the same rule should apply to authors of books as well. I attempted to bury my disappointment in Mr. Fredericks's fussy manner and lackluster appearance and made another attempt at enthusiasm.

"Indeed I am. Perhaps you've read my latest work *A Comprehensive Travel Guide for Discriminating Sensitives*?" He leaned back in his chair and drew his fleshly, moist lips into a broad smile. He tented his fingers over his spindly chest and fixed his watery blue eyes upon my face. I glanced at the door eager for the two remaining guests to make a last-minute appearance. Honoria surveyed the room and after raising an eyebrow at the empty spots at my table reached to depress a bone button mounted upon the dining room wall. A moment later the swinging door leading to the kitchen pushed open and the serving staff appeared with broad trays held aloft.

"I am afraid I have not had that particular pleasure." Any travel guides Father would have sanctioned would have more likely borne the title *One Hundred Best Places to Fleece the Masses*.

"An easily remedied misfortune, I assure you." Mr. Fredericks reached into an inside pocket of his dinner jacket and withdrew a mercifully slim volume, which he presented to me with a flourish. He then withdrew a fountain pen from his waistcoat pocket and opened the book to the title page. I watched as he inscribed the book with fanfare before handing it to me. "I look forward to discussing it with you at length as soon as you have familiarized yourself with the information therein."

Fortunately, I was spared any need to formulate a response, by Mr. Fredericks himself. He commenced to sputter and gasp before releasing another bone-rattling sneeze.

"Excuse me, miss." He snapped his fingers at a member of the serving staff, a very young girl who had begun employment at the Belden only a few days before. "Please remove the vase of flowers from this table immediately. As a matter of fact, I insist that you rid the room of all the others as well." He gestured at the other tables in the room before he turned back to me. The serving girl, Frances, stood looking at me as if rooted to the spot with indecision. I, too, was taken aback. After all, what possible grievance could anyone have against flowers?

"Have the floral arrangements offended you in some way?" I asked.

"Not in the way I'm certain you mean." Dewitt dabbed at his red nose with his handkerchief before tucking it back into his pocket. I shuddered to think of his poor laundress. "As a point of fact, I am a card-carrying member of the Hay Feverists Society."

Out of the corner of my eye I noticed Frances's lower lip beginning to wobble. The poor girl was torn between continuing her serving duties and Mr. Fredericks's unusual demand. No wonder she looked ready to cry. I reached for the offending bouquet and placed the vase on Frances's nearly empty tray.

"Frances, you go ahead and remove the vase from this table. Mrs. Doyle will have to be consulted about the other bouquets. Please hurry back to complete your serving duties." Frances bobbed her head at me and scurried away with the offending vase. Mr. Fredericks rolled his eyes and sighed extravagantly. He was a man in need of a soothing distraction. "Hay Feverists Society, you say. Is that a sort of medical organization?" I asked.

"We are a group dedicated to seeking out and preserving those environments which provide sensitive people such as myself relief from the onslaught of seasonal attacks of catarrh." Mr. Fredericks pulled a fresh handkerchief from the depths of another pocket and applied it vigorously to his nose. "We have a large and enthusiastic membership."

"Really, how fascinating. How does one become a member of your society?"

"While technically, membership is open to anyone with the means to pay the five-dollar-per-year dues, hay fever is felt by only a certain sort of person. Those who are true sensitives are the only ones who are stricken." Dewitt nodded to himself.

"One of the staff here at the hotel is afflicted by trouble with her breathing," I said, thinking of Millie. "Is it possible that she suffers from the same affliction?" Perhaps Mr. Fredericks's unpleasant company would be worth enduring not only on behalf of the hotel but for my friend's health as well.

"I would not be at all surprised for those as sensitive as the metaphysical practitioners here at the Belden to be often laid low by hay fever."

"I'm afraid I haven't made myself clear. Millie is one of the maids," I said. I nodded to the waiter who appeared at my elbow offering a platter of asparagus on toast. I looked up as Mr. Fredericks let out a sort of strangled cough.

"I'm sorry to say there is no possibility of your maid experiencing hay fever. The lower classes simply don't have characters of sufficient refinement to be afflicted." Mr. Fredericks scowled at the food being offered then waved the waiter away without partaking. "Which is why I feel privileged, quite privileged indeed, to be a sufferer. It assures me of the company of those people in the highest strata of the arts and intelligentsia and ruthlessly sorts out those of the lower classes, like hotel maids." Mr. Fredericks inspected his water glass with a gimlet eye before condescending to take a sip.

"I am ashamed to admit to you I myself am not a sufferer of hay fever. I fear you will find me unworthy of sharing your table." I felt a spark of pleasure at the blush creeping up his scrawny neck. People, even those who consider themselves to be a part of the intelligentsia, do so often speak without thinking. I had a particular dislike for those people who believed and decreed themselves to be superior.

"For some sufferers the seaside is a great aid as well. Perhaps you were amongst those fortunate enough to have found a remedy before any difficulties could be perceived."

"Perhaps I should mention that to my aunt. Maybe we could include information about how good the fresh air here on the coast would be for other Hay Feverists." Yet another waiter arrived with a tureen of soup and I gladly availed myself of the generous portion he offered. I was happy to see Mr. Fredericks finally accepting something to eat as well. It would never do for Mrs. Doyle to hear from the servants that a guest had refused to eat. She might feel honor-bound to terminate her employment.

"You certainly could. Although I will say it is inferior to the purity of the air in Bethlehem, New Hampshire. Which is why the Hay Feverists hold their convention there every year."

"Is there something special about Bethlehem, New Hampshire, for sufferers such as yourself?"

"I would have thought someone working in the hospitality business would know all about those summer resorts in direct competition with your own."

"I have only joined my aunt here at the Belden a few weeks ago. Before that I lived with my father in Canada. I'm afraid I am new to the business."

Every time I felt I was becoming comfortable in my new role as a member of Honoria's household I ran straight up against a reminder of how little practical experience I truly had. I cringed on the inside every time I had to make an excuse for a lack of knowledge. And not only because I hated to feel incompetent but also because I wished it were possible to forget my time before the Belden had ever happened. Even when the skills I had learned during my old life helped me to succeed in my new one it pained me to think of it.

"That explains your ignorance. Bethlehem and some other locales in New Hampshire's White Mountains are free of noxious pollens most likely to bring on attacks. There is something about the high altitudes which renders the air purer than that in the lowlands." DeWitt's attention turned to the plate of soup in front of him. "But, as I said, the seaside is also excellent for avoiding the onslaught of symptoms."

"Was it the sea air or an interest in metaphysical practices that prompted you to stay here at the Belden?" I asked. Everyday conversation was one of the quickest, most effective ways to gather such information as might help me to do my job as the hotel medium. Learning as much as I could about the people who would likely ask me for a reading during the course of their stay most certainly was in my best interest.

"I am here working on another book and enjoying the opening of the pier like everyone else in Old Orchard this month." Mr. Fredericks cast his gaze about the dining room. "Besides, I am a great supporter of suffrage and wished to attend the events planned by Miss Foster Eldridge."

"I noticed that you spoke with her when you entered the dining room. It appeared you were acquainted." I raised my soup-spoon to my lips and enjoyed a taste. Cream of lettuce was one of my favorites. My life on the road with Father had not included meals like the ones Mrs. Doyle provided at the hotel. Burnt biscuits and vats of flavorless beans were the staples of the cook tent and something as sublimely silky as a creamed soup was a delight I had known of only through the pages of books.

"I am happy to say that is so." Dewitt poked at his own soup with his spoon before setting it down. "Miss Foster Eldridge is herself a Hay Feverist. As is Miss Rice. In fact, they were the ones who assured me the Belden was just the place to spend the month of July. At least it would be if the establishment wasn't so blighted by the unnecessary profusion of flowers." He pushed his soup plate away barely touched. Mrs. Doyle would not be pleased.

Food returning to the kitchen, plate untouched, sends her into apoplexy.

"Since it appears the serving girl is not the one in charge of such details, with whom should I speak about making the hotel suitable for sensitive guests such as myself?" I thought about letting him off the hook by offering to take care of it personally. But who was I to deny Mrs. Doyle the pleasure of someone to complain about? I was delighted to think that the someone was not going to be me.

"It is clear to me that you are a man who likes to speak to the person in charge. You should make your case directly to Mrs. Doyle, our cook and housekeeper, straight after dinner."

CHAPTER ELEVEN

YANCEY ARRIVED HOME LONG AFTER SUPPERTIME. THE RUCKUS at the rally had been only a small part of a long and tiring day. Fistfights under the pier, more reports of pickpocketing, and a lost child had kept him on the dead run since he left the amphitheater many hours earlier. He let himself in through the kitchen door and looked around. His mother often waited for him to return before she served dinner but it was clear from the plate and cutlery stacked in the sink that she had already eaten. Yancey had no cause to complain. His job meant he often missed suppertime by hours and hours. At such times his mother or Lucy always thoughtfully left a covered dish for him in the warming oven. He could not recall a time since returning from the army when he had arrived home and no supper was prepared.

His mother appeared in the doorway clad in her nightclothes and a wrapper despite the warmth of the evening.

"Hello, darling." She crossed the room and opened the icebox for a bottle of milk. "There's a plate of ham and new potatoes for you in the oven if you're hungry." He nodded and she busied herself pulling the dish from the oven and jars of relish from the icebox.

He settled at the end of the old wooden table, out of the way, and drew his pipe from his vest pocket. He'd barely had time to tamp fresh tobacco into the pipe's bowl before Orazelia placed a heaping plate before him. She piled a few leftover breakfast biscuits onto a plate and plunked them down on the table next to the relish tray before lowering her comfortable bulk into a wooden chair opposite him. He was still tucking a napkin into his collar when he heard the stairs creak and footsteps upon the hallway's wooden floorboards.

"Is that you, Warren?" Lucy called out. Not waiting for a reply she burst into the kitchen, her face all aglow. From the way she was dressed Yancey suspected she had not been home long herself but rather recently returned from the Belden or some other respectable dining establishment. She wore a dressing gown but her hair was still pinned up in a complicated configuration held aloft by delicately wrought metal combs. Usually by this time in the evening Lucy's hair would be confined in a single long braid snaking down her back. It wasn't unheard of for Miss Proulx to invite Lucy to the hotel in an evening but he couldn't help but worry after the morning's events that the two of them were up to something.

"You haven't told him my news, have you, Mother?" Lucy asked as she took the third seat at the table and helped herself to a plate of ham and biscuits slathered with butter and drizzled with molasses.

"Of course not. I knew you'd want to tell him yourself." Yancey's sense of trouble increased as he shifted his gaze between the two of them.

"I've been invited to work as a sort of a secretary for Sophronia Foster Eldridge," she said.

Yancey lowered his forkful of ham and returned it to his plate untouched. His feeling of hunger had entirely deserted him.

"You haven't agreed to do so, have you?" He looked from his sister's face to his mother's, hoping one of them would smile as if Lucy were jesting.

"Of course I have." Lucy shot Yancey an exasperated look. "It is a tremendous honor to be asked to help someone who is on the front lines of the cause."

"What exactly are you expected to do for Miss Foster Eldridge?"

"I'm to help with correspondence, with names of local women whose acquaintance she should make, and also to act in a sort of understudy capacity," Lucy said. "Most of all she is relying on my help in organizing a march to bring attention to the cause."

"A march?" Yancey asked, his throat suddenly dry.

"That's right, a march. She told me all about it this evening during dinner at the Belden. Sophronia has the whole thing planned out brilliantly. She's even alerted the newspapers." Lucy's eyes shone in the low light of the candles.

Much of the house had been wired for electricity but his mother had insisted that the kitchen could wait for such modernizations. Yancey found some comfort in the kitchen remaining just as he had known it as a boy. Especially on evenings like this one where the world and the roles assigned to its inhabitants seemed to change more quickly than he could get used to. For just a fleeting moment he wished his father were there to act as the voice of reason in his stead. Yancey dismissed the thought as quickly as it flitted in and took up the part of protector he had assigned himself since returning to the bosom of his family.

"I cannot support this decision." Yancey cleared his throat and prepared for the onslaught of arguments from his nearest and dearest. "I don't think either of you realizes what sort of risk you are assuming by participating in this sort of event." Yancey leaned across the table and reached for his mother's hand.

"See, Mother, I told you he would try to dissuade us from helping with this." Lucy abandoned interest in her biscuit and glared at Warren instead.

"The crowds at those marches are agitated, violent, even. Their behavior makes what happened at the rally this morning look like a church service." Yancey could hear the pleading tone in his voice but he couldn't control it. "People are always hurt. You'd be far safer staying home."

"I should think in your capacity as a police officer you would realize how often women are hurt in their homes. The vote is the only way women will be able to help themselves get out from under the yoke of men." Orazelia's usually gentle voice took on a strident note.

"That changes nothing about the danger to you during a suffrage march. Especially one when there will be so many people visiting the town." Yancey could feel his argument falling on deaf ears. Orazelia had managed to survive the last twenty years in a small town where her husband had been at the center of a horrific scandal by shutting out words she would rather not hear. She was an expert at ignoring things. She looked over at Lucy and some sort of signal passed between them.

He often felt like an outsider when he was with the pair of them. Ever since returning to Maine after his years in the army he realized how little he had to say in how his family comported itself. He had no reason to believe either his mother or sister would humor him about discontinuing their association with Miss Foster Eldridge or the suffrage movement simply because he asked. But, if he held his tongue and then something happened to either of them, he would never be able to forgive himself.

"Women are already in constant danger. The rally certainly won't make that worse and maybe it will make it better in the end," Lucy said.

"Please, don't allow this." Yancey addressed his mother. "You know how reckless Lucy can be."

"You are the one who went off and joined the army and now are part of the police force. How can you possibly say that I am the reckless one in the family?" Lucy jabbed at a slice of cold ham with a fork, and Yancey thought it likely she was imagining him on the plate instead.

"For young women like Lucy the vote matters even more than for women my age. They have their whole lives in front of them. I would not deny your sister the opportunity to make history."

"That's exactly what I am afraid of. Lucy making history is a terrifying prospect." The image of Lucy tied to a stake with a gaggle of men with torches circling her feet flitted through his mind.

"I've promised to be one of the organizers. I intend to fulfill that commitment whatever the risk to myself," Lucy said.

"So you admit there is risk involved?"

"Only because you insist that it is so. I have no worries as to my safety and neither does Ruby." Lucy delicately sliced a sliver of meat from the larger piece and brought the morsel to her mouth. "If there were anything to worry about I am sure her spirit guide would have warned her."

Yancey shifted in his chair. Of course Miss Proulx was involved. Somehow she was always involved when there was trouble afoot. While he was glad his sister had made a friend he did wish that it had been someone less likely to encourage her to give her adventurous side its head.

"Somehow I am quite certain that will only make things worse. You and Miss Proulx act as a tinderbox whenever you are in each other's company."

"I think Miss Proulx is an entirely wonderful influence upon your sister." Mother gave him a pointed look. "In fact, she seems to have worked a bit of magic on us all."

"Speak for yourself, Mother." Yancey felt himself growing warm beneath the collar. His mother's matchmaking was legendary. He had no intention of encouraging her. Best to change the subject. "It isn't just Miss Proulx who I am afraid will encourage Lucy to be reckless. I understand trouble follows Miss Foster Eldridge wherever she goes."

"Worse things have been said about us."

"Were you aware that this woman that you both seem to admire so much has been arrested? Repeatedly." Yancey knew he was fighting a losing battle but he just couldn't seem to concede.

"I've never been one to brand someone a criminal simply because the police seize upon the notion to arrest her." Orazelia let out a deep sigh and slowly shook her head as if disappointed in him. "Before the week is out you may be forced to arrest Lucy and me, too. You can think of it as a sort of family tradition."

Yancey thought of his father's disastrous run-in with the law. In fact, the family scandal and the mistreatment his father had received from the police, headed by Chief Hurley, was the primary reason Yancey had joined the force in the first place. Still, he was going to have to let his boss know what was in store for

Old Orchard even if his family found it hard to forgive him. A suffrage march would require police presence, and the chief was the only one who could authorize the extra manpower.

"I've said my peace." Yancey stood, then bent over his mother and deposited a kiss on the top of her graying head. "If things go as badly as I fear they will, just know I'll be there if you need me."

CHAPTER TWELVE

CLANGING FROM THE FIRE ALARMS HAD ROUSED THE ENTIRE hotel. Sadly, fire is a constant worry in the town and on more than one occasion flames had consumed whole blocks of buildings in mere moments. I had retired to my room only long enough to exchange my evening dress for a nightgown. In fact, I was seated on the tufted stool in front of my vanity table still working the pins from my hair when the sound first rang out.

I hurried to the turret window and stuck my head out. Under the glimmering light of the moon I could see dark waves lapping against the shore and shadowy figures hurrying along the sand but I could not see the source of the alarm. I heard doors banging closed all along the corridor and voices of guests hurrying past. I felt a panic rise within me. Was the fire within the Belden or without? I sniffed the air and believed I smelled the acrid tang of smoke mixing with the salt breeze.

I reached for my dressing gown, slid my arms in the sleeves, and tied the sash on my way to the door. The rules of society would have to give way to common sense. I only hoped most guests would agree that safety was more important than dying of smoke whilst demurely struggling into a gown deemed worthy of public viewing.

By the time I made it from my third-floor room to the lobby it was clear that most of the other Belden inhabitants were willing to risk a similar state of dishabille. Except for Honoria, who stood in the center of a large group of staff and guests, still wearing her gown from dinner. I would have been concerned by my own appearance except that Mrs. Doyle had appeared with her hair tucked inside a frilly nightcap. It was shocking to see her without her apron and stays. She almost looked like an approachable grandmother. Almost.

"Please, everyone, return to your rooms. I have it on good authority that the source of the fire is up near the amphitheater. One of the homes near there has caught fire but I have been assured the blaze is contained and we will not be impacted in any way." Honoria smiled wearily at the guests filing past her and up the stairs. Mrs. Doyle let loose a tonsil-baring yawn she hadn't the will to stifle then turned on her heel and trudged back toward her personal quarters at the back of the hotel, leaving me alone with my aunt.

"Aren't you heading back to bed yourself?" I asked, surprised to see Honoria standing motionless near the front door.

"I have the feeling I should wait up a little longer. But you go on, Ruby dear. There's no need for both of us to be tired come morning." Honoria peered into the darkness at Seaside Avenue. Her back turned toward me and her shoulders slumped a bit now that there was no one to keep up appearances for but me. There was something in the familiarity that gesture implied that made me feel at home in a way nothing up to that point had done.

Honoria had welcomed me with open arms when I had first arrived as the only child of her long-lost sister. She had claimed me as her family, sheltered me beneath her roof, and even imperiled herself with the law when she thought I was at risk of being arrested. But none of those things spoke as eloquently of her feelings for me as the simple act of releasing her role as hostess. I moved to the door and tucked my hand into the crook of her arm.

"I couldn't possibly go back to sleep if I were wondering what you were waiting for down here all by yourself," I said. "Does this have anything to do with your dream?"

"I don't believe so but I expect we shan't have to wait any longer to find out. Look." Honoria pointed out the door. A carriage clattered to a stop right in front of the hotel. A shrill woman's voice and a harsh-sounding man's cut through the night air, and two figures hurried up the steps to the Belden, followed reluctantly by a third person. Honoria slid aside the bolt and pulled open the door.

A matronly woman wrapped in a wet dressing gown stepped inside and stood dripping on the hall carpet. Smears of soot adorned both her cheeks. She put me startlingly in mind of a disgruntled eagle. A miserable-looking man of middle age stood beside her shaking his head. George brought up the rear. He slunk into the lobby looking even more like a walrus with dyspepsia than usual. His luxuriant mustache drooped at the ends and, unless I missed my guess, appeared shortened.

He turned his sad eyes on my aunt and slowly shook his head.

"We are here to throw ourselves upon your mercy, Honoria." George reached up and touched the end of his mustache, and a queer expression passed over his face. Indeed, the mustache did appear abbreviated.

"Because of my imbecilic brother's latest ill-considered exploits none of us has a place to hang our hats," the man said.

"Or even a hat left to require hanging," the woman said. That explained it. This was George's brother, Osmond Cheswick, and his wife, Phyllis. Even without being introduced it was clear to me why George had not been eagerly awaiting his brother's arrival. I took a moment to evaluate the couple from afar.

The man had likely been slim in his youth but was now running to the sort of soft physique that spoke of a life spent indoors indulging his appetite for rich foods and strong drink. A prominent nose and a sparse mustache that would have been better off being put out of its misery by a sharp razor dominated his face.

"George," Honoria said, turning her back to the other two and giving him her full attention, "what exactly has transpired that I find you in my hotel lobby in the middle of the night?"

"I've had a misadventure." George's voice rose barely above a whisper. Honoria nodded at him like he was a small boy who needed encouragement. "You know how I have been looking to develop my spiritual gifts beyond the practice of automatic writing?" Given that George's messages from beyond often read like unspoken desires of his own heart, it did not surprise me that he continued to seek new forms of connection with the other side.

"You've mentioned it to the Divination Circle from time to time."

"I recently read an article in the *Golden Beacon* concerning the practice of smoke painting. Have you heard of it?"

Honoria looked at me and we both shook our heads. "I cannot say that I have," Honoria said.

"It is a technique for delivering messages that involves a flame and blank sheet of paper."

"How does it work?" I asked. Mr. and Mrs. Cheswick snorted simultaneously in a show of marital harmony.

"The querent chooses a sheet of paper and inspects it to be sure no mark is upon it." George paused as if to allow us to keep up. "He presses the paper to his solar plexus while he brings to mind an image or a message he would like to receive."

"How is the flame involved?" I asked.

"The querent waits for spirit to urge him to approach the flame. He then holds the paper over the flame and moves it slowly in a circle until he feels the image has appeared," George said.

"Some people would realize it would be best to practice the technique out of doors until you have a feel for how quickly the paper can catch fire," Mr. Cheswick said.

"Oh dear. You don't mean you tried this inside your house?" Honoria asked.

"Of course he did. The man is an utter simpleton," Mrs. Cheswick said.

"Did the house burn to the ground?" I asked.

"It was gone in the blink of an eye. I can only rejoice that no one was hurt and that no other structures were damaged." George shook his head woefully. "I haven't even a change of clothes left to my name."

"As my brother no longer has the ability to offer us his hospitality, we shall require rooms for the duration of our stay," Osmond said. His wife nodded. Although from the pursing of her mouth as she looked around the lobby I could not help but feel the Belden was not up to her usual standard.

It was true that the Belden was not the largest hotel along the beach. In fact, its limited size and a total inability to increase the size of the building had led Honoria to reimagine her business as a sanctuary for spiritual seekers. She decided in what I could only consider a flash of genius that while she could not hope to compete with her neighbors in terms of size or amenities she could offer guests a thoroughly unique experience.

While the Sea Spray next door or the Old Orchard House up on the ridge impressed with on-site ballrooms, bowling alleys, and bathhouses, Honoria had refurbished the hotel and had hired a full faculty of metaphysical practitioners. The guests could book appointments with Nell, the palm reader, Ned, the numerologist, or Cecelia, the astrologer. Amanda could divulge a person's secrets if she wrapped her small hand around an object they owned. Everett MacPherson could find water or even gold with a pendulum or a pair of rods. It would not be modest, but it would be the truth to say mine was the most requested service. If the guests wanted to develop their own ability to read tea leaves or tarot cards they could sign up for lessons. It had proved extremely popular and if we could avoid any reason for guests to cancel their reservations we should be well on the way to repaying our creditors in a couple of years' time.

The pleading look on George's face gave my heart a squeeze. Because of the opening of the pier all rooms had been sold out. Considering the magnitude of the occasion, even if the weather turned unfavorable there was little likelihood there would be cancellations.

"That is quite impossible, Osmond. I believe all our rooms are filled for the entire summer and have been for months."

"No vacancies? You've done well for yourself with this psychic nonsense, haven't you, Honoria?" Osmond waggled his finger in Honoria's face. "You always were clever. For a woman."

"It isn't nonsense at all," George said.

"I haven't found it to be so," Honoria said as she stiffened her posture and added a chill to her tone I had yet to hear her use with guests.

"How can either of you possibly believe any of it? After all, aren't we standing here with nothing but the clothes on our backs?" the man asked. "If spirits could be called upon to predict the future my brother would have known not to play around with that smoke painting foolishness. He would have been warned that he was about to burn his house down." He smiled and looked around as if hopeful his words were being heeded. This man reminded me of my father and his constant desire for an audience.

My stomach tightened and I was glad Honoria said we had no space for him or his wife. That was until I noticed the pleading look in George's eyes. Honoria must have noticed it, too.

Without warning Ben appeared from the room behind the reception desk. Honoria acknowledged him with a slight nod. I was not sure I would ever grow used to the way Ben simply arrived without warning, indeed without a sound, wherever he seemed needed.

"Ruby, was it my imagination or did I notice two empty seats at your table this evening at dinner?" Honoria asked.

"There were two. They belonged to a couple by the name of Clemens, if I recall correctly," I said. Honoria turned to Ben, who ran a white finger down a column on the large leather-bound guest register. He confirmed my memory with a nod at Honoria. He beckoned her to his side and pointed at an entry in the ledger.

"Mr. and Mrs. Clemens canceled at the very last minute. We can offer you their room for the week. If your stay in Old Orchard will be longer than that I trust you will make other arrangements before that time is up," Honoria said.

"And what if there are no other accommodations to be had?" Mrs. Cheswick asked. "Would you throw us out on the street?"

"Osmond has always been such a worldly man. I would be very much surprised if he couldn't find a way to come out on top of whatever sort of difficulties he would manage to place himself in," Honoria said. "Wouldn't you agree, George?" Honoria and George exchanged meaningful looks. Mr. Cheswick cleared his throat loudly. Unless I missed my guess he was hoping to keep his wife from hearing any more of the conversation passing between George and Honoria. Mrs. Cheswick appeared to have heard them anyway.

"He is a very resourceful man but any troubles that enter his life are entirely of someone else's making," Mrs. Cheswick said. "Tonight's situation is a perfect example of this sort of a thing." Mrs. Cheswick scowled at George. I had the feeling Mrs. Cheswick was a woman who was used to getting her way.

"If you will just follow Ben, he will take you up directly." Ben glided up as silently as ever and motioned for the Cheswicks to follow him. Honoria waited for them to pass the first landing on the wide front stairs before speaking to George again. "Oh, my dear friend, what a thing to have happened." Honoria tucked her arm in his and made warm noises. "As soon as Ben returns from installing your odious family in their room we shall rearrange the furniture in the family parlor and put you in there. I am afraid it will have to suffice. We really are completely full at present."

"I am most grateful for whatever you can provide. I feel such an utter fool."

"Nonsense. This was meant to be." Honoria reached up and touched the end of his mustache. "You singed your mustache, too, didn't you?"

"That was the worst thing of all." George shook his head again.

"But there is an upside to everything, you know," Honoria said.

"I can't imagine what that might be."

"Now you have nowhere for Osmond and Phyllis to stay," Honoria said. "With any luck they will both have to return home at the end of the week." George broke out into a beaming smile. His back straightened and the set of his shoulders squared.

Chapter Thirteen

EVERY MORNING MY FIRST SITTERS OF THE DAY ARE THE VEL-mont sisters. The two of them had invested in the hotel at the beginning of the season, much to Honoria's great relief. As part of the return on that investment they were assured daily readings with me.

Each time, Elva arrived for the daily sitting two minutes early. Invariably, Dovie arrived ten minutes late. How it happened that way every day was a constant source of irritation for Elva and bafflement for me. They shared a room only one floor above the séance room and neither had mobility problems that would preclude them from arriving simultaneously. But today, they arrived together and were accompanied by Sophronia. It would seem the three of them had gotten along at dinner the night before exceedingly well.

"Good morning, Ruby. I hope you don't mind that we have invited Sophronia to sit with us this morning," Dovie said.

"I am delighted to include whomever you would like in one of your readings." Strictly speaking, that was not the truth. I felt a surprisingly fierce case of nerves. It wasn't every day that I conducted a reading with someone famous. It was even less usual for me to do so for a famous medium. After all, if she believed me to be a fraud there would be dire consequences for the hotel.

Many people relied on the Belden for their livelihoods, myself included. If she discredited me we would all suffer. Even the Velmont sisters, who had invested so much of their money, and even their reputation, in the hotel. I felt as though everyone's future rested with me. I wiped my clammy hands as discreetly as I could on the back of my cotton day gown and gestured to the séance table in the center of the room. Sophronia bestowed a dazzling smile upon me as she approached.

"I feel quite certain you possess an unusual level of talent," she said, pulling out a chair and placing her hands in her lap. "These ladies both speak very highly of your ability to connect with their father." It still felt strange to have champions, people who believed in me and told others how they felt. It was a support I was loath to lose. But delaying the experience would not make things easier. I took myself in hand and forced a smile to my own face.

"Why don't you tell me what you would like to consult your father about today?"

"We do not wish to speak with Father. We are well aware of his thoughts on the subject of women and the right to vote." Elva shook her grayed head. "No amount of transmuting powers of the great beyond would change his opinion on that subject, we're afraid."

"Dear Sophronia has been urging us to join the cause of suffrage. She suggested we consult the spirits since we are still undecided," Dovie said.

"I think today it is high time we ask you to try contacting someone else entirely for an opinion."

"Who would that be?" I was aquiver with curiosity.

"Our mother," the sisters said in unison.

I had never given any thought whatsoever to Mrs. Velmont. Her daughters had expressed such utter devotion to the memory of their father that I had simply forgotten that another parent had ever existed. I felt rather foolish and I found myself apologizing.

"I should have thought to offer to seek her before," I said. "I am very sorry not to have done so."

"We didn't like to ask," Dovie said.

"Whyever not?"

"We thought it might be painful for you," Elva said.

"Because of your own mother," they said in unison.

"That is very thoughtful of you but you needn't have tried to spare my feelings. I have absolutely no recollection of my mother."

"Neither do we. The similarities are striking."

"We lost her before we were out of the nursery," Dovie said.

"In fact, I was still less than a year old when she slipped away during Dovie's arrival."

"It was easier to pretend she had never existed than it would have been to acknowledge the gaping hole where a mother should have been," Dovie said. "We thought it likely you would feel the same." She blinked her light blue eyes at me from behind her wire-rimmed spectacles. Their thoughtfulness touched me deeply and I felt my throat burn with unshed tears. Dovie seemed to sense them and leaned across the table to cover my hand with her own.

"I know just what you mean but I must confess, I longed for my mother every day for as long as I can remember."

"Then you are just the person to help us get into contact with our own. Will you try?" I nodded but felt a heavy heart as I did so. My readings for the Velmonts and their father were based heavily on all the emotion they brought forward about him as well as the tidbits of information they dropped in casual conversation.

I had not had the opportunity to glean anything about their mother, not even her name. I could only hope that between the voice and the tarot cards that they would find themselves satisfied with the reading in the end. I shuffled the deck, cut the cards into three stacks, and asked the voice for guidance.

The cards felt lifeless, as they sometimes do. It doesn't happen often but when it does the reading does not tend to go well. I wondered why the voice was silent and my own intuition had abandoned me. I was going to have to rely on the showman's box of tricks to prime the pump. After all, it wouldn't do for the hotel's investors to lose confidence in my abilities to connect with the dead. I ran through my usual list of leading questions for sitters. I felt nudged to think about the woman they asked about and about mothers in general. I thought about the sorts of things I might want to hear from my own mother on the subject of suffrage.

I closed my eyes and placed my hands shelteringly over the cards. "The cards are cold. She does not need them." I pushed them into a pile at the center of the séance table. "She wishes to communicate more directly with her beloved daughters." Through slitted eyes I noticed the hopeful glances exchanged between the sisters. Even at their advanced age it was clear they longed to feel like someone's cherished child. It didn't require any form of metaphysical ability for me to understand how they felt or what they most desired to hear.

"I hear her faintly. She seems like a gentle spirit." Considering the way opposites attract and the information I knew to be true of Mr. Velmont, she would have had to have been a mild-mannered person to garner his attention.

"So everyone who knew her has said." Elva sounded so hopeful. I almost felt bad about deceiving her but since the deception increased her happiness and cost her nothing I told my conscience to quiet itself down. "What else does she say?"

"She speaks of watching you both throughout your lives. Even though she could not make herself felt in the physical realm, she hopes you were aware of her constant, loving presence."

"We have been, haven't we, Elva? Haven't I always said I could feel her in the very air around us?" Dovie gripped her sister's hand and shook it.

"She asks if you noticed any signs of her here in the Belden," I said. "Anything that answers the question you have set before her?" I watched through the barest crack between my eyes for the exchange between them.

"The cycling suits." Elva nodded at Dovie. Without thinking I opened my eyes in surprise. Cycling suits had not been at all on my mind.

"You mean like mine?" I asked.

"Yes. And Lucy's and Miss Rice's."

"Don't forget the catalogue, sister," Dovie said.

"We received a Sears and Roebuck catalogue in the post a few days ago," Elva said. "One of the pages was folded down at the corner as if it had been marked."

"When we opened it we noticed the illustration showed a pair of women, arm in arm, wearing matching cycling suits."

"And you believe this is a message from your mother?" I asked. It was not what I would have expected but the sisters seemed surprisingly pleased.

"It most certainly is." They nodded at each other again in that way they had, as though they knew exactly what the other was thinking without any words passing between them. "She planned to dress us alike, you see," Dovie said.

"You sound quite certain," I said.

"Oh yes. Mother was an avid needlewoman. Even before I was born she created clothing that matched in a variety of sizes," Elva said. "She sewed little dresses and knitted little shawls and caps. They were always in light blues and soft yellows and there was always one that was larger and one that was smaller."

"There was enough to keep us clothed for several years," Dovie said. "The nurses and nannies that cared for us after she died followed her wishes and dressed us in matching outfits every day." I didn't have the heart to mention to the ladies that it was likely their mother was simply a thrifty woman who wanted to use up the bits of material left over from creating a larger garment to produce a smaller one as well. If it pleased them to believe their mother had planned for them to dress alike it did no harm for them to continue to think so.

"Once we had outgrown the clothing she had made, Father made a point of having the help replenish our wardrobes with things that matched," Elva said.

"We could never see a reason to discontinue the practice so we dress alike even now," Dovie said. That explained it. I had been curious as to why two adult sisters would dress identically all the time. In fact, when I had first met the pair it had been difficult to tell them apart. Elva was slightly older and just a bit smaller. Dovie walked at a more leisurely pace and was inclined to smile more. But everything they adorned themselves with matched exactly from their shoes to their hatpins to their spectacles.

"It is said that if you see or hear something three times it is a sign," I said.

"Exactly. First we received the catalogue, then we saw you and Lucy leaving for your outing sporting your matched suits," Elva said.

"Don't forget meeting Miss Rice in the lobby just now," Sophronia said. "She was asking Ben if he knew of a seamstress she could call to make some alterations to her cycling outfits. Miss Rice can't even thread a needle."

"That was the third incident," Dovie said. "Obviously, Mother has something to say."

"Which is what prompted our desire to contact her as well," Dovie said. "Could you ask her if she wants us to procure cycling outfits of our own?"

"More important, should we join the suffrage movement?" Elva asked. Both sisters leaned toward me, their eyes shining and their crepey cheeks pinked with excitement. There was no doubt in my mind which answer they hoped their mother would give them.

At our first sitting together, with a great deal of help from the voice, I had convinced the sisters of my ability to channel messages from their father. I had used that complete faith to convince them to follow their own instincts on many occasions. They only needed a bit of ghostly approval to push them in the direction they wanted to go in the first place.

I should probably have felt guilty about devising such falsehoods but they were happier and more confident in their own decision-making abilities than they were when first we met. They had taken up swimming, learned to manage their own investments, and had allowed themselves the pleasure of reading popular, sensationalized fiction. My readings for them were something the highly critical Mrs. Doyle would have described as white lies. Even though I knew it to be fraud, I fully intended to continue to encourage them to trust in their own minds until such time as they seemed to have no need of such support.

I closed my eyes once more and swayed gently back and forth in my chair. I cocked my head to one side as if catching a message in my left ear. I nodded to the unseen speaker and then opened my eyes and smiled at the sisters.

"Your mother wishes you to know that she approves of whatever it is the two of you desire to do, as long as you do it together."

"So she approves of us joining the suffrage cause?" Elva asked.

"She does if you are in agreement." The sisters nodded their heads simultaneously and pushed back their chairs at the same time. I looked over at the ornate silver clock on the mantelpiece. "You still have time left in your session."

"Thank you, Ruby, but we have much to do today."

"We have to seek out a pair of cycling suits. Before the march." They rose and flitted away. I watched their retreating backs as they went through the door arm in arm and I wondered, not for the first time, what it would be like to have a sister.

CHAPTER FOURTEEN

SOPHRONIA WAITED UNTIL THE VELMONT SISTERS HAD PASSED through the midnight blue portiere before speaking.

"I am impressed," she said. I felt the knots in my neck and shoulders ease. Perhaps I had succeeded in convincing her of my abilities after all. "You have as rare a gift as the Velmonts, and your aunt, say that you do." I felt my cheeks warm. It was pleasant to receive such a compliment but I was still learning to offer a gracious response.

"Your good opinion leaves me overwhelmed. I am still quite new to mediumship and am exceedingly grateful for any encouragement but from someone as respected as you it is even more valued." Ever since arriving in Old Orchard my ability to hear the voice had strengthened. Honoria and Mrs. Doyle had given me advice on building my skills but neither of them was a medium and neither was clairaudient. I would dearly love a mentor to assist me in making sense of my gift. A flicker of hope swelled in my heart that Sophronia might be just such a teacher.

"You give me more credit than I deserve, Ruby. Tell me, do

you try to use these in all your readings?" Sophronia pointed at
the stack of tarot cards placed in the center of the table.

"Not always. I use them when the situation seems to call
for it." I didn't say that I also used them when I felt unsure. My
cards were like a child's favorite stuffed toy or doll. They brought
me comfort when I needed to be soothed by something familiar. Half the deck had belonged to my mother and I had used
it for years to earn the extra pennies that had kept food on the
table when Father wasted his earnings on wild schemes or strong
drink.

The other half of the deck had been in Honoria's possession
and I had only recently begun to use both halves together. I had
never had a guide other than the voice I heard in my head to advise me on the true meaning of the cards. Instead, I had always
used my intuition and imagination to interpret the images on the
cards querents chose during the readings. Unsure how best to
proceed I determined I'd let Sophronia decide.

"Would you like me to use them with you?" I asked.

"Perhaps another time. Today I would like to become more
acquainted with you. Tell me, how do you manage to give such
satisfactory readings to your sitters?" There was a conspiratorial
tone to Sophronia's voice that set my heart pounding and lifted
the fine hairs along my forearms.

That was just the sort of question that I most wanted to
dodge. I worked in the hotel as the medium and I prided myself
on the helpfulness of the readings I gave to the clients. Honoria
reassured me that what I did was genuine but I still could not say
with any surety that I truly believed I was a medium at all. Hearing a voice was not the same, in my opinion, as seeing spirits or

even hearing a multitude of different voices of dearly departed individuals. I heard only one. One that always felt like the same exact advisor. It was a fine line between what I did and what the clients believed me to be doing and I was not sure how much of the truth I should reveal to Sophronia. I swallowed a dry lump in my throat and asked the voice for guidance.

"Tell her about me."

I had made a point in recent weeks to follow the advice the voice gave me no matter what. Even when I trembled at its suggestions. Even when I felt certain it must be wrong.

"I hear a voice," I said, looking at the table. Sophronia reached across the space between us and took my hand. She did so in a comforting, reassuring way and I felt oddly at ease despite my usual reluctance to discuss such things.

"Why do you say this like it is something to be afraid of?"

"There is an inherent danger in admitting to hearing voices. Asylums are filled with people who make such claims." I had never told anyone about the voice until I arrived in Old Orchard. In fact, if Mrs. Doyle hadn't suggested she had expected me to inherit my mother's gift of clairaudience, I likely never would have done. All my life I had suffered from a dread of being shut up in the sort of lunatic asylum I had read about in books. I would not have mentioned it to Sophronia if it had not been for the voice's urging.

"You are right to be cautious when sharing such a secret. It is far too easy for men to confine independent and inconvenient women to such places." She shook her head so swiftly a hairpin escaped its mooring and clattered onto the table. She picked it up and winked at me. "In honor of your confidence in me shall I entrust you with a secret of my own?"

The voice spoke again. *"Accept this offer."* I nodded.

"Do you really believe I see visions of the dead floating in front of my eyes when I am holding a rally or giving a public presentation?" She released my hand from her grasp.

"Don't you? That is your reputation within the Spiritualist community," I said, trying to keep my voice even. I could hardly hear my own words over the swishing of blood in my ears as I thought of Lucy and the disappointment she would feel knowing Sophronia was a fraud. "It is part of the way you bill your public appearances."

"Very effective it is, too. I was quite pleased with myself when I decided to add the theatrical flair of Spiritualism to my presentations."

"Are you entrusting me with the confidence that you are a fraud?" I was flabbergasted. Sophronia had so much to lose if I were to share her secret with the world.

"Certainly not. It's just that there is a narrow gap between what the audience would like to hear I can do and what I actually do. It seems remarkably similar to what you do."

"What is it that you do if you don't see spirits of the dead?" I asked. I wasn't sure if I should be hopeful or even more worried by her admission.

"I see not the dead but a vision of the future with such clarity it often feels more real than the present circumstances in which I find myself. Women will have the vote. They will even be elected to public office. I daresay one day even the highest office the land." Sophronia gazed off toward the ceiling as if that bright future called to her from the plaster medallion ringing the small crystal chandelier dangling above our heads.

"Why don't you simply share that vision with the public?

Wouldn't your supporters be overjoyed to hear such things from you?"

"For the simple reason that I have found one of the most effective ways as a woman to be heard is to not seem to be the one speaking at all." Sophronia leaned across the table and drummed the top with her slim fingers. "If I say what I see or even what I think I am demonized as a woman who has forgotten her place. If I share messages from those who have passed into the wisdom of the great beyond, rather than it coming directly from a mere woman, the message becomes far more palatable. Especially with those who believe in the possibility of spirit communication far more than they believe in the capabilities of the female population."

"So you billed yourself as a medium?"

"Exactly. Most men prefer to think of women as passive channels. Or empty vessels into which something of value can be poured. The majority of them don't care to entertain the notion we can be the source of power or ideas. It was a very simple thing to convince them that a woman, any woman, could be overpowered by spirits," Sophronia said. "Surely you cannot deny you have felt the difference in reception of your ideas between those you speak as young Ruby Proulx and those you impart as the celebrated medium at the Hotel Belden?"

Sadly, Sophronia spoke an undeniable truth. I had long understood the power of the otherworldly. A rootless girl in a traveling show had little chance of her voice being heard and if it was, even less chance that it would be respected. But when I donned the guise of a gypsy fortune-teller by blackening my lashes with a burnt match end or draping my head with a dark lace shawl and altering my accent to that of an exotic stranger, suddenly my words had weight. Could I really fault Sophronia for wanting to bolster the cause of suffrage? Was she really doing anything so different than I when I smoothed the path for the Velmont sisters to follow their own desires?

"I see from your expression that you know quite well what I mean," Sophronia said. I nodded.

"That does not mean that I am not genuinely hearing a guiding voice," I said, hoping I sounded more convincing to her ears than I did to my own.

"I meant no offense. It is just that after watching the reading you just gave the Velmonts I believe you are someone who, like me, exercises a certain leniency with the truth if it serves the greater good . . ."

"Are you implying that you believe me to be a fraud as well?"

"Please do not be offended. You have my greatest admiration. You needn't try to convince me of your talents. I assure you I do not care what part of what you do is genuine and which part requires a well-honed knack for observation and lucky guesses. What I do care about is how we could help each other to have what we both want most." She gave me another of her smiles but this time it left me feeling chilled.

"What is it that you think I want most?"

"The ongoing success of this hotel? Being seen as the premier Spiritualist hotel in the nation, perhaps. Possibly something as humble as simply preserving its reputation as a place of genuine metaphysical marvels?" If Sophronia were not channeling spirits and hearing voices she was as adept at reading people as I was. I squirmed under her intense gaze and felt reluctant to answer. She tilted her head to the side and raised her eyebrows.

"Perhaps." I doubted a lie would deceive her but I did not wish to elaborate. I was too busy worrying about what sort of an arrangement she wished to create. "How is it that you propose we help each other?"

"How do you feel about platform readings?"

"You mean readings in a public forum? Conducted from the stage?"

"Exactly. You are ideal for the role. You're young, pretty, and very talented. The cause will benefit greatly from the participation of a modern young woman like you," she said. "As compensation for adding your performance at the march tomorrow I plan to recommend the Belden as the preferred hotel of discriminating suffragists in all my interviews and advertisements. Before you know it you will be as widely recognized across the country as I am myself."

My stomach fell to my feet. I had spent all of my childhood working the medicine show circuit with Father so it was not as though I suffered from stage fright. What made my knees wobble was the idea of calling such attention to myself.

It was one thing to work with individuals at the hotel in private. In that capacity it was unlikely anyone would connect me with the girl who was on the run from the medicine show where Johnny accidentally met his death while testing a new product for Father. If I stepped onto the stage all bets were off. Even though I would be using my real name and not one I had ever used on the road there was no guarantee no one would recognize my face, my mannerisms, or even my tone of voice. After all, only weeks before I had been recognized by a man who knew me from the medicine show. His eye for faces had almost been my undoing.

After all, New Brunswick and Quebec were not that far by train. In fact, a great many of the visitors to Old Orchard were Canadians. I had heard at least as much French spoken in Maine as I had across the border. Before, I'd worried Sophronia would cause problems if she thought I was not genuine enough. Now I wished she had not been quite so impressed. I needed an excuse and it had to be reasonable and inoffensive.

"I shouldn't want you to feel I am not grateful for your offer. However, I cannot possibly commit to any public appearances without first speaking with my aunt. Part of the draw here at the Belden is the exclusive access our guests have to the services we provide. I'm sure you understand my need for Honoria's permission." I hoped that would be enough to close the matter, at least until I could come up with another excuse.

"Your businesslike attitude and devotion to your aunt do you credit. I am even more convinced that your appearance onstage tomorrow will stir additional interest in the event." Sophronia pushed back her chair. "I'm sure you will be pleased to know I discussed it at length with Honoria after dinner and she eagerly accepted the proposal on your behalf. In fact, your name should already be mentioned in the newspaper article announcing tomorrow's march."

"You are certain Honoria said I should do this?" I asked. It wasn't like Honoria not to consult me on something that involved me so directly. To have been so forgetful she must have been even more preoccupied with her prophetic dream than I had realized. Either that or she really was convinced I would have no objection and felt confident that accepting on my behalf would make for a pleasant surprise.

"Just think of it, Ruby, with all the press in town for the pier opening there is sure to be comprehensive coverage of the march." She flashed me a final bright smile of the sort that reminded me disconcertingly of my father. "By tomorrow evening newspapers from New York to Montreal will have mentioned our names and printed our photographs. Won't that be wonderful?"

CHAPTER FIFTEEN

FOG BILLOWED UP FROM THE SHORE AND BLOTTED OUT YAN-cey's view of the buildings all up and down Old Orchard Street, creating ideal conditions for pickpockets to have a banner day in their chosen profession. He stopped at the walk-up eatery nearest the station and bought a box of corn fritters. Truth be told, he had hurried out of the house without breakfast to avoid encountering either his mother or Lucy. They had all gone to bed in a bit of a huff and he had no interest in reviving the argument of the night before.

He felt certain telling the chief about the march was in the best interest of the women involved but he still felt disloyal about carrying tales. Halfway down the sidewalk he pushed open the glass door of the police station. The air in the small office was humid and smelled of stale sweat and the remains of an aging fish dinner.

Yancey offered the box of fritters to the other officers scattered around the room before taking one for himself. As he chewed slowly he tried to convince himself someone would have broken the news about Sophronia's planned march to the chief already. By the time the last bite of his fritter had landed with a heavy thump in the pit of his belly he had reconciled himself to the fact his conscience would not allow him to shirk his responsibilities to the public or to his ungrateful family. He steeled himself for what would likely be an unpleasant encounter and knocked on the chief's door.

"What do you want?" Chief Hurley lowered the morning paper and scowled over the top of it at Yancey.

"Are you aware of the suffragist Sophronia Foster Eldridge's plans to organize a march here in Old Orchard?" Yancey asked.

"It's right here at the end of this article about that rally she held yesterday." Hurley slapped the paper onto his desk and jabbed a blunt finger down onto a block of text. "It says here she's planning some kind of a big hoopla with a march through town, a speech, and even a performance by that pretty little medium from the Belden," Chief Hurley said. "You know the one, Honoria Belden's niece?"

Yancey's pulse began to pound. The march was enough of a worry without the added concern of Miss Proulx standing onstage offering her person as a target for any angry bystander with a rock in his or her hand. He was just as irritated at himself as he was with her. This was exactly the sort of stunt he should have expected from Miss Proulx. After all, she was a professional mountebank. Why would he not have expected her to climb up onto a stage and advertise herself?

He was more convinced than ever that she and Lucy were headed for a world of trouble. Her plans to appear gave him all the more reason to convince the chief to send men to the march. "We need something like that in town right now about as much as a dog needs a second tail." Hurley shoved back his chair and crossed his hands on his paunch. "You're going to have to make sure Miss Foster Eldridge doesn't do anything to make even more of a nuisance of herself than she has everywhere else she's gone."

"It's likely she'll draw a large crowd," Yancey said.

"It says right here they had nearly a thousand people attend her speeches up in Portland last month." The chief shook his head and groaned. "I see no reason to expect we won't have at least a few hundred."

"Do you plan on hiring extra officers to police the march?" Yancey asked. "We're stretched to the breaking point with the pier opening and I don't think we can pull anyone off other duties."

"Like I keep telling you, there isn't any money in the budget for more officers. You're all just going to have to do your jobs without whining about it." The chief slammed his hand down on the desk. "After all, how hard can it be to keep a bunch of women in line?"

"It wasn't the women I was thinking about so much as the mobs that always seem to gather at suffrage events. The marchers are likely to be hurt by protesters if it doesn't look like we are there keeping an eye on things."

"I have no intention of wasting our budget on them. In fact, I am looking forward to seeing them get their comeuppance when things get ugly." The chief flashed Yancey a rare smile. "Should be a good show. I plan to have a front-row seat."

"So you don't care if people get hurt?" Yancey knew he shouldn't feel surprised, but he did. The chief was a hard man and a self-serving crook but he wouldn't have thought he'd be so outspoken about his willingness to shirk his duty. There had to be something more behind his attitude. Knowing Hurley, it came down to a payoff or a political alliance. Hurley hadn't kept his job for as long as he had without some well-connected politicians supporting him for reasons of their own. Yancey was going to try like hell to find out who was the one doing the paying.

It was no surprise the chief was unwilling to expend resources. After all, if he used money to pay the officers there would be less left in the coffers to line his own pockets. But surely even that greedy bastard wouldn't want out-and-out rioting in the streets. At least not just days before the pier opened. What would his cronies on the board at the pier company or the board of selectmen think if the town garnered the sort of bad press such a thing would produce? Surely no one would want that just before the biggest event in the town's history was scheduled to take place?

"If those women haven't sense enough to stay home where they belong instead of making a spectacle of themselves in the streets I'd say society will be better off with a few of them put out of commission." He pointed a stubby finger at the door of his office. "You take Frank and whichever other officers are on duty tomorrow and make do or I'll replace you with someone who will." Hurley lifted the paper in front of his face again and gave it a thorough shake. Yancey knew there was no arguing with him. There never was.

Yancey pulled the door behind him hard enough that the plate glass window in the front of the station rattled in its pane. The other officers looked up but no one said a thing. The chief had that effect on most of the members of the department but he got under Yancey's skin worst of all. He tried not to let the corrupt bastard get to him but every time he saw his face, instead of the podgy middle-aged man before him his memory supplied the image of a much younger man. The man who had arrested Yancey's father for the murder of Gladys Willard, a young singer at a local dance hall.

There had been no doubt that Oren Yancey had been romantically entangled with Miss Willard at the time she had been found strangled in the grubby little room she shared with another girl. There had also been no doubt about the heated argument that had taken place between the elder Yancey and the victim not long before her death. The two were overheard by other residents of the rooming house quarreling about Miss Willard's refusal to leave town with Mr. Yancey in order to start a new life together funded by the money he had embezzled from the bank where he worked.

What had been surprising was Oren Yancey's shock at her death and his subsequent arrest. He had proclaimed his innocence right up until it appeared he took his own life by hanging himself in a cell at the jail in the neighboring town of Saco. Yancey could still see the sly look on Hurley's face when he had accompanied his mother to the station to retrieve his father's effects. He didn't believe his father killed Miss Willard then and he didn't believe it now. He was even less convinced that Oren Yancey had killed himself.

Yancey had joined the army in a cowardly attempt to leave the gossip and the reputation his family endured as far behind him as he possibly could. But there was at least as much to try to forget from his time in the army as his childhood in Old Orchard. When he'd found he had his fill of making bad memories, he came home determined to lay his father's ghost and Gladys Willard's to rest by joining the police force and poking into the cold case. He'd been surprised when Hurley had hired him on but

Yancey figured if he was given a chance to access files and the authority to question people he wasn't going to second-guess the chief's motivations. Still, despite himself, everything about his boss rubbed him the wrong way.

Frank stood at Yancey's desk, fishing the last fritter out of the box. Not that Yancey cared. He'd lost his appetite completely.

"What's got you so riled up?" Frank asked through a mouthful of fried food.

"There's a suffrage march scheduled for tomorrow and the chief won't authorize any additional officers to help keep the peace," Yancey said. "He's got to have a reason for being so irresponsible, hasn't he?" Frank often had more insight into the chief's motivations than Yancey did. Ever since Frank had been involved in the death of a prisoner he had been tucked right down in Hurley's pocket. Yancey was never sure anymore where Frank's loyalties lay but he was content to make use of his insider knowledge whenever possible

"He's a member of one of those anti-suffrage organizations. Rumor has it his wife has joined the suffrage movement. I'm thinking he's hoping if things get too ugly she'll scurry back where she belongs. He's made several mentions lately of meals left in the oven for him while the missus went out to some meeting or other." Frank gave Yancey a smile. "Glad my wife knows her place." Yancey's stomach tied itself into a double knot. The chief could say what he wanted about hoping the crowd got out of hand but Yancey doubted his boss would hold that position when he witnessed the danger to his wife. He hated to consider the sort of dressing-down in store for an officer who allowed harm to come to Mrs. Hurley.

Yancey's thoughts turned to what he knew of Frank's young

wife, Sadie Nichols. From what he had observed from infrequent invitations to dinner at the Nichols home, he was certain her lack of involvement in the cause of suffrage was purely her own decision. She deftly allowed Frank to think he was in charge while always doing exactly as she pleased. Even their daughter, who was barely walking, had more say in the household than Frank did.

Yancey kept his thoughts to himself about the balance of power in the Nichols marriage. After all, with no wife of his own he was hardly the one to venture an opinion on that state of affairs. Besides, he and Frank had managed to patch together an uneasy peace after Frank had been involved with violence against a suspect that left him beholden to the chief in ways that worried Yancey. While he still couldn't quite dismiss the idea that Frank was keeping an eye on him for their boss he didn't need anything rocking the leaking boat of their partnership. Sharing a confidence might go a ways toward mending fences.

"My mother and my sister are involved with organizing the march. In fact, Lucy is acting as Miss Foster Eldridge's personal secretary while she's in town." Yancey felt a vein in his forehead twitch as he said the words aloud. In his mind's eye he could see his mother and little sister sailing up Washington Avenue on the way to a rally, their chins held high, daring jeering men standing along the sidewalk to pelt them with rocks or rotted produce. He was especially irked to realize his thoughts turned also to the image of Miss Proulx striding alongside them with her deep red parasol held at the ready in case of trouble.

He had no reason to think the unsettling Miss Proulx had changed one whit in the weeks since she had struck her head on the pavement after fighting off a pickpocket with that very same parasol. He doubted very much she would accept harassment any more demurely than anything else. Having had more than enough experience with angry mobs out West, his guts churned at the notion of those three ladies putting themselves in harm's way.

"Then that Miss Proulx is sure to be in the thick of things as well, isn't she?" Frank asked, winking at Yancey. "I expect her involvement worries you at least as much as your womenfolk's."

"Miss Proulx is no special concern of mine other than the fact that she is my sister's closest friend. Any particular attention I pay to her is to ensure she does not have the opportunity to lead Lucy astray. Unfortunately, they seem to egg each other on."

"I saw the two of them dressed in them cycling getups whizzing down Old Orchard Street." Frank shook his head. "I'd be careful about getting any more involved with a girl like that if I were you. Have you seen them in that nonsense? A woman should look like one, as far as I'm concerned."

Yancey had seen them in their matching cycling outfits. After all, the two of them had taken turns standing on a wooden stool in his family's parlor, his mother crouched before them, her mouth filled with pins, fitting them in the tight-waisted jackets and matching knickerbockers. He distinctly remembered enjoying the unobstructed view of Miss Proulx's well-turned calves in her dark stockings when his mother tacked up the hem on the cuff of Miss Proulx's pair. Just thinking of it tightened his throat.

"What Miss Proulx does or doesn't wear is no concern of mine."

"You keep telling yourself that and maybe you'll be able to convince someone that it's true." Frank elbowed Yancey in the ribs. "Every time that girl is anywhere in range you look like you're having some sort of a fit."

"I certainly do not." Yancey had suspected Frank wasn't particularly observant for a policeman and here was the proof. There

was no way on God's green Earth Miss Proulx could reduce him
to fits. No matter how shapely her calves or how expertly she
fended off attackers armed with nothing more than determina-
tion and an unorthodox wielding of a lady's accessory.

"You do, too. Whenever Miss Proulx shoves into view you
start blinking like you're cutting onions and your posture straight-
ens like your trouser seat's been showered with sparks from a
passing train."

Yancey stepped away and pulled some messages from the nail
on his desk. He thumbed through them in an effort to discourage
Frank from venturing more unwanted opinions. But the content
of the messages simply didn't register. The words swam before
his eyes and were replaced by first the memory of Miss Proulx's
delicate ankle bones and then the thought of her, ankles and all,
being trampled in a crush as scores of terrified women fled down
Grand Avenue barely ahead of an armed mob.

Chapter Sixteen

A LITTLE BIRD TOLD ME YOU'VE BEEN INVITED TO MAKE A DIS-play of yourself before the suffrage rally by our celebrated guest." Mrs. Doyle, the Belden's formidable cook and house-keeper and Honoria's trusted advisor, rocked a large knife over a pile of onion slices, cutting them aggressively into fine pieces. I didn't like to imagine what Mrs. Doyle thought about while she was chopping things. I often caught myself wondering if it was me she was imagining under her glinting blade.

Mrs. Doyle and I had gotten off to a rocky start when I had first arrived at the hotel. She had informed me that she was keep-ing a sharp eye on me to be sure I was not as lacking in morals as my father. Then she fixed me with a soul-singeing scowl. It wasn't until sometime later that she revealed her sharp looks were not meant to convey dislike. Rather, she was evaluating my aura.

Mrs. Doyle's psychic talent lay in the reading of auras. She claimed she could see lies. Nothing about her suggested to me she was making such a thing up. In fact, she had known from the color of my aura about the voice without my saying a thing about it. It was from her that I first learned that others had heard voices and had not been sent to the lunatic asylum. *Clairaudient* she had called that ability and she told me my mother had experienced it, too.

While we had come a long way because of our shared allegiance to the hotel and Honoria and even a surprising degree of affection, I was wary of losing her hard-won good opinion of me. I wasn't sure if she approved or disapproved of the idea of suffrage.

"Was your little bird a person here at the Belden or an article in the newspaper?"

"Your aunt may have been a bit distracted since her dream but she wouldn't neglect to tell me something as important as that. Why don't you seem more pleased to be offered such an opportunity?"

Mrs. Doyle squinted at me as she always did when assessing my aura. She checked my aura the way some women check children's faces for milk mustaches. Even though I understood what her piercing look meant it still made me cringe. I couldn't help but feel far too exposed whenever she turned her attention fully on me. I knew better than to lie so I stuck to the truth no matter how little of it I divulged.

"I'm flattered that Sophronia has taken an interest in me and wants to provide more publicity for the hotel. It feels like a once-in-a-lifetime opportunity and one that could help to keep the Belden profitable by being associated with someone as well-known as Sophronia," I said. "But, I do feel uncomfortable standing in front of a crowd and having them all looking at me. The idea of public scrutiny disquiets me. I wanted to leave all such displays behind me when I left the medicine show."

"I can see that you're bothered by this," she said. Mrs. Doyle laid the knife aside and reached onto the counter behind her. She flicked a dampened tea towel off a plate and offered me a jam tart. "As well you should be. I told Honoria so myself when she came in all aflutter with the idea of you parading about in front of the masses." I bit down on the small tart.

The flavor of tiny wild blueberries bound together with a sugary thickened juice burst upon my tongue with a brightness that should have made me forget my troubles, if only for a moment. But instead, the scowling look on Mrs. Doyle's face made me worry all the more.

"Do you have reservations about suffrage for women?" I asked. I knew a little of Mrs. Doyle's history and would have expected her to be all for a cause that allowed women better control of their destinies.

When Honoria and my mother were small girls Mrs. Doyle had bundled up her own daughter and slipped out in the night to escape from a husband who was quick to turn to the bottle and even quicker at turning his fists on his wife. She sought shelter with my grandparents at the Belden and had been there ever since. It had been a lucky thing for her that Mr. Doyle had been claimed by the sea the very night she left him.

"I have no disagreement with women speaking up and asking for what should have always been our due."

"What is it, then?" I asked. "You don't seem pleased about my involvement with the cause."

"My reservations concern that Foster Eldridge woman, not suffrage itself." Mrs. Doyle swept the onions into a large pot then seasoned them with a generous amount of salt. "Her aura is too muddy for my liking."

Mrs. Doyle had explained to me how she saw the lies once

before. According to her, the aura should be made up of clear bright color. When a person lies to spare someone's feelings or to make life better for another their aura gets lighter and harder to see. Which she claims is where the term *white lies* comes from. But the other sort of lies, those that people tell for gain or to wriggle out of responsibility for their actions, those are blacker, grayer, or even brown. All are muddy auras and raise a red flag with Mrs. Doyle.

"She lives a controversial life. And she seems to spend her time steeped in animosity. Could her aura be caused by that rather than by lies she tells?" I asked. Mrs. Doyle peeled butcher's paper from a beef tongue. She lowered it onto the onions and reached for a bundle of herbs hanging from a hook above her head.

"I suppose there could be many reasons for what I see with my own two eyes. Lying is the most common cause of an aura like hers but in rare cases other unpleasantnesses can account for it, too." She hoisted the pot and lugged it to the deep sink, where she filled it with water. "Still, none of the reasons she might have for a muddy aura will be good for you."

"I don't suppose they are good for Sophronia, either."

"Sophronia's troubles are none of my concern. But yours are yoked together with the Belden's and that makes them mine."

"Did you tell Honoria what you thought of the idea of me conducting platform readings?" I asked. I felt a small surge of hope. Mrs. Doyle's opinion meant a great deal to Honoria. It was a rare thing for my aunt to discount it. The last time she did so was when Mrs. Doyle suggested Honoria leave me to find my own way in the world when it looked as though the Belden might be forced to close.

"Indeed I did. I told her I didn't like to think of the sort of influence Sophronia might gain over you. You are at an important stage in developing your gift. I don't want to see it tainted by such a person." Mrs. Doyle turned her back to me. I could still hear her as she banged the pot down on the stove and added a lid to the pot. "Honoria said our notorious guest has brought a great deal of prestige to the Belden by choosing to stay with us. She said we still need all the help we can get to overcome the difficulties we endured last month." Honoria was right about that. In June the hotel's reputation had been thoroughly besmirched by criminality and if it had not been for the generosity of the Velmont sisters, Honoria would have lost the hotel. I felt the last flicker of hopefulness die out. If Mrs. Doyle couldn't change Honoria's mind there would be no changing of it at all.

"It looks like I will be giving platform readings whether I am afraid to do so or not," I said. Mrs. Doyle waved her red hand in front of her face as if to physically brush away my words.

"I wouldn't be sure about that. A great deal can happen between now and the time you are expected to take the stage."

"But Honoria has committed me for the march tomorrow. What could possibly happen to intercede between now and then?"

"A great deal, if I have my way. But, I think it best that you not go asking too many questions." Mrs. Doyle turned her back to me. "I think we'll start by keeping you too busy to spend much time with Miss Foster Eldridge."

I felt my heart sink. I had no desire for Mrs. Doyle to be thinking of extra things for me to do. I already had a full schedule between tarot card readings, séances, and the ways Honoria required my help entertaining the guests. Still, it was never good to rile Mrs. Doyle and if there was a chance I could get out of the platform reading without alienating Sophronia I was willing to do most anything.

"What did you have in mind for me to do?"

"That man with all the hay fever notions is not satisfied with the way his room is being dusted. Since I understand you are the one who sent him to me with his concerns, you may go into town to fetch a new feather duster just for him." Mrs. Doyle gave me a final scowl and then shooed me off. "Millie needs it as soon as possible so you'd best get going straightaway."

Chapter Seventeen

Old Orchard Street was busier than I'd ever seen it. Bicycles, carriages, and automobiles clotted the length of the street with activity and people of all ages did likewise along the sidewalks. I thought I had grown accustomed to the cheerful merrymakers and the air of excitement the coming of the pier created but as I moved along with the tide of people my heart lightened and I struggled not to begin whistling.

The words of a cook from one of the medicine shows I'd worked with Father came back to me at times like these. "Whistling girls and cackling hens all come to very bad ends." I stopped dead in my tracks and felt jostling from people behind me who hadn't expected an obstruction in their path.

This was exactly the sort of thing Sophronia was working for. It wasn't just the vote. It wasn't just big things suffrage was trying to address. It was the small, everyday slights and inequalities. Why should boys and men be allowed to express happiness by whistling but girls and women were told to keep their happiness to themselves? And at the same time we were relentlessly told to smile should our faces take on a serious expression.

I looked around me at the people going about their business, women shaded in extravagant hats walking sedately under the weight of their garments, men hurrying to and fro in seersucker trousers and straw hats. It struck me as inordinately unfair and my temper started to flare. It was as if all the things Sophronia had said to me were crystalizing in that one old rhyme learned long ago. I was overcome with the urge to throw my own hat in the air and take off running down the long stretch of beach just like a small boy would be permitted to do. The temptation was almost overwhelming.

But while I was feeling sufficiently emboldened to buck the conventions of society in general, I was not feeling brave enough to thwart Mrs. Doyle. I turned my wandering feet away from the shore and up toward Palmer's Mercantile, where a new feather duster was sure to be in stock. As I approached the shop a familiar figure caught my eye. Sophronia, clad unseasonably all in black, was making her way determinedly up the hill. Surely she must have suffered in the heat despite the parasol she held above her head and the fan she waved in front of her face.

She stopped abruptly a few paces away from the man I was surprised to recognize as the one who had heckled her at the rally. He seemed to be waiting for her and took a few steps into a secluded alley leading away from the main thoroughfare. I watched as she closed the distance between them in a few quick strides and addressed him. Given the outburst at the rally I decided in that moment it might be in Sophronia's best interest to keep an eye on her so long as she was in his company.

I moved up the street doing my best to keep them in sight without appearing to do so. As I drew closer, I saw the congressman's expression. His eyes were narrowed to angry slits and a deep groove appeared between his brows. With the distance and the clamor of the passing carriages and motorcars on the street I could not hear what was said. Congressman Plaisted held out both hands in front of his chest in what looked like supplication.

Sophronia smiled, shook her head slowly, then leaned toward him and tapped him square in the center of his chest with the edge of her fan in what could have been interpreted as a playful gesture. Without hesitation the congressman used both hands to shove her away. She stumbled backward and her head struck the brick wall of the adjacent building.

He looked down at her with an expression of surprise, as though he could not quite believe what he had done. I reached for the edge of my skirt to rush up the street to her aid. But then Plaisted turned on his heel and set off back down the street quickly enough to garner attention from passersby. I started once more in her direction to ask if she was all right but the voice spoke in my ear.

"Watch instead."

I held my ground and kept my eyes on Sophronia. She stood watching Congressman Plaisted's retreating form until he was out of sight. Rather than the look of pain I expected to see on her face there was a look of satisfaction instead. She reached up to adjust her hat then stepped out of the alley and headed off in the direction of the Belden.

I considered hurrying down the wide avenue after her but thought better of it. Sophronia's affairs were none of my concern. Honoria had impressed upon me how important it was to draw a line between providing guests with every comfort and meddling in things we ought not. Besides, Mrs. Doyle would be wanting the new feather duster she had requested. There would be no peace at the Belden until the persnickety Mr. Fredericks was satisfied that his room could be kept absolutely dust free.

CHAPTER EIGHTEEN

I F IT WOULD NOT HAVE ATTRACTED UNWANTED NOTICE I WOULD have run all the way back to the Belden. Between Sophronia's announcement that I would be expected to conduct a public reading and the emotions brought to mind by the violence I had witnessed I was desperate to hide away until I had gained mastery of myself. Arriving at last at the hotel I had the good fortune to hand the feather duster over to Millie rather than to Mrs. Doyle, lest she find more errands for me to run. Still finding myself of agitated mind and spirit I did what I found most soothing and headed for my beloved bedroom sanctuary.

Even though I do not remember her, the idea that the space belonged to my mother long before I arrived to enjoy it, comforts me. Ever since arriving at the Belden the pleasure of having a room of my own has been amongst my favorite experiences of my life. I adored the furnishings, the draperies, the view of the beachgoers in all their finery, and the sparkling sea. But most of all, I cherished the lock.

Life on a medicine show is grueling. The days are long and the conditions are harsh. Grime and hunger and discomfort are constant companions. Privacy is as scarce as lasting results from the bottles of cure-all my snake oil salesman father had hawked day after day. Tents and the backs of wagons afforded no privacy. There were no doors to close and so there were no locks to secure them.

I wish I could report that there had been no need for such security but in truth, that was just not so. Thieves and swindlers, drunkards and men with thoughts of violence pricking at the corners of their minds provided a steady supply of worry. But no matter how much a young woman might wish she could secure a door against all such dangers, she simply could not do so. Instead, one had always to be vigilant, to be on guard against those seeking to take advantage of her inattention. At any moment one could lose the contents of her purse. Or far worse.

Every time I turned the lock I held my breath to better hear the click as it secured the heavy walnut door. As I did so, I sent up a word of thanks to whatever power might be responsible for my change of fortune. While I did not believe in any particular deity, I did believe in being grateful. I had not missed my father for a moment since we parted ways. In fact, I had come to realize I was thoroughly relieved to be rid of his constant presence. Seeing Sophronia on the receiving end of a violent outburst brought unwanted memories flooding into my mind.

I crossed to the bed and climbed up onto its firm mattress. I lay on my side and curled into a ball, suddenly overcome with a chill despite the warmth of the day. I slipped my hand beneath my pillow and reached for the familiar feel of the timeworn envelope I always kept there. I told myself I needn't pull it out and look over the letter contained within. I knew it by heart just as surely as I could picture the photograph it also held.

When I was a young girl the letter, a missive from Honoria to my mother, as well as the photograph she had enclosed of the two of them smiling as they posed arm in arm in front of the Belden, had been my only knowledge of my mother's life. The only knowledge, that was, besides the scraps of information that stuttered and slipped from my father's lips when he had consumed far more whiskey than any man ought, and forgot himself completely. A bitter taste rose in my throat as I remembered the many times I had endured the same sort of treatment I had witnessed between Sophronia and Congressman Plaisted just to hear a word or two about the woman who had given birth to me.

I lay there contemplating the change in my circumstance and how eager Honoria had been to tell me all about her sister. Everything about my new life filled me with gratitude and I did not want to imagine losing any of it. I stared at the heavy wooden door with its shiny brass lock and I felt an almost overwhelming urge to break down and cry. Sophronia's invitation and Honoria's acceptance of it might cost me everything. A sob started to make its way up my throat. I felt heartily ashamed. I was well aware that I was guilty of many things but I was loath to think self-pity might be amongst them.

I closed my eyes and a picture of Johnny, my friend from the medicine show, filled my mind. I could envision his warm, wide smile, his long black braid, the look of his strong hands as he shuffled my tarot deck when day in and day out he asked for a reading. Before I could stop it I imagined, too, his body prone on the floor of the show tent, electrocuted by my participation in my father's latest get-rich-quick scheme. There was nothing to do but to let the tears flow. For Johnny, for myself, for all the women denied the rights that could keep them safe from treacherous men like my father.

I had just gotten myself in hand once more when I heard a knock land on the door. I sprang from the bed to answer it. I felt exceedingly guilty at lying down in the middle of the day and foolish for giving in to my tears, and the knock startled me to action. I turned the lock and pulled open the door. Lucy, clutching an envelope, stood on the threshold. While it did me no credit I admit I was relieved that she seemed too distressed herself to notice my red eyes or rumpled bed.

"I have to show you something," she said. She closed the door behind her and locked it once more. She held out the envelope. "This came in the morning post. I wasn't sure what to do with it." I slid a piece of cheap stationery from the envelope and stared down at the message printed in block letters across its surface in heavy black ink.

> *Your threats to expose men in power will amount to nothing. You are a disgrace to the nation and to the sacred state of womanhood. Cancel the march or you will not live long enough to be sorry.*

I turned the envelope over to inspect it more closely. It was addressed to Sophronia in care of the Belden. There was no return address, no stamp, and no postmark, either.

"Where did you find this?" I asked.

"It was in the bundle of mail addressed to Sophronia that Ben handed to me when I arrived this morning. Why do you ask?"

"Because it must have been hand delivered. See?" I pointed at the front of the envelope. "No postmark and no postage."

"That means whoever sent it is here in town." Lucy bit her lower lip.

"Has Sophronia seen it?"

"No. She asked that I deal with the correspondence while she is in Old Orchard." Lucy bit her lower lip again. "Do you think it's just someone making idle threats or should I be concerned?"

"I have no idea. But I am inclined to take it seriously. It would be better to take precautions than to expose Sophronia or any of the marchers to danger." I felt worried about Sophronia's safety and Lucy's. In fact, I worried for the safety of all the women who were planning to attend the march the next day.

"Do you think we must report it to the police?" Lucy plucked the letter from my hands and looked it over once more like it held the answer to her question.

"Maybe it would be best. It wouldn't do the suffrage cause a great deal of good if Sophronia comes to harm." I crossed the room to the turret and pulled back the curtain to look at the sparkling sea. On the sand below, children, tin pails clutched in their hands, ran ahead of their mothers. Men clad in woolen bathing costumes strode purposely toward the beach and slowed as their feet touched the frigid water. I wondered how many of those men shared the letter writer's sentiments about the place of women.

"But if Warren finds out he will say he was right to object to me associating myself with Sophronia and will have even more to say about my participation in the march. Besides, I don't feel right about going to the police without Sophronia's consent." I could see her point. Officer Yancey had been high-handed and, in my opinion, unsupportive at the rally. As much as I wished my part in the march might be called off, I made it a rule to avoid involving myself with the police whenever possible. But maybe Sophronia would feel inclined to call off the march herself if she knew about the letter. That thought made up my mind.

"Of course you mustn't do anything behind Sophronia's back. Do you know where she is right now?"

"She's in her room practicing her speech for tomorrow."

"Then, by all means, let's show this to her."

CHAPTER NINETEEN

Sophronia had returned from her trip into town and from the sounds of it, was unruffled by her encounter with Congressman Plaisted. Her impassioned voice penetrated the door as Lucy and I approached her room. I worried she might not hear my knock. But after a pause in the sound from behind the door I knocked again and she bid us enter. We did so and found her holding a sheaf of papers, her back to the sea, a glistening bit of perspiration dampening her hairline.

"Forgive me, I was practicing my speech for tomorrow and as usual found myself caught up in the urgency of the cause." She sat on the edge of the bed and drew a deep breath. More than ever she reminded me disconcertingly of my father and the energy he had expended to give a well-received performance. It was not a comforting thought. "What brings the two of you to my room looking so disquieted?"

Lucy held out the letter, envelope and all. Sophronia slipped out the thin paper and read it over quickly.

"You weren't worried about this, were you, ladies?" Sophronia gifted us one of her charming smiles and even gave a little laugh.

"We were, rather," Lucy said, blushing a little. She looked at the floor and I noticed the skin on the back of her neck reddening.

"While I am touched by your concern, you needn't give things like this a moment's worry." Sophronia said. "In fact, I am over-joyed that this has happened." I thought I must have misheard her. Surely no one would take pleasure in a letter such as that? Lucy seemed to be thinking the same thing from the darting glance she gave me.

"How can you possibly be pleased by this? Aren't you fright-ened?" I asked.

"Certainly not. It just confirms that the article in the newspa-per this morning about the march is having the intended effect." She crossed to the desk and set her sheaf of notes on its polished surface. The top of the desk was littered with towering stacks of paper and discarded candy wrappers. Vases of flowers dropped withered petals on the nightstand. I caught myself wondering what the fastidious Mr. Fredericks would have to say about dead flowers in a bedroom. "I'm sure the newspaper would be eager to run a follow-up article reporting how I have been threatened with violence as a result of my willingness to take a stand for my beliefs."

"I think you should take it more seriously than that. The letter was hand delivered. Whoever sent it is near enough by to actually do you harm." I thought again of the scene I had witnessed be-tween Sophronia and Congressman Plaisted. "Perhaps it would be best to consider postponing the march until tempers are not quite so inflamed."

"I've received dozens of letters just like this one over the years and they've never amounted to anything. I use them to bring a bit of attention to the cause whenever they occur." Sophronia's hand reached up and gently touched the back of her head. A flicker of pain passed over her face and I wondered how injured she actually had been when the congressman threw her against the wall. Perhaps she had been too stunned or too scared to let it show in the alley. "I have never canceled before and a letter such as this one gives me no reason to do so now."

"Have you ever threatened to publish an exposé of men in power before now?" I asked.

"I have not. I didn't want to lower myself to such ugliness if it could be avoided, but over time I have become convinced it is necessary to use whatever weapons one can lay hands upon in this fight for our rights."

"Then you might consider the possibility that the writer may have more reason to threaten you than any other anonymous man with a poisoned pen in the past."

"You might be right. Maybe this time we'll be lucky and the letter writer will actually try to make good on his threats. Imagine all the press coverage an out-and-out riot would garner."

I stared in surprise at Sophronia, whose eyes shone like she had contracted a fever. I stole a look at Lucy, whose expression registered fear followed immediately by admiration.

"You can't mean that. All sorts of people could be hurt if someone makes good on those threats."

"Of course I mean it. One cannot expect great rewards without being willing to make great sacrifices."

"Then won't you at least notify the police ahead of time?" I asked, surprised to hear myself making such a suggestion. Sophronia's eagerness to incite a riot had me thoroughly rattled. "To alert them to the threat and ask for additional protection?"

"I have never relied on protection from the police or anyone else in the past. I am more than capable of protecting myself, no matter what the circumstances." Sophronia patted a thick stack of paper perched precariously on the top of the desk. "Now you'll both have to excuse me. I have a telephone call to place to the newspaper straightaway. If this is to be a help stirring even greater interest in the rally tomorrow there is no time to waste."

Chapter Twenty

It was all well and good for Sophronia to throw caution to the wind concerning her own safety but it was an entirely different matter to endanger her supporters. My mind whirled and I found my thoughts turning once again to the counsel my deck of cards had provided. I made my way down the wide front stairway. Light streamed in through the tall window overlooking Saco Bay. As I hurried past I recognized Henry, one of the boys who drove a Peanutine cart along the beach. An eager gaggle of children had flagged him down just in front of the Belden and I wished for a moment I had as few cares as those little ones holding out their pennies in exchange for some candy.

I slipped down the hall and into the séance room. I opened a drawer in the small walnut desk at the end of the room and withdrew a satin drawstring bag. My tarot cards were the one thing that always brought me comfort when my mind was ill at ease. I took the deck to the cloth-covered table in the center of the room and sat in one of the chairs. As I shuffled the deck I felt a familiar sense of calm descend upon me and before long I focused my thoughts on a single question.

"What should I do about Sophronia's threatening letter?" I whispered aloud. I shuffled again and again until three different cards urged me to tug them from the deck. I lay them one by one, facedown in front of me. I exhaled a long, slow breath then turned over the first card.

I stared at the image before me and waited for an interpretation. Five of Swords. *"Chaos, confusion, strife,"* the voice explained. It appeared my worries were justified.

I reached for the next card. Eight of Wands. *"Swift communication."* The voice spoke clearly into my left ear.

I hesitated before flipping the last card. I felt my breath catch in my throat when I saw the image. This card needed no explanation even though it was one that had not been part of my half of the tarot deck but rather had belonged to Honoria's portion. The Knight of Swords. It was a card I had pulled time and again in readings for Lucy or her mother, Orazelia, and it stood for Officer Yancey. I never would have thought myself as someone who turned to the police for help. But it looked like that was exactly what I should do.

The telephone at the Belden sat just off the lobby in a tiny room built under the stairs. A quick glance up and down the hall assured me no one would question what I was up to. Then I knocked on the telephone room door to be sure not to interrupt someone else's call, and hearing no response, let myself in. The operator's voice came on the line and for a moment I thought about replacing the receiver, the call abandoned. But the image of the Knight of Swords flashed through my mind and I requested to be put through to the police station. Officer Yancey, I was told, was out on patrol but was expected to call in for messages within the hour. I asked for him to meet me in the Belden's side garden at his earliest convenience. I added that I would appreciate it if he did not announce his presence. The man on the other end of the line sounded more amused than concerned. I was almost certain from his voice that it belonged to Mrs. Doyle's son-in-law, Frank Nichols. I thanked him and replaced the receiver. There was nothing to do now but wait.

Y ANCEY CONSIDERED WHAT COULD HAVE MOVED MISS PROULX to request him to pay a call, and a clandestine one at that. Frank had made it sound as though she were quite desperate to see him. He hadn't much cared for Frank's tone, either. He played out several unpleasant scenarios involving Lucy on his way to the hotel. By the time he reached his destination he felt overheated and out of sorts. He wished he had not just missed the dummy train and had been forced to hurry on foot. He wished even more that Hurley would allow the officers to patrol on bicycles. It would be much faster and cooler, too.

He hurried to the gate at the side of the Belden property and lifted the latch. The ocean breeze passed through the lavender and brought the musty scent mixed with the salty smell of the sea to his nose. The garden was not a large one, just large enough to supply blooms for the hotel and herbs for the kitchen.

Still, it took a bit of wandering through the tidy beds to find Miss Proulx. He saw the toe of a small brown boot sticking out from beneath an arbor smothered in some sort of twining vine, and without calling out headed toward it. Grass clippings muf-fled the sound of his footsteps and he came quite near before she looked up with a start.

"You said not to announce myself," he reminded her as he took a seat on the stone bench next to her. "I'm sorry if I frightened you." In truth Miss Proulx did look remarkably unsure of herself. Worried, in fact. Of all the things he had pictured on his way from the police station this had not been something he had envisioned. Truth be told, he thought he preferred her to display a defiantly raised chin rather than the hunched shoulders he saw before him.

"It isn't you that troubles me. Actually, I am very much afraid that I am about to be a bad suffragist and a worse hotelier," she said. "I wouldn't have called if it weren't for Lucy."

"Do you wish to report a crime?" Yancey knew it. His stomach knotted up as he pulled his small notebook from his jacket pocket. Miss Proulx laid a staying hand upon his forearm and slowly shook her head.

"Not as such. And I wish there to be no record of our conversation." She dropped her voice even lower. "Lucy found a threatening letter amongst Sophronia's correspondence today. The writer says if the march goes on there will be violence. It goes so far as to threaten Sophronia's life." Even with the cool breeze, small beads of perspiration formed along Miss Proulx's hairline. Yancey exhaled slowly as he watched a trickle make its way along her slim neck.

"Do you have the letter?"

"No. Sophronia kept it. It hadn't been posted, just slipped in through the letter slot."

"So the sender had to have been in town earlier at least."

"Yes. I mentioned that but all Sophronia did was laugh. She said she is used to such threats and isn't in the least worried."

"But you are?" Yancey was surprised. Miss Proulx was far more likely to take risks than he approved of. If she was concerned there had to be more to the story. She nodded.

"Were you listening to her speech at the rally when she threatened to expose some men in power and make examples of them?"

"Yes. It made quite an impression."

"I wonder if it was directed at Congressman Plaisted. I saw him with Sophronia earlier today in town and the conversation turned ugly."

Yancey thought of his conversation with Thomas. "Ugly how?"

"She said something to him that I was too far away to hear. He looked like he was pleading with her and when she shook her head he shoved her hard enough to throw her against the brick wall behind her."

"Did she seem injured?" Yancey asked.

"She didn't react at all at the time but when I saw her in her room later I noticed her feeling the back of her head like it bothered her," Miss Proulx said. "What worried me more though was the look on her face. She looked triumphant. It was as if she had been trying to provoke him to violence."

"Why do you think she would wish to anger him?" Yancey felt even more ill at ease than before.

"When Lucy brought the letter to Sophronia she said she was delighted with the attention it would bring to the cause and that she was pleased to have garnered a passionate reaction. She was positively cheered at the prospect of how much press coverage a riot would attract."

"Your Miss Foster Eldridge sounds quite ruthless. I'm not sure I'd be willing to trust her if I were a suffragist."

"I don't doubt her commitment to her cause. But it seems almost as though it is the ideal and not the individuals that interests her. If she needed to use someone to further her purpose she would not think twice about doing so. Nor would she feel remorse about whatever befell them."

"Is that why you wanted to see me?"

"I'm worried about Sophronia but I'm also worried about all the marchers," she said. "I fear there is the likelihood of real danger for all those involved."

"I think you have every reason to worry. People can become violent when they feel threatened," Yancey said.

"You think men feel threatened by a group of innocently marching women?" Miss Proulx asked.

"I would hardly describe Sophronia and her supporters as innocent." Yancey looked directly into her eyes and was surprised to see a look of guilt rather than fear. It was gone as quickly as it appeared. "At least not if the term implies naïveté. I think you should be prepared for more aggressive behavior than that exhibited at the rally."

"You think it could get as out of hand as that?"

"I do. I am concerned for Lucy and you and all of the other women involved. I spoke with Chief Hurley this morning to ask for extra officers to be assigned to patrol the march," Yancey said. "Not only did he flatly refuse, he said he had no intention of protecting any of you should the crowds turn ugly."

"So we shall have to fend for ourselves?" Miss Proulx's posture straightened even more. There was something about that girl that seemed to rise to a challenge. This time, Yancey worried the challenge might be too much for any of the people involved, himself included.

"I'll be there along with Frank and Officer Lewis." Yancey thought it best not to mention the chief planned to attend.

"Is that all?"

"There may be one or two others I haven't heard about," he said. "I wish you would assure me neither you nor Lucy will take any unnecessary risks. I can't shake the feeling something bad is in the offing."

"Do you often have a predictive gift, Yancey? I thought you had no truck with the metaphysical." Yancey was gratified to see the sparkle return to Miss Proulx's eyes. It was worth being the butt of some good-natured teasing to see her looking more like herself.

"I may not hold with claiming to speak with the dead but I never discount my instincts."

"Never?"

"Perhaps 'never' is an overstatement." Yancey's face clouded over. "Never that I have not soon regretted."

"Your instincts tell you something will happen at the march?"

"They do."

"Unfortunately, so do mine."

CHAPTER TWENTY-ONE

SOPHRONIA APPROACHED ME AS WE LEFT THE DINING ROOM.
"Ruby dear, I feel the need of some air to aid my digestion.
Will you take a stroll with me along the beach?" Her eyes were
sparkling and I felt quite sure digestion was not behind her request.

"Let me fetch my shawl and I will join you directly," I said. I
did not want to hear whatever it was that Sophronia wished to
confide. I dragged my feet all the way to the back hall cloakroom,
where a woolen shawl that had belonged to my mother was hanging on a peg. Honoria had kept all of my mother's clothing and
since I had arrived with nothing besides the garments on my
back I was grateful that she had done so. The shawl was a light-
weight confection of white, cobwebby lace. It was one of the pret-
tiest things I had ever seen.

Mrs. Doyle had been responsible for much of the finery found
in my mother's wardrobe. She had created a veritable fleet of
beautiful, if dated, hats complete with tiny flowers and satin and
velvet ribbons. She had added beaded stitching to delicate gloves
and even edged handkerchiefs with lace. Most miraculous of all

were the knitted items. I hardly dared to wear them for fear they would be damaged. Honoria convinced me Mrs. Doyle's well-hidden feelings would be hurt if I did not adorn myself with all her handiwork and so I had taken to wearing what seemed to me like something fit for a ballroom to wander the beach.

Sophronia stood pacing the veranda when I pushed open the French doors and stepped out into the night air. The breeze off the water made me glad I had taken the time to fetch the shawl. Sophronia tucked her arm through mine and drew me down the steps and onto the sand. We walked along silently until we had passed several other hotels and were out of earshot of any other promenaders.

"I wanted to speak with you about the platform reading to-morrow," she said, looking over her shoulder. "I don't wish to get in the way of your communing with the spirits but I would be very much obliged if you could be sure to mention one or two things during your reading. Whether a spirit moves you or not." My sense of disquiet increased and I thought once more of my conversation with Yancey. Still, if there were no way out of my obligation without telling Honoria why I was so eager to avoid the public eye I would have to acquiesce to her request. At least she was offering to trade favors rather than to blackmail me.

"What sort of things did you have in mind?" I asked.

"I have a phrase or two I would like you to slip into the overall reading. I completely trust your discretion as to how best to do so."

"And what are the phrases you wish a spirit to convey?" I stopped walking and faced her.

"I would be very appreciative if you would mention February the fifteenth." Sophronia looked me in the face. The bright light of the nearly full moon shone down on us and made it easy to see her persuasive smile. "I also would like you to mention bribery and unfaithful partners. Do you think you can work those into your routine?" I was uneasy. I could certainly incorporate such broad ideas into any reading whatsoever. But despite my lack of confidence concerning the source of the voice or the insights it provided to those who consulted me I was loath to call what I did a routine.

In the time I had been at the Belden my understanding and acceptance of my abilities had grown. When I first arrived I had worried that my readings were based entirely on my ability to read people rather than on any contact with anything truly otherworldly. I was unsure of the source of the voice I heard and more than that, I was frightened to admit to anyone that I heard it.

As my faith in the possibility of the metaphysical grew I came to believe what I did was more than simple chicanery or even finely honed observational skills. When Mrs. Doyle told me my aura was that of a clairaudient I felt a profound sense of relief and of belonging.

I had never considered the possibility that what I was experiencing was a gift to be valued rather than a form of insanity or a grubby knack for trickery. Hearing what I did called a "routine," as if it were a medicine show performance, felt tawdry and wrong. I felt an overwhelming desire to vigorously defend myself against Sophronia's assumptions.

"Hold your tongue."

Despite my conviction the voice was mistaken to counsel me to essentially admit to wrongdoing by not contradicting Sophronia, I did as the voice instructed. But I didn't have to like it.

"You wish me to mention all three of those topics at the march tomorrow?" I asked, working to keep my voice neutral.

"Yes, if you can manage it." Sophronia squeezed my arm. "But what am I saying? A talented young woman such as yourself will accomplish this request with remarkable ease."

Without another word we turned back toward the Belden, reaching the veranda once more in only a few moments. Despite the warmth of the shawl and the mildness of the evening I felt chilled to the bone. Sophronia bid me a good night's sleep and left me alone with my thoughts as I looked out over the dark waters of Saco Bay.

I STOOD ON THE VERANDA UNTIL THE DAMP NIGHT AIR HAD soaked through my shawl and onto my skin. Even then I was not eager to step away from the soothing sound and smell of the sea. Ever since arriving in Old Orchard I'd been startled to find a comfort in the proximity of the ocean. I had never seen it before I had come to the Belden but now that I had it was as though an ache I never knew I experienced had eased.

Finally the cool damp was too much for me and the body demanded more than the spirit. I headed for the kitchen with the anticipation there would at least be residual heat from the cookstove to warm myself a bit before I made my way up to bed. I was in no hurry, being certain I would find it difficult to fall asleep after my encounter with Sophronia. I wandered listlessly down the back hallway and into the kitchen.

Mrs. Doyle sat in an old maple rocker in the corner as if waiting for me to arrive. She looked up from a sock she had stretched over a darning egg. A large hole marred the toe and she was busy pulling a fine, threaded needle through the gap. She waved me toward her and gave me her customary squint.

"You look all off-kilter, child. Is that woman still bothering you?" She laid the wooden darning egg in her lap and gave me her complete attention.

"I wasn't entirely honest with you before. I didn't lie but I didn't tell you the whole truth about what was said when Sophronia asked me to serve as a platform reader."

"I told myself at the time you held something back. Your aura wasn't really muddy but it was very faint." I knew there was no way to withhold information from Mrs. Doyle entirely. It was simply bound to come out no matter how well I thought I parsed the truth. "What is the trouble, girl?"

"It wasn't just that I had no desire to make a spectacle of myself upon the stage once more. It was also that Sophronia confided to me that she is not the medium she purports to be."

"Is that what's bothering you, child?" Mrs. Doyle waved her hand as if such a confession was of little consequence. After all, Sophronia wasn't plying her trade at the Belden and the reputation and success of the hotel was most often all that mattered to Mrs. Doyle.

"No, it wasn't that. She told me that she knew me to be a fraud and that she wanted me to use my performance skills to convince the crowds at the rally of the righteousness of the suffrage cause." Mrs. Doyle's lips thinned as she clamped them together. I decided to risk telling her a bit more. "Tonight she asked me to include three specific things in my readings tomorrow. She implied it would be worth our while for me to be sure to do so."

"She did, did she?" Mrs. Doyle set her mending aside in a basket on the floor next to the rocking chair and drew herself to her full height. "What did you say to that?" Mrs. Doyle crossed her thick arms over her pillowy chest and stared up at the tin ceiling like the answer to my dilemma was written in a code made of pressed leaves and ornate stars.

"I agreed to do as she asked." When Mrs. Doyle squinted at me once more I felt I needed an excuse. "The voice told me to fall in with her plans."

"Voice or no voice the Hotel Belden does not need favors from the likes of her." Mrs. Doyle untied her apron and hung it on a peg near the door. "I want you not to worry about this anymore. Mark my words, Miss Foster Eldridge is going to regret placing you and the Belden in such a position."

Whatever Mrs. Doyle was planning, I was quite sure I didn't want to know the details. It occurred to me, and not for the first time, that of all the people I had ever met, Mrs. Doyle was the one I would least want to have as an enemy.

Chapter Twenty-two

T HE MARCHERS LINED UP FOR THE LENGTH OF THREE BLOCKS down Grand Avenue. I had been prepared for a great number of participants but must confess that I had no real idea what more than five hundred women in a group would look like. A lump swelled in my throat as I looked at the Velmont sisters in the group in front of me, staring straight ahead and ignoring the jeers and cheers of the spectators.

The crowds that had gathered to watch were almost entirely composed of men. Nothing could have prepared any of us for what such a circumstance would feel like. As the drummers at the front of the line started tapping out a beat, and the marchers moved slowly forward, the noise from the bystanders increased in volume and hostility.

A few rows ahead of me Sophronia stood at the front of the line, holding a brightly colored standard that fluttered in the stiff sea breeze. With a clammy hand, I clutched the edge of the banner Orazelia had created and hoped I looked more confident than I felt. Even the stage at the medicine show had felt less intimidating.

Yancey had been right to be concerned about the threat of a mob. The language spilling from the mouths of well-dressed men I recognized as prominent local business owners would have put the medicine show roustabouts to shame. I felt rather than saw Lucy move closer to me as the line pressed ahead.

Dewitt Fredericks marched directly behind them. I imagined he was taking note of the sights, sounds, and smells for his book. As we drew closer and closer to the pier the crowds grew larger and spilled from the sidewalk. Men pressed in closer than polite society would ever allow and some even reached out their hands and snatched at the women's sleeves and the backs of their gowns. I wished I had thought to bring along my trusty parasol as protection. I looked right and left and behind but could not see Yancey or any police officers in sight.

We picked up speed as the jeers grew louder. I thought fleetingly of a pack of dogs and how the worst thing one could do was to break into a run and activate their instinct to chase. A woman bumped into me from behind and I stumbled. If I had been wearing a full-length gown I would have tripped and likely started a chain reaction. As it was, the cycling costume saved me from a fall.

Elva looked back at me and gave me a reassuring nod. I kept my eyes on Elva and Dovie. As the crowds grew increasingly rowdy I regretted telling the Velmonts their mother supported their plan to march. If anything happened to them I would not forgive myself.

Old Orchard Street hoved into view and the pier rose up on the right. Sophronia had arranged for a makeshift podium to be placed at the foot of the pier, and she intended to deliver her speech from there. It was also the place I was to use for the plat-

form reading. The lectern looked like it had been borrowed from
a local church. It sat upon a riser swathed with a deep blue fabric
hiding the underpinnings. I was reminded of the many stages I had
worked with my father in the medicine show over the years and I
was reminded once more of the similarities between Sophronia's
ability to attract an enthusiastic audience and Father's.

Even a seasoned showman like Father would have been impressed by the numbers Sophronia drew. The crowds at the junc-
tion of Old Orchard and Grand Avenue were larger than any I
had ever seen. They were so large, in fact, I felt a moment of
panic that we would be crushed to death. Even with the breeze
blowing about I suddenly was overwhelmed by the feeling there
might not be enough air to breathe.

I looked over at Lucy but she had eyes only for Sophronia,
who had come to a halt. Before the rest of the line was stopped
she was energetically mounting the steps to the podium. I made
my way through the crowd to the edge of the platform and she
beckoned for me to join her onstage. As I forced myself to mount
the first step I heard the voice.

"Stop. Look around. Remember what you see." The voice came
clearly into my ear despite the deafening noise of the crowd and
the background sound of waves crashing upon the nearby shore.

I swept my gaze all around the square. Standing near to the
podium up on a raised platform of his own was George's brother,
Osmond. Immediately to his left was Yancey's boss, Chief Hurley. They stood watching Sophronia and leaning toward each
other to exchange words. All at once, Henry, a young boy who
drove a Peanutine cart on the beach, darted up to the chief. He
yanked his cap off his head as he approached the older man. The
chief bent down and seemed to be speaking to him. I couldn't be

certain but I thought the chief handed him something. Henry nodded and ran off.

I strained to keep an eye on him as he approached a group of boys about his same age. After a moment the group disbanded and the boys scattered to the four winds. Something in their looks of excitement left me feeling uneasier than anything else I had witnessed during the march.

"Friends, I want to thank you for coming out today to support the cause of women's suffrage. It is with great pleasure I look out over such a robust army of women. I also feel overwhelming gratitude for the courageous support of the men in this community." Sophronia turned on a smile that would have outshone one of my father's and raised both her hands, spreading them out toward the crowd. The jeers increased in volume and it occurred to me that she was deliberately agitating her detractors.

From the sidelines photographers and men with notebooks chronicled the day's events. I felt more certain than ever from the gleam in her eyes that the safety of the marchers was of little consequence compared to the value of the press coverage for the cause.

"It is also clear that those who would deny us the same rights they enjoy are here in force as well." Sophronia paused and turned her gaze toward Chief Hurley and Osmond. I felt certain something unexpected was about to unfold. "My spirit guides assure me their time of unchecked and corrupt power is almost at an end." She turned to me and motioned with her hand that the time had come to join her in the center of the stage.

At Sophronia's words cheers went up from the marchers. A roar emanated from the crowd assembled around the edges. Flashes from the photographers' cameras went off in every direction. I looked out, hoping for some sort of sign all would be well. Mrs. Doyle appeared at the edge of the stage and instead of scowling at me like always she just stood there staring intently at Sophronia. Mrs. Doyle had promised she would get me out of the platform reading obligation. Unless she had a very last-minute plan it seemed as though it was a promise she would not be keeping. My throat became drier and the flutters in my stomach more insistent when I spotted Honoria standing near the Velmont sisters, all three wedged into the center of the marchers. I felt a squeeze in my heart as I considered all I had to lose if the newspaper coverage connected me with Johnny's death.

I took another step up the stairs that led onto the stage. Out of the corner of my eye I saw something soar through the air coming right toward me. Something hard struck me on my temple. I reached up as I felt a trickle of blood running down my cheek. Before I understood what was happening, all around me rocks and bottles and rotted pieces of fruit began to fly through the air.

Popping, sparking sounds like firecrackers erupted throughout the crowd. I frantically looked down at the marchers. They lurched and leaned, some even lost their balance completely and toppled to the ground. I tried to see the cause of the turmoil, and there in the middle of the chaos I noticed a number of young boys running through the assembled marchers, jostling and shoving them as they threaded through their midst. Little puffs of smoke followed on the trail of several of them.

I searched the crowd for those most dear to me. Lucy stood hunched over, protecting her head with her arms. Before I could spot any of my other friends I felt a tremor beneath my feet. My attention snapped back to the center of the stage. Sophronia's eyes widened and her mouth formed a circle of utter surprise. With a *whoosh* the stage, and the stairs leading up to it, collapsed beneath us both.

I lay stunned, splayed on my side, a wooden stair tread pressing into my rib cage. I tried to draw a breath and realized the fall had knocked the wind right out of me. Fleetingly, I wondered if Mrs. Doyle had knocked over the stage armed only with the power of her stare. The stampeding mob looked even more terrifying from the ground than it had from the stairs.

I ventured to sit up but the sharp pain from my ribs stopped me in my tracks. I sagged back down against the ground and then thought better of it as I realized several pairs of men's feet were running toward what was left of the stage. I winced with pain as air rushed back into my lungs.

"Miss Proulx, are you injured?" A pair of sturdy brown boots stopped just short of my head. Officer Yancey crouched over me, a look of earnest concern upon his face. "Can you move?"

"If you give me a hand I think I can stand." I hated to admit it but there was something very comforting about Officer Yancey's presence. He slipped an arm beneath me and helped me to my feet. The pain in my ribs caused me to flinch as I tried to turn. "Is Sophronia all right?" I asked.

The stage lay in a heap upon the brick square at the base of the pier. "I have no idea. Shall we find out?" he asked, offering me his arm. I hoped he was too distracted by the continuing turmoil to notice that my whole body seemed to be shaking. A ring of people, including several photographers and men with notebooks and pencils in their hands, crowded around what was left of the stage. With Officer Yancey's help I squeezed through the throng and peered into the center of the wreckage.

Sophronia sat on the ground. Blood oozed down her face from a long, jagged gash to her cheek. One of the men stepped forward and offered her a hand. She shook her head and scrambled to her feet unassisted.

She turned toward the photographers and journalists and gave a little wave. "I think it is safe to say someone doesn't want people to hear my message. But it will take more than a little tumble like that to get rid of me, gentlemen."

Chapter Twenty-three

YANCEY STOOD AT THE EDGE OF THE SALT POOL, WISHING HE could be in two places at once. He would give a great deal to be keeping another set of eyes on Lucy and his mother. The owner of the bathhouse, Pinckney Ferris, had turned away and brought up more of his breakfast. Not that Yancey could blame him. If he had managed to choke down more than a black cup of coffee before the call had come in he might have had trouble with his own stomach.

The pool sat in a courtyard sheltered from public view, next to the Sea Spray Hotel. Rumor had it that Robert Jellison, the owner of the Sea Spray, had been trying for months to convince Pinckney to sell him his popular bathhouse and pool. Water was let into the pool every couple of days and the sun heated it to a much more pleasant temperature than that of the open ocean.

People were willing to pay a pretty penny to soak in waters warmed by the sun that still contained the perceived benefits of the sea. Yancey had enjoyed the pool himself during his infrequent days off on a number of occasions since his return to Old

Orchard. He was sorry to think he would never be able to do so again without thinking of the body splayed inelegantly before him.

Sophronia Foster Eldridge looked far smaller in death. Perhaps it was her unusual clothing that created that impression. He knelt over her body and noticed a dark patch on her fair head.

"Did you see this, Frank?" he asked. "It looks like blood."

"I'm sure it is." Frank pulled a cruller from a paper sack in his hand and took an enormous bite, cascading powdered sugar onto the straining buttons of his uniform and onto Sophronia's corpse. "A woman like that was always going to come to an end like this."

"A woman like what?" Yancey looked up at Frank and wondered how they were going to be able to impartially pose questions when clearly his partner didn't care about the victim. He didn't even want to think about how all the ladies at the Belden would react to the news. Maybe Frank would get called in to help with something else and he'd be free to take Lewis with him to inform Honoria instead.

"An unnatural one. As far as I'm concerned she belonged in a nuthouse and the only mystery here is why we're even looking into this when she obviously killed herself."

"I think you've been spending too much time with the chief." Yancey looked up at the man he used to consider a friend. "You're starting to sound just like him."

"And I think you've been spending too much time in a house full of womenfolk." Frank crossed his arms over his broad chest and scowled. It wasn't likely that they were going to start getting along much better, so Yancey asked a question he knew wouldn't go over well with Frank.

"Has anyone gotten ahold of Thomas Lydale yet?"

"You aren't planning to call that ghoul in on every investigation from now on, are you?" Frank said. Frank had never gotten over his mother hiring Thomas to take a memorial photograph of Frank with his dead father. From what Yancey had heard, Frank had not reacted well to the experience and instead of owning up to his own fear had blamed Thomas for his discomfort.

"You seem to have forgotten how much he assisted in solving our last murder case," Yancey said. "Besides, with the department being stretched so thin lately I'm happy to make use of any technological assistance I can muster."

"You want him, you call him." Frank stomped off to the far end of the pool. Yancey spotted Lewis, looking eager to please, hovering near the still-queasy Pinckney Ferris. Yancey waved Lewis over.

"I'm going to send you out to telephone for Mr. Lydale, the photographer, but before I do, tell me what you see when you look at this body." Yancey leaned away to give Lewis a complete view of the deceased.

"She appears healthy, well formed. She's suffered a blow to the head but I think it took her by surprise." Lewis pointed to the side of her head where something clung to her hair, darkening the blond strands.

"What makes you say that?"

"She looks peaceful, not frightened." Lewis shrugged as if to apologize for having an opinion of his own. The kid was new but he had sharp eyes. Given enough time he'd make a far better detective than Frank. Maybe better than Yancey even.

"What else do you see? You can take a closer look if you'd like." Lewis knelt on the side of the pool.

"She's wearing a gentleman's coat. Not only is that a bizarre choice for a woman but it's been far too warm lately, night or day, to have need of a heavy layer."

"Check the pockets," Yancey said.

"May I touch her?" he asked. Yancey nodded then watched as Lewis gently laid his hands over the bulges Yancey had noticed in Sophronia's large overcoat pockets.

"Rocks?" Lewis asked.

Yancey nodded and pointed to the lumps around her ankles. "A whole lot of them. Designed to keep her body underwater once she went into the pool, I'd say."

"Do you think she drowned herself?"

"She might have done, but how do you explain the blow to her head?"

"She could have hit it on the edge when she entered the pool."

"It's a stretch but it is possible." Yancey straightened. "I had gotten the impression that she was the sort of person who would consider it a sin to rob the world of her presence."

"Are you going to interview the owner? He found the body." Lewis inclined his head to Pinckney, who was still bent at the waist, gripped by dry heaves.

"I suppose it would be shoddy policing not to," Yancey said. "While I do that you go get Lydale and ask him to hurry. And ask him if he has time when he's done to develop anything he's got from the march yesterday." Lewis nodded and broke into a trot. Yancey admired the younger man's energy and enthusiasm. He wished for a moment he hadn't lost his on a broad plain far out West. He also appreciated the fact that the kid did as he was asked and didn't waste time questioning a more experienced officer. Yancey approached the bathhouse owner again, keeping a bit of distance in deference to his shoes.

"Pinckney, I need to ask you a few questions about this morning. Do you think you can answer me if we step outside?" Yancey asked. Pinckney struggled into a standing position and followed Yancey through the seaside door and into the fresh air. Yancey waited while the older man drew in a few deep, ragged breaths and then pulled out a notebook and a pencil.

"Tell me, if you can stand to, what you saw when you arrived at the bathhouse this morning."

"I don't know what you want me to say."

"Just tell me what you did and what you saw to the best of your abilities, from the time you arrived."

"Things seemed much as usual until I got right up to the edge of the pool. I always check the pool first thing in the morning when I come in to make sure no animals have wandered in during the night and managed to get themselves stuck."

"Does that happen often?"

"More than I'd like the bathers to hear about. Not that it will matter now." Pinckney's face blanched again. "This will ruin me."

"I wouldn't count on that. People love a good scandal." Yancey could tell from the expression on Pinckney's face he hadn't considered that. He looked almost animated for the first time since Yancey had arrived. "You'll probably be turning them away by the time this reaches the papers."

"I hadn't thought of that. Do you think I should be more forthcoming about the mice and the dogs, too?"

"I think you might want to keep that to yourself. So, what happened next?"

"I looked in the pool and saw a shape at the bottom of it, just splayed out on the bottom."

"It wasn't floating?"

"No. It was flat on the bottom. I leaned over to get a better look at it and as soon as I realized it was a person I jumped in and pulled her out."

"I assume she was dead at the time? There was no hope of reviving her?"

"She was completely beyond help. For such a little bitty thing her body was surprisingly heavy."

"Did you see anything else unusual?"

"Not a thing."

"How do you think she managed to get in here when the pool was closed?"

"It isn't locked."

"Not ever?"

"No. There's no need. There's nothing here to steal and no one wants to use the place when the sun goes down." Pinckney's voice betrayed his belief that Yancey was a fool for asking such a thing. Yancey remembered a time as a youth when he and friends would sneak into the bathhouse after dark for a free swim without the prying eyes of the adults upon them. The water had retained its warmth from the day and the bathhouse had been a favorite haunt for many of his friends. Perhaps Pinckney needn't hear such a thing, though. He'd had enough of a shock for one day.

"Thanks for all your help, Pinckney. We'll get out of your hair as soon as the photographer has had a chance to document the scene and once the body is removed."

"Will I be able to open for business today, do you think?" Some might think it a crude question but having grown up in town Yancey understood from where it sprang. With only a single season to earn a year's income, each and every day mattered.

"That will be in Frank's capable hands but I'm sure he'll have you up and running before noon." Yancey hoped he was telling something like the truth.

"You're not leaving before this is all cleared up, are you?" Pinckney looked like he might be sick again.

"As much as I'd rather stay and keep an eye on things here, someone's got to let them know over at the Belden what has happened to their famous guest." Yancey patted the older man on his bony shoulder and set off down the beach.

Chapter Twenty-four

THE MORNING AFTER THE MARCH I LAY ABED LONGER THAN was my habit. The bruising to my ribs had caused me to pass a restless night. If I were honest, nightmares filled with the violent memories of the march had roused me whenever I managed to drift off.

Throughout the night images of smoke and sirens, shouting and terrified expressions on the marchers' faces filled my mind. Over and over I startled myself awake with the sensation the stage was collapsing beneath me. Every time I stretched or turned the soreness in my ribs made me almost cry out in pain.

Ben stopped me on the way to the dining room for a late breakfast. He handed me a message slip indicating I had received a telephone call from Officer Yancey, who wished to interview me about the events of the previous day. He planned to be at the Belden within the hour.

Within a half an hour I found myself sitting across from him in the hotel dining room. Providing him with a hearty breakfast was the least I could do after he had helped get me back on my feet at the march. Even the events of the last few days did not explain the change in his manner. His eyes bore deep shadows beneath them and his shoulders looked rigid under the cut of his uniform.

He accepted a cup of coffee but seemed reluctant to partake of any nourishment. I managed to persuade him only by mentioning Mrs. Doyle would be most put out if he refused to partake of her excellent breakfast. His grip upon the spoon whitened his knuckles and I feared he would snap the piece of cutlery as he stirred two spoons of sugar into his coffee. It was as if it had done him an affront. I was glad all of the guests had either already eaten or had decided to have a tray taken to their rooms. Some were not completely recovered from the terrors of the march.

"You seem out of sorts, Officer," I said. "Is your investigation off to a difficult start?"

"What investigation?" Officer Yancey stopped stirring and gave me his complete attention.

"The investigation into the stage collapse and the chaos caused during the march yesterday."

"I'm not here to investigate the stage collapse." He sawed back and forth maliciously on a burnt sausage. It would seem Mrs. Doyle was perhaps as rattled by the events of the day before as the rest of us. "That case is not going to have priority."

"What do you mean there is no investigation? Elva Velmont was knocked to the ground. Miss Rice has taken to her bed. There's been no sign of Sophronia so far today. Those are just the injuries I witnessed." I could not believe my ears. "Has your chief told you not to look into it because he was the one involved?" I kept my eyes firmly focused on his face and was gratified to see his own eyes widen in astonishment before he tucked his surprise back under his police officer demeanor.

"That is a bold charge. Are you able to provide proof of such an accusation?"

"Proof, no. But I can tell you what I saw." I leaned forward and lowered my voice. "Just before the collapse I saw your boss having a quick word with Henry Goodwin. Almost immediately after I saw a group of boys, Henry included, weaving in and out through the ranks of marchers, jostling and shoving. They are what started the chaos."

"It is quite a leap between a quick chat and soliciting a bunch of youngsters to incite a riot."

"I watched as Henry ran straight up to him as though he were expected. We both know Henry is not the sort of boy to pass the time of day with the police for no reason." Henry's brothers were infamous in Old Orchard for entanglements with the law. His brothers were both serving time on burglary charges, amongst other things. "Chief Hurley was up on a raised area and in plain view. He reached out his hand and pulled Henry up beside him. I saw the whole thing as plainly as I am seeing you here now."

"You seem very sure the collapse wasn't simply an unfortunate accident that resulted from shoddy workmanship." Officer Yancey reached for a piece of toast from the silver rack on the table between us. "Is there a reason you suspect it was intentional?" Officer Yancey bit down on his toast with a will, sending a dribble of strawberry jam cascading down his chin. I felt an unreasonable urge to dab his face with a napkin. Fortunately, I resisted such nonsense and kept my attention firmly on the matter at hand.

"Have you forgotten the threatening letter Sophronia received?" I asked. "Of course the first thing I thought was that the collapse was planned."

"Did anything strike you as strange besides Henry speaking to Chief Hurley?" Officer Yancey asked. His tone was urgent and I couldn't help but wonder what was really behind his questions.

"The only thing that struck me, Officer, was a rock. I still have a lump on the side of my head." I reached up and moved my hair back from my face. Officer Yancey looked slightly green at the sight of the lump. It wasn't a very polite thing to display at the breakfast table. "If you aren't here to investigate the stage collapse why are you asking so many questions about what led up to it?" Officer Yancey returned his toast to his plate and sat up straighter. His eyes looked sorrowful and I didn't want to hear whatever it was that he had to tell me. No one with that sort of look in his or her eyes was ever going to deliver good news.

"I am sorry to inform you that Sophronia was found dead in Pinckney Ferris's plunge pool just a couple hours ago." My first thought was one of guilt. I am sorry to say the second was of relief.

I knew I should have done more to convince her to take the threats to her life seriously. On the other hand, the wanton disregard Sophronia had for the safety of the other suffragists would no longer put anyone else at risk. I could stop worrying about Lucy and the Velmonts. I could also stop worrying about myself since I would no longer be expected to give any platform readings in public. The mixture of emotions was powerful and confusing.

"How did she die? Do you think the person who wrote the threatening letter actually killed her?"

"We don't know yet. We know she drowned but there were some indications she may have wanted to end her own life," Yancey said. His voice carried very little conviction.

"You don't believe that, do you? She'd received a threatening letter. She issued oblique threats herself in two different public forums. I saw her being assaulted. On top of it all, I would in no way characterize her as despondent."

"I have to investigate based on the evidence. I've only heard about the letter and only have your word for it that Congressman Plaisted got rough with her."

"Are you saying I made those things up? What about her manuscript?" I could hear the tone of my voice rising but I couldn't seem to stop it.

"I don't mean to insult you. I just have to pursue an investigation based on facts. Especially if it involves a volatile public figure and a seated congressman."

"I didn't think you were the sort of man who would let things like that influence you in carrying out your duties."

"I am not trying to shirk my duties. But with a case like this, especially one where the chief of police may also be involved, I have to be sure I cover all angles." Officer Yancey's voice was firm but not unkind. "I'm going to need a great deal more than hearsay and your opinion of Sophronia's character in order to be persuasive at an inquest. After all, you've only known her for a few days."

"So you are saying you are planning to investigate this as a murder?"

"I'm saying I need to have more facts. I will need to speak with the other guests. But first I need to search her room." Officer Yancey pushed his chair back from the table. Whatever I had thought today would bring, I had been wrong.

"I'll get the key."

CHAPTER TWENTY-FIVE

IT'S JUST ALONG HERE," I said, leading Officer Yancey down the hallway on the second floor. I stopped in front of Sophronia's door and turned the key. I stepped inside and even though Sophronia couldn't have left the space for the last time more than a few hours ago the room had already taken on the stuffy, forlorn air of an uninhabited place. I couldn't help but feel that Sophronia's spirit lingered in the room watching our every move and willing us to understand what had happened to her.

"What exactly are we looking for?" I asked.

"*We* aren't looking for anything. Your part of the job ended when you let me into the room," Yancey said. The look on his face, however, said he was not sure where to start. I couldn't blame him in the least. But I could use his uncertainty to my advantage.

"I'm sure you'll want to finish up here and get on with

questioning the guests as soon as you can. Do you have another officer available to help you get through all this before noon?" I asked.

Sophronia had not been a tidy woman. Books and handkerchiefs cluttered the bedstand, and jackets, shirtwaists, and skirts were draped over the backs of chairs and heaped upon the bench placed at the foot of the high bed. The door of the drop-front, carved walnut desk lay open, exposing pigeonholes crammed with papers and envelopes. It looked like Millie had never been by to work her magic. In truth, I, too, felt daunted by the prospect of searching the space for information that would explain Sophronia's death.

"All the other officers are either assigned to the pier or are busy with other aspects of this investigation."

"Then you should be happy for an extra pair of hands. Besides, a woman is more likely to notice if something is amiss."

I noticed Officer Yancey averting his eyes from a pair of drawers heaped on the floor next to the nightstand. "I am happy to say I have rarely had the experience of a room such as this one."

"Then my assistance is all the more useful. I'm sorry to say scenes such as this are all too common in the hospitality business. There is just something about staying at a hotel that brings out the worst in some people." I closed the door behind me and turned the lock. Officer Yancey looked at me with a distressed expression on his face.

"Miss Proulx, what will people say if we are discovered in a room such as this, completely unchaperoned?"

"Unless one of the hotel guests killed Sophronia, no one else in the building knows she isn't the one in here. If we work quietly and keep the door shut I see no reason for concern," I said. I pointed to the wardrobe. "So, are you prepared to tell me what you are looking for?"

Officer Yancey glanced at the door once more then spoke softly. "I am looking for a note. Most people who decide to take their own lives leave one. We didn't find one at the plunge pool, which makes this the next place to look." Officer Yancey looked at me and shook his head. "I'll start with the desk. Would you look over near the nightstand?" And just like that, I was once again helping the police with an investigation.

We both turned to our respective areas and began the sad task of sifting through items Sophronia would never have need of again. It made me think about the things that my mother left behind when she died. I had believed all that remained of her by the time I was old enough to think of such things were a few pieces of jewelry, a letter from her sister, and a half a deck of tarot cards. By the time my father and I had parted ways even the jewelry was gone. Father sold it off one piece at a time as each of his business ventures failed.

When I arrived in Old Orchard with only her letter, her tarot cards, and the clothing on my back, Honoria had surprised me by offering me the hotel room that had belonged to my mother. Honoria had preserved everything as she had left it when she snuck out of the house, with her shoes in her hands in order to elope with my father.

By living for the last few weeks amongst her clothing and hairbrushes, her books and her furniture I felt like I knew her in a way I never had before. Looking around Sophronia's room I wondered if she would have left it the way it was if she, like my mother, realized she would not come back.

"I've had no luck. How about you?" Officer Yancey asked me about half an hour later. I shook my head.

"Nothing at all. There are plenty of digestive aid packets and peppermint candy wrappers but no notes of any kind." Apparently she enjoyed reading poetry. I held up a slim volume of verse I recognized from the hotel library. Which brought something to mind. "What about her manuscript? Have you seen that?" I stepped toward him.

"No. Nothing that looks like a manuscript. Just drafts of her speech for the march." Officer Yancey stepped aside to give me room to see for myself.

I looked at the top of the desk for the stack of papers Sophronia had caressed like a good luck charm. Nothing but more dust and debris. Where could it have gone? Had I just assumed it was the manuscript because of Sophronia's behavior? Had there ever even been a manuscript or was announcing one simply another one of her tactics for stirring up interest in the press?

Officer Yancey and I proceeded to look into every possible hiding space. I riffled through the wardrobe, searching the folds of her clothing. Officer Yancey crawled under the bed and tapped the floor and the paneling for loose boards behind which to hide something. Long before I had shed three hairpins and Officer Yancey's hands were covered in a fine layer of dust I had despaired of finding the reputed manuscript.

"No note. No manuscript. What's next, Officer?" I asked, throwing my hands in the air.

"What's next is that I start interviewing the guests. Alone."

"Miss Rice was Sophronia's close friend. I happen to know she is still abed as a result of some minor injuries acquired during the march. I suggest we start with her."

"Perhaps I need to be more clear. While I appreciate your help searching this room, I will be interviewing Miss Rice and all the other people on my own."

"I doubt that very much. Unlike me, I am quite certain Miss Rice will not be willing to be alone with you in a bedroom. I shall have to chaperone."

CHAPTER TWENTY-SIX

MISS RICE SAT PROPPED UP AGAINST THE HEADBOARD OF THE high bed in her room. She was in no way dressed to receive visitors, and just as Miss Proulx had predicted, had been extremely resistant to receiving Officer Yancey. But a murder inquiry cannot stand upon social niceties and so Yancey had to admit he was glad of Miss Proulx's presence. Not that he thought it likely anyone would imagine anything untoward would occur between himself and the paragon of virginal rectitude, Miss Rice.

While Miss Rice did indeed show signs of her ordeal the day before, in the form of bruises all along the left side of her face, she still looked more than capable of defending herself if she felt an imminent assault upon her virtue. Her sharp glances and pursed lips as well as the way she crossed her stout arms across her expansive chest gave the impression that while she was wounded she was not down for the count. Even from the confines of her bed she seemed a force of nature.

"If you are here to finally take my statement about this"—she touched the side of her head and winced—"I can't say I am impressed with your enthusiasm for the task." Miss Rice nodded to Miss Proulx and her face softened slightly.

Yancey was even more relieved Miss Proulx had insisted on accompanying him. Not that he liked to encourage her in her high-handedness with the police or everyone else, for that matter. She was already quite comfortable enough with investigatory work, as far as he was concerned. Still, her assistance was most welcome in this interview. Ruby shook her head slightly and he waited for her to break the news.

"Miss Rice, Officer Yancey is here on an entirely different matter. One that I am afraid may prove distressing." Ruby moved to the edge of the bed and took Miss Rice's hand.

"Has something happened to Sophronia?"

"Why would you ask that?" Yancey rarely found loved ones in the least prepared for tragic news. They were even less likely to suggest such a thing themselves.

"Surely you aren't foolish enough to believe what happened at the march was an accident? Sophronia stirs up controversy wherever she goes. I have long been expecting she would come to harm."

"Any reason you can think of that matters would worsen at this time?" Yancey asked.

"There is no doubt in my mind that now that Sophronia has announced her memoir is forthcoming things will escalate even further." Miss Rice hugged her chest even more tightly. "You aren't here to finally suggest police protection are you?"

"That won't be necessary, I'm afraid," Yancey said. "I'm sorry to say Miss Foster Eldridge's body was discovered at a local bathhouse this morning." Yancey kept his eyes firmly on Miss Rice's face as he delivered the news. It could be that their relationship had turned lethal.

"Sophronia's body?" Miss Rice's eyes widened and she sat bolt upright. She turned to Miss Proulx and clutched at her as if trying not to lose her balance. Miss Proulx's small frame wobbled then stiffened to help support them both. As much as he found it hard to admit, even to himself, Miss Proulx was a remarkable woman. "You mean to say Sophronia is dead?"

"Yes, I'm afraid that is correct." Yancey hated this part of his job. Grieving people made him squirm and he could feel his desire to flee increasing with each passing moment he spent with them. He always felt the best way to honor the victims and to bring solace to their loved ones was to get on with the job of solving their murder. But hurrying the bereaved was never the right thing to do.

"Someone finally killed her?" Miss Rice turned her head slowly to Ruby and then back to Yancey again. Yancey wasn't sure he understood the look playing across her features but he thought for just a second he saw a flicker of guilt before it was replaced by sorrow. Not that guilt was a rarity when a sudden death occurred. More often than not it was based on words left unsaid or those that never should have been but were and then regretted.

"The investigation is in its early stages but her death doesn't look like an accident."

"How did she die?"

"She drowned. There's a wound on the side of her head and her clothing was weighed down by rocks before she went into a saltwater pool at a bathhouse down at the beach," Yancey said. Miss Rice gasped and fell back against her pillows, then covered her face with her hands. Yancey wondered if she was trying to block out the news or to keep him from seeing her reaction.

"Did Miss Foster Eldridge ever give any indication of being in low spirits? Melancholy in any way?" Yancey slipped his small notebook and a pencil from his pocket and quietly opened the notebook. Miss Rice lowered her hands from her face, a spark of anger shining from her eyes.

"What are you implying?"

"From the way she died it is possible that she inflicted harm upon herself. Officer Yancey has to ask such things, Miss Rice," the younger woman said. "Otherwise he won't be doing his job properly and that is no way to honor her." Miss Rice shrugged but then nodded.

"Rather than feeling melancholy, Sophronia was elated. She considered the march a tremendous victory despite the way it ended," Miss Rice said. "She said it showed that the cause of suffrage had a real chance of success if some in the crowd felt threatened enough to resort to sabotage."

"She thought the stage was rigged to collapse?" Yancey asked. He started to lean forward, then checked himself. There was no need to lead Miss Rice in an opinion. It wouldn't help him get to the truth to do so.

"She had absolutely no doubt. As she herself suffered no real injuries, she considered the whole incident a blessing. She was certain it would make the papers all over the eastern seaboard."

"Did she suspect anyone in particular of having a reason for carrying out an attack against her?" Yancey asked. He couldn't help but notice Miss Rice's posture stiffening and the way she protectively crossed her arms over her chest.

"If she did, she didn't make any such accusations to me."

"Do you have any ideas of your own?" Yancey asked.

"I am not inclined to indulge in idle speculation. I am feeling most unwell now and would ask that you leave me in peace to grieve for my dear friend." Miss Rice turned her head away and closed her eyes. Yancey thought she did look unwell but it wasn't just from grief. He was certain that Miss Rice looked frightened.

CHAPTER TWENTY-SEVEN

"YOU KNOW YOU SHALL HAVE TO QUESTION YOUR SISTER, TOO," I said as I closed the door of Miss Rice's room behind us. "Other than Miss Rice, Lucy was the one who spent the most time in Sophronia's company."

"I don't suppose she is already here, is she?" he asked. After checking with Ben as to Lucy's whereabouts, he confirmed she could be found in one of the small rooms off the lobby practitioners used for a variety of readings. Lucy sat at a small table in the center of the room but instead of a crystal ball or dowsing pendulum she sat busying herself with a gleaming black typewriter. As we entered she looked up and the clattering of the keys tapered off.

"I wondered where you had gotten off to so early. What are you doing at the Belden?" Lucy asked, looking over my shoulder at her brother. I stepped aside to allow him to be the one to deliver the news.

"I have something to tell you that I know you will not want to hear," he said. He spoke softly, like one might to a frightened child. Lucy's eyes widened and her hands dropped to her lap.

"Has something happened to Mother?" she asked with a quaver in her voice. I was suddenly reminded that her father had suffered a sudden death and that perhaps she lived in fear of losing her mother as well.

"Mother's fine but Miss Foster Eldridge, I'm sorry to say, is not. She was found drowned this morning in Pinckney Ferris's plunge pool."

"That can't be. She asked me to come in today to attend to her correspondence." Lucy looked from Officer Yancey to me as if I would contradict him. I slowly shook my head and approached the table.

"I'm sorry, Lucy, but she is no longer with us. I know you are shocked. We both are but your brother needs to ask you some questions and the sooner the better if he is to find out exactly how she died," I said.

"Is there some question as to what happened?" Lucy asked. "Wasn't it just an accident?" The question was a natural one to ask, I suppose. With seven miles of beach on the Atlantic Ocean, Old Orchard was no stranger to the idea of accidental drownings. Swimmers were overcome by cold and cramp, fishing and pleasure vessels were caught in storms and sank to the bottom of the sea. Occasionally someone even toppled over in an inebriated state, despite prohibition laws, and drowned in shallow water.

"I am trying to determine the exact cause but it seems unlikely it was an accident. Rocks weighted down her clothing."

"You don't think she killed herself, do you?" Lucy's eyes filled with tears and I was once again reminded of her father's untimely passing. With every surprising death, suicide would spring to mind. Officer Yancey reached for her hand and held it in his own.

"It's possible that she may have done so. Or someone may have wanted her dead. Which is what I wanted to ask you about."

"Do you think it was the hate mail?" Lucy asked. She turned to me. "I knew we should have forced her to cancel the march." Lucy's tears spilled over onto her cheeks. Officer Yancey pulled a pressed white handkerchief from his back trouser pocket and handed it to her.

"We tried our best, Lucy. There was no chance we could have persuaded her to cancel the march. She was completely determined to go on." I was gratified to see her give the slightest nod of her head in acknowledgment of my words. "The best way to help her now is to answer your brother's questions. We've already spoken with Miss Rice but she was of little use."

"Did she ever give any hint as to who she thought had sent the threatening letter?" Yancey asked.

"I'm sorry, but she didn't."

"What about the manuscript she mentioned? Did she entrust it to you?" I asked.

"No, she did not. I've never even seen it," Lucy said.

"Did she say anything to you about the stage possibly being rigged to collapse yesterday?"

"I didn't see Sophronia after the stage collapsed to discuss it. Mother wanted to go straight home and, I confess, I was too rattled by what had happened to argue with her. Do you really think the stage was sabotaged?"

"It may have been. It was such a gimcrack job that when we checked it over there was no way to tell by what was left of it if someone had done it on purpose or if the stage just couldn't bear weight," Officer Yancey said. "Is there something about that you think I should know? Any small thing might be of assistance."

"I don't want to cause someone's reputation harm if the stage wasn't sabotaged."

"Trust me to decide what is or isn't important, Lucy. You know I am never eager to tarnish anyone's reputation," he said. A look passed between them and I wondered once more what it would be like to have a sibling.

"I hate to say it because it seems so disloyal but one person does come to mind," Lucy said. "George Cheswick."

"George?" I asked. I couldn't believe my ears. "Are you quite certain?"

"I'm afraid so. I didn't want to say anything to you, Ruby, because it all seemed so gossipy when Sophronia mentioned it and in truth, I found it all quite embarrassing."

"What did Miss Foster Eldridge confide?" Officer Yancey sounded encouraging rather than impatient. I was impressed with his attitude as I was having trouble with my own.

"According to Sophronia, George made rather a fool of himself at a Hay Feverists convention held in New Hampshire a couple of years ago," Lucy said. "Everyone else there was focused entirely on improving their health and alleviating their symptoms. George's attention was unfortunately pointed elsewhere."

"George attended a Hay Feverists convention? I had no idea George is involved with the organization," I said.

"Yes, he did. Sophronia said he was there with his brother and sister-in-law. Apparently, he used to be very active in the organization but he isn't anymore. Sophronia told me he made rather a nuisance of himself through his bothersome and entirely unrequited interest in her. In fact, the president of the Hay Feverists Society felt compelled to ask him to desist in his attentions toward her."

I was astonished. It had been my understanding that George was and always had been utterly devoted to Honoria. The idea of him showing any interest in another was incomprehensible. He was the very picture of a devoted suitor.

"George is such a mild-mannered gentleman. What could he have done to merit a sanction?" Officer Yancey asked.

"Sophronia said a secret admirer insisted on showering her with inappropriate tokens of affection and handwritten poems." Lucy shook her head. "She believed that George was responsible. She went to the president of the organization and complained. When the president asked George to apologize for his actions he simply packed his bags and quitted the hotel without a word. To my knowledge he's never participated in the organization since."

"Why was it thought that George was the one responsible?"

"Because once Sophronia began to complain of the unwanted gifts, the society president took it upon himself to discover who was sending them. The gifts were all charged to accounts at the shops in town in George's name."

"And you think that would be enough to sabotage the stage over?" Yancey doubted George would be moved to action over a bit of embarrassment.

"I shouldn't have thought so except he has had a great deal of trouble in his life lately. Between his brother showing up to visit and the house fire, he can't have been too happy to end up lodged in the same hotel as a woman who humiliated him. He may even have been certain she would tell Honoria about what had happened," Lucy said. She looked at me and I nodded vigorously.

"Why should Honoria knowing matter in the least to George?" Officer Yancey asked.

"You cannot possibly call yourself an investigator if you can honestly say you've never noticed George's feelings for Honoria," Lucy said, sighing. "No wonder you are still unmarried at your advanced age."

Officer Yancey withdrew his hand from his sister's and cleared his throat. "If there is nothing else you can tell me I think I should be going."

"Are you going to question George?" I asked.

"George will be questioned eventually. But I have a couple of other lines of inquiry to follow before I get to him."

"Would you like me to ask him about his unrequited feelings for Sophronia?" I asked. "It would save you some trouble and as Lucy says, you may not be particularly well suited for such a task as that one." I held my breath waiting for him to answer. A pained look flitted over his face.

"I may not be the person in this room the most attuned to the personal lives of others but I am the only one authorized to ask questions in a police investigation. Your assistance is not required." Officer Yancey returned his hat to his head and left the room without a backward glance.

CHAPTER TWENTY-EIGHT

I DECIDED TO TAKE ADVANTAGE OF OFFICE YANCEY'S ABSENCE BY asking some questions on my own despite his assertions that it was not my place to do so.

George had made himself at home in the family parlor. I shouldn't like to speak ill of a dear friend of Honoria's or second-guess her decision to offer him shelter but there was no denying George had made his presence felt. I had to wonder if his tendency to sloth had played any role in Honoria's refusal of his alleged repeated offers of marriage. If it had, I could not blame her.

As I picked my way between piles of socks and discarded sweets packets I was reminded of my father's tendency to try my patience in the housekeeping department. Life in a tent is grubby at best. Conditions are crowded and dust is a constant companion. Father's native untidiness was another cross to bear and one I did not shoulder without feeling decidedly put upon. Not that it would have been prudent to display such feelings to Father.

George lay sprawled across the sofa in his stocking feet, gently snoring. The singed ends of his damaged mustache fluttered in the steady breeze issuing forth from his large nose. At rest George looked like an elderly baby with luxuriant facial hair. That might be another reason for Honoria's polite but persistent refusal. It would be a rare woman who found such a comparison romantically appealing.

I considered returning later to ask my questions but thought better of it. As was so often mentioned in detective fiction, it did not do for a case to be allowed to grow cold. Surely Sophronia's death could be no exception. I approached the side of the sofa and feigned a delicate sneeze. George blinked rapidly then struggled upright with all the grace of a beached merman.

"You've caught me resting my eyes, Ruby dear." George looked at his feet and planted them firmly on the floor. "A pitfall of age I'm afraid."

"I think it more likely a symptom of hay fever." Even with all the mess strewn about it was impossible to harbor hard feelings toward someone whose wispy hair stood on end like a puff on a spent dandelion. Everything about his appearance made me want to pat him on the shoulder and hand him a teething biscuit. "I understood you attended a Hay Feverists convention some time ago."

"I have attended but if you ask me the whole thing is no more than an excuse for a bunch of self-absorbed laggards to idle about during some of the best weather of the year. They install themselves in luxury hotels in bucolic locations and then set about to suffering as if it were a paying job." George's face had purpled and a vein throbbed valiantly in his forehead.

"I was given to understand that your brother and his wife accompanied you to the convention. Were they similarly disappointed in the experience?"

"Not in the least. They fell for the whole of that nonsense, hook, line, and handkerchief. I'm sorry to say it was a sore spot between us for some time. In fact, this is the first I've seen of them since the convention."

"I'm sorry to hear it caused a rift. It must have been quite a while since last you saw them."

"Around two years. Not a word from either of them until they appeared without warning on my doorstep when they couldn't find a hotel room in Old Orchard in time for the pier opening." George shook his head. "Cursed uncomfortable that was, I can tell you."

I made a soothing, clucking sound as if George were a tiny chick with ruffled feathers. It seemed to do the trick so I steered the subject back to hay fever. "So Mr. and Mrs. Cheswick still take their hay fever seriously, then, do they?"

"Like religious zealots. I would have expected such nonsense from Phyllis, who has always been too careful of her health for my taste. Usually Osmond can be counted on to be more sensible. But not this time."

"He was the instigator?"

"No. I wouldn't say that. But he took to it like a duck to water. He went on the hikes, took the alternating hot and cold water treatment baths, and booked rooms for the same time the following year before the first week was out."

"Something about the whole experience must have appealed to him."

"Or someone." George said this under his breath and then clamped his lips together as if to keep more words from spilling out.

"Your brother found the company at the convention to his liking?" I asked. "I shouldn't have thought he had particularly, since he didn't appear to recognize either Sophronia or Miss Rice."

"Perhaps he had simply forgotten." George refused to meet my gaze. George was as bad a liar as I was an accomplished one. Between his darting glances, nervous foot shuffling, and the sheen of perspiration, which had misted his face like a soft, spring rain, there could be no doubt he wished to play down his association with the dead women. The question had to be asked why that would be so.

"I was surprised that I never saw you speak to either of them here at the hotel. Surely that is odd?"

"I can see how it would seem that way. Age dulls the memory as well as increasing the tendency to nap." George looked as though he wished to be anywhere but with me. It pained me to press him but if George had anything to do with Sophronia's death, I couldn't allow societal niceties to coerce me into cowardice.

"I suppose it is all for the best that you weren't on close terms, considering the news I've just heard," I said. I hated myself for suspecting him but I kept my eyes on George's face, looking for signs of surprise or guilt. I was sorry to see a wariness in his eyes that left me with uncomfortable doubts.

"Which news is that?" he asked.

"I'm very sorry to say that Sophronia was found drowned this morning in Mr. Ferris's plunge pool." This time George's face took on its customary expression of mild befuddlement.

"Was she there for a hay fever treatment and something went wrong?" he asked.

"I'm afraid not. She was found dressed in street clothing and her pockets were weighed down with rocks." I shook my head with genuine sadness.

"Do you have any idea why someone could have wanted to

harm her?" I asked. "Or why she might have decided to harm herself?"

"As you so astutely pointed out, we never even spoke during her stay here. I could not possibly speculate on this tragedy."

"What about your brother? Do you think he might be able to shed some light on the situation?" I asked. George paused as if considering his options, then let out a slow sigh.

"I have never been good at speaking to or for my brother. Or his wife. I suggest you ask them yourself." With that mild-mannered reproach George lay down once more on the sofa and closed his eyes. I had been dismissed.

CHAPTER TWENTY-NINE

YANCEY STOMPED ALONG THE SHORT STRETCH OF SIDEWALK between the Belden and its neighboring hotel the Sea Spray. Why should he care what Miss Proulx thought of his ability to pick up on something so outside of his purview as George's romantic interests? Everywhere he turned in this case he kept running up against romantic entanglements.

And now he had the misfortune of needing to ask a congressman about a broken engagement to a dead woman. He had the irrational thought all of it was Miss Proulx's fault. He reached for the brass handle of the Sea Spray's lobby door and told himself to be reasonable. He simply needed to keep his attention on the job at hand.

At the front desk he inquired after the congressman and was led by a chatty young man in livery to a darkly paneled room at the back of the hotel. The congressman sat silhouetted against a long window with a stack of papers in his lap and a silver fountain pen in his hand. On a white linen–covered table at his side sat a steaming cup of coffee and plate of nut bread.

"Congressman Plaisted, my name is Warren Yancey and I'm

an officer with the Old Orchard Police Department. I need to have a moment of your time."

"You're here about Sophronia, aren't you?" Nelson Plaisted tapped his spoon against his coffee cup and placed it on the tablecloth, leaving a dark stain on the white linen for someone else to clean up. "I heard about what happened." The congressman gestured to the deep leather chair opposite him. Yancey thought that he could get used to such comforts. Not that he was likely to be able to afford them if he remained an honest police officer.

"What specifically did you hear?"

"That the poor woman had become unhinged after the scene at the march and had thrown herself into a pool at the bathhouse next door. Someone said her pockets were weighted down with rocks."

"We haven't released such information to the public at this time. Would you mind telling me with whom you've been speaking?"

"I shouldn't like to say. But it would be fair to say I've had my information on very good authority." The congressman gave an insincere smile. "How is it you think I can help you?"

"Your behavior at the rally suggested you had strong opinions about suffrage and even about Miss Foster Eldridge herself. It seemed prudent to ask you why that might be."

"*Strong* isn't the word. Sophronia was a blight on the face of our nation and I think I speak for men everywhere when I say I will sleep more soundly knowing she is no longer walking amongst us."

"You sound as though you wanted her dead," Yancey said.

"Are you accusing me of something?"

"Not yet. I'm a fair man. I'd like to give you the opportunity to present your side of the problems you had with Miss Foster Eldridge in a calm and reasonable manner." Yancey settled back deeper into the recesses of the chair. No sense not to be comfortable or to make it look like he didn't have all the time in the world to dog Plaisted's footsteps. "Because from what I remember at the rally, you looked anything but reasonable."

"Obviously you did not know Sophronia like I did. If you had you would have considered that I was behaving with a great deal of self-control."

"That is one of the more interesting things I have heard in a long while. You must have really disliked her."

"Sophronia was the most ruthless person, man or woman, I have ever had the misfortune to meet."

"I've heard from another source that she could be single-minded in pursuit of her cause. That it meant more to her than anything else in the world. I also heard that at one point the two of you were on the same side of the prohibition issue."

"We were. In fact, it was how we met. She had a passion and a dedication to causes that won one over, convinced one to embrace her view. It was exhilarating to be in her presence when she was fired up about one thing or another."

"It sounds like you didn't always dislike her. Is it true that you were once engaged to be married?"

"I don't deny it. I was a foolish, besotted youth when I asked for her hand. When it looked like I had a bright future she was happy to plan a future with me. But when my fortunes changed with the economic collapse she suddenly found we were incompatible."

"My source told the story differently," Yancey said.

"If Sophronia is your source, she would have. The truth made her look like a shallow, grasping social climber. I expect you have heard what everyone who meets her first hears. I'm certain she would have said she became convinced that suffrage, not prohibition, was the way to solve society's ills and that I was too narrow-minded to consider that point of view."

"You sound quite sure of Miss Foster Eldridge's opinions," Yancey said. Far more certain than Yancey was himself, considering his source of information concerning the broken engagement was Thomas Lydale, not Miss Foster Eldridge.

"I put up with listening to them long enough that I consider myself an expert. I expect she also said I was the one who ended our engagement?"

"I was told you would no longer allow your name to be linked with hers and you withdrew your proposal."

"Sophronia returned my ring right after she somehow heard my bank account was as empty as her promises to me."

"That would have made many a man bitter," Yancey said. "Did her change of heart have that affect on you?"

"Not in the least. In truth, some of Sophronia's single-mindedness could be quite terrifying." Yancey felt a stir as Plaisted lowered his voice and bent toward him. "There was little she wouldn't stoop to in order to advance her plans."

"What sort of stooping?"

"I cannot remember details. Just a general impression. It was a long time ago and I've moved on."

"But did you leave the past behind entirely?"

"Why would I not? Eventually I amassed another fortune, even greater than the first." Congressman Plaisted smiled and crossed his hands over his vest. "I even found the courage to give my heart away once more to a far more deserving woman."

"I understand that Mrs. Plaisted was once also a close associate of Miss Foster Eldridge. Did that make things difficult for you?"

"Why should it? My dear wife had no desire to continue her acquaintance with Sophronia after we became engaged. As for me, I have always found it an easy thing to leave the past behind."

"Your behavior toward Miss Foster Eldridge at the rally did not look like that of a man who had left things behind," Yancey said.

"Chief Hurley and I have enjoyed renewing our friendship and our commitment to the common cause of traditional family values. Did you ask your superior about your plans to question me?"

"Causes like anti-suffrage?" Yancey asked.

"You've heard of us. Are you considering becoming a member yourself?"

"I'm afraid even if I shared your beliefs there would be no peace for me if I acted upon them."

"You have the look of a man who is married to an opinionated woman."

"No, I'm not married. I live with my mother and my younger sister, both of whom are ardent suffragists. In fact, my sister took on the role of Miss Foster Eldridge's secretary as soon as she arrived in town."

"You have my pity. Women are natural rulers of the domestic sphere. They degrade us all when they turn their backs on their birthright and reach out with sticky, grasping hands for that which they are biologically unsuited."

"So your disruptive attendance at suffrage rallies is wholly motivated by your desire to keep women from degrading themselves and the rest of the nation? None of your interest has ever been in striking out at an individual woman whom you feel wronged you?"

"Sophronia wronged herself. If she had remained faithfully at my side during my times of difficulty she surely would not have died such an untimely death." Plaisted pushed back his chair. "Should you have any more questions about my character or the workings of my organization I suggest you take them up with Chief Hurley. After all, he is one of the founding members."

CHAPTER THIRTY

Yancey was certain as soon as he turned his back on the Hotel Belden Miss Proulx would take it into her head to continue to ask questions of the guests and the staff. There was not a single thing he'd be able to do to prevent her. If he were honest he would admit he was happy to have some help, especially since there were other interviews he felt were more pressing.

He doffed his hat as he entered Thomas's photography studio. The wall opposite the door was covered with images, and Yancey wished, not for the first time, that he wasn't there on business. Before he turned to the reason for his visit he lingered for just a moment looking at photographs that captured the pier in various stages of completion. A swell of pride caught him off guard as he remembered what the beach had looked like before and how the pier stood as a symbol of economic hope for all the townspeople.

"I've got the photographs of the march ready. The ones of the crime scene will still be a little while yet," Thomas said as he stepped through the swinging door at the far end of the studio. He pointed to the long counter at the center of the small shop. Photographs covered its wooden surface. Yancey leaned over the offerings for a better look. Thomas had captured a surprisingly complete record of the event. And he had arranged the photographs chronologically on the counter.

Images of crowds lining the street before the march began lay on one end of the counter and at the other were photographs of the collapsed stage and the ambulance wagons arriving. Through it all he had stayed at his task, snapping picture after picture regardless of the commotion around him.

"How did you manage to keep taking photos with all the turmoil around you?" Yancey was impressed. "I shouldn't have thought owning a studio would have prepared you for something like that." Yancey lifted an image of a woman splayed on the ground with a man standing over her, jeering.

"I haven't always worked in a studio. I've done all sorts of different photography work. In fact, I've seen a lot worse than this during my time overseas."

"I didn't know you spent time abroad," Yancey said. He was surprised. It was the sort of thing many a man would have boasted about to all and sundry.

Thomas shrugged. "It never came up before now. Besides, many of the memories are not ones upon which I wish to dwell." Yancey thought back to his time in the army and felt a surge of connection and respect for Thomas. He spoke very rarely of such things himself and esteemed those who did likewise. He considered it something akin to sin to romanticize conflicts, especially those that had escalated to violence.

"Where did you go?"

"Africa, Europe, South America. A decent photographer can find work almost anywhere."

"Well, I appreciate the benefit of your experience. I never expected so many photographs or ones of this quality when you offered to show them to me." Yancey leaned over the counter again and perused the scenes more slowly. "Did you notice anything strange about the collapse of the stage?"

"What did you have in mind?"

"I was considering if it could have been deliberately knocked down," Yancey said.

"You think it may not have been an accident?" Thomas sounded surprised. "Do you think someone tried to kill Sophronia by rigging the stage and when it didn't work they drowned her instead?"

"Let's say at this point I am keeping an open mind."

"These photos are of the stage and these are of the crowd around the time of the collapse. I don't remember seeing anything that indicated deliberate sabotage but maybe the camera caught something I failed to notice at the time." Thomas handed Yancey a magnifying glass from a tray on a shelf behind him and took another for himself. Both men bent over the display and began a methodical search.

Photograph after photograph showed crowds and horses and hats knocked to the ground. They showed angry faces, determined expressions, and raised fists. Yancey couldn't help but notice that Miss Proulx featured in more of the photographs than anyone else, including Sophronia. By a large number. He did not wish to consider why that knowledge made him feel less kindly toward his companion.

While he wasn't happy with his suspicions about Thomas's interest in Miss Proulx or even worse, why it mattered to him in the least, it did make him aware that she was in the thick of things the entire time. With a good view of the action. He hoped Thomas had photographs that supported her story.

Yancey held his magnifying glass over an image of the chief looking in the direction of the stage. There beside him was Henry Goodwin. They stood quite close together but nothing in the photograph indicated they were interacting.

"You don't have any other images of these two together, do you?"

"Let's see. Here's one." Thomas tapped his finger against a photograph in front of him. Yancey took it and inspected it carefully. Sure enough, his boss and Henry were turned toward each other and appeared to be conversing. He would have given a lot to know what had been said.

"Does the collapse come shortly after this photograph in the sequence?" Yancey handed it back. Thomas placed it in the right spot and nodded.

"It was taken only moments before, at most. Do you think those two were involved in what happened?" Yancey liked Thomas and had appreciated being able to rely on his help. But he would be a foolish man to share his suspicions about his chief with anyone until he had much more proof. Lucy knew what he was up to by working for the chief only because she knew Yancey so well. And because she was an excellent guesser.

"For now, I'm just hoping they may have seen something since they were so close to the action. I'll ask Chief Hurley what was going on at the time."

"Here's another one with the chief." Thomas handed another photograph to Yancey. The chief stood near the stage in that one as well but his companion was a man Yancey thought he should recognize but didn't. There was something familiar about him but he just couldn't put his finger on why. There was no doubt that Chief Hurley was having a conversation with the man, though. The photograph clearly showed the man pointing to something near the stage and the chief leaning to the side to get a better view.

"Do you mind if I borrow these two to show him?"

"Take any of them you would like. I have the plates and can make copies of any of them."

"I'll bring them back within a day or two. I appreciate all your help."

Yancey pocketed the photographs. He was about to take his leave when his glance fell once more on a particularly fetching photograph of Miss Proulx.

"I'd like to thank you for all your help and to impose on you for one more favor?" he asked. Lucy was an attractive young lady, too. There was no reason she wouldn't also capture Thomas's notice. Especially since he seemed keen on feisty damsels in distress.

"I had the unpleasant duty of informing my sister, Lucy, of Miss Foster Eldridge's death earlier today. She was quite distressed by the news. There's little chance I'll be able to get home to check on her myself and I wondered if you would be willing to do so in my place?"

"It would be my privilege to do so on your behalf. But are you certain I should intrude upon her at what will likely prove a difficult time?" Thomas asked. Yancey took another look at Miss Proulx's dark eyes staring intently at him from yet another of Thomas's photographs.

"On the contrary, I am certain we will all feel better if you did."

CHAPTER THIRTY-ONE

HONORIA TOOK THE NEWS OF SOPHRONIA'S DEATH MORE CALMLY than I might have expected. In fact, she seemed almost relieved.

"I can't say that I am entirely surprised," she said when I located her in the family parlor, where she was tidying up a bit. George's presence could still be felt in the neatly folded blanket at the foot of the sofa but the gentleman himself was nowhere in sight. Honoria seated herself on the sofa and patted the spot beside her. Her face still bore signs of strain I attributed to the harrowing events of the prior day. I doubt she slept any better than the rest of us had or likely would that night, either, considering what had happened to Sophronia.

"Do you believe Sophronia's death is the reason for your prophetic dream?" I asked. A shiver ran between my shoulder blades and I understood better why my aunt had looked so distressed when her dream had first occurred. It was an unsettling thing to see such evil events before they happened. Honoria's gift seemed more like a burden. I felt a wave of gratitude that my own experiences with things I could not explain were rarely so grim.

"I hope so but I cannot be sure. Prophetic dreams are much like other dreams. They fade as time passes and they return in snatches of memory when something in the immediate environment causes recall. I am still piecing it all together."

"Do you have any better sense now of what the warning was for?" I asked. "Are there any other misfortunes we can expect to endure?"

"I confess, this dream has been particularly muddled." She gave me a long look.

"Why do you think that is?" I asked, not sure I wanted to know the answer. I hoped her look had not meant it was my fault in some way but I was afraid that was exactly what it meant.

"I have not had such an intense dream as this one was since your mother passed over to the other side. I think this dream is personal and I think you are what is making it so."

"Am I in danger?" I felt my heart lurch in my chest. I had just settled into a life I wanted to live. I had no desire to lose it anytime soon. But looking at Honoria's face I knew she was worried about exactly that.

"I wish I could say that I am not worried for you. The things I've remembered of the dream disturb me still. They are not entirely reconciled with what has happened to Sophronia."

"What else have you remembered?"

"I'm not sure I should tell you. Saying terrible things out loud always feels to me like I am daring them to come to pass." Honoria reached over and touched my cheek with her plump hand.

"I have a very vivid imagination. I think I would find it easier if you shared what you've seen rather than letting me create even worse things in my own mind." I wasn't just curious about her dream. My mind's eye was picturing all sorts of horrors, from a fire ravaging the Belden and trapping me on the third floor to a disfiguring incident between my bicycle and an inexperienced automobile driver. Honoria must have sensed my agitation.

"I've seen you struggling mightily to breathe," she said. "It is as if the air was being pressed out of your lungs by an outside force." Honoria twisted the rings on her hands like she always did when she became unnerved.

"Maybe you dreamt about Mr. Fredericks's concerns for my chances of contracting hay fever. According to the book he authored and so generously gave to me, those who suffer from catarrh often struggle to breathe. Sometimes it feels as though the air is shut completely off at their throats."

"It wasn't just that. The next image I remember is that of us facing each other. You open your mouth to speak and as soon as you do the ground between us rumbles and shakes. An enormous chasm forms with you on one side and me on the other." Honoria looked so distressed I felt soothing her was beyond my ability.

I tried another tack. "Would you like to speak to Officer Yancey about your concerns? Would that help to put your mind at ease?" I asked. Honoria let loose a most unladylike snort.

"I doubt very much that the police would take such a thing seriously. Can you imagine that Chief Hurley, or Yancey for that matter, would start an investigation based on a dream?"

"No, I suppose I can't. Do you have anything to share with them that they might be more willing to consider?"

"Like what? A suspect based on something I witnessed with my waking eyes?"

"Something like that would prove ideal."

"No, I don't. I was hoping you had seen something yourself."

"I was too busy trying to keep to my feet to see much of anything clearly. I've already told Officer Yancey what I did see."

"What did you tell him?"

"I remember seeing Chief Hurley speaking with Henry Goodwin only moments before the collapse. Henry and some other boys scattered into the crowd and that's when all the pushing and shoving started."

"Did you have the impression the boys were responsible for the chaos?"

"At the time I thought maybe they were just being boisterous. In such a tightly packed crowd their rambunctiousness could have easily led to accidents."

"But now you think more may be involved? You think it was deliberate?"

"I don't know. What I am sure of is that Officer Yancey and I searched Sophronia's room and were unable to discover the manuscript she claimed to have written."

"Do you think it was stolen?"

"I'm not sure it ever existed in the first place. Apparently even Miss Rice hasn't seen it. She says Sophronia told her it would be safer for her if she remained unaware of its contents."

"You seem remarkably well-informed. Are you assisting with the investigation in some way? Don't tell me you've convinced young Yancey to ask for help beyond the world of the physical?"

"No, I simply provided a chaperone when he interviewed Miss Rice and assisted with the search of Sophronia's room." I debated whether or not to mention what Lucy shared about George. I decided Honoria had endured enough terrible news for one day.

CHAPTER THIRTY-TWO

YANCEY STEPPED INTO THE STATION THINKING ABOUT WHO TO question next. He really ought to head back to the Belden to talk with the Cheswicks. From what Lucy had said, all three of them might be able to provide him with some much needed answers. But first he wondered if there were any messages from his mother or sister. No sooner had he walked to his desk to check than the door to the chief's office opened and Robert Jellison, followed by Frank, filed out. Both men were smiling. Without even a nod of acknowledgment to the officers in the room Robert Jellison strode out of the station, banging the door behind him.

Robert Jellison, known to his many detractors as Jelly Roll, owned the large luxury hotel next to the Belden. He was a prominent local businessman with properties scattered all over town, including bathhouses that competed with Pinckney Ferris's own elaborate establishment. He also happened to be married to the chief's sister.

"The chief wants to see you," Frank said as he sauntered to his desk.

Chief Hurley's office smelled, as it always did, of stale smoke and fried fish. The chief sat behind his desk, turning a paper knife over and over in his hands. He used it to point at the chair opposite him. Yancey sat.

"I want you to pull all available officers off other duties and put everyone, you included, on safety patrols around the pier. With the opening happening tomorrow we need to keep focused on what's important."

"What about the case I'm working on?

The chief raised his great tuft of an eyebrow. "What case?"

"The unexplained death of Miss Foster Eldridge." Yancey was sure he didn't like where this was going.

"There is no case. The poor woman was clearly out of her mind when she dressed herself in a man's coat, loaded her pockets with rocks, and jumped into the plunge bath."

"You believe she committed suicide?" Yancey's mouth went dry and his stomach stopped rumbling and knotted up instead. He could feel righteous indignation fill his belly like a steaming bowl of stew.

"Of course she did. I should have thought it would be obvious."

"Not to me it isn't," Yancey said. "What are you basing that decision upon?"

"The woman believes women should have the right to vote, for starters. She was convinced she was in contact with spirits of the dead. She was found wearing men's clothing, for God's sake. What more proof do you need that the balance of her mind was disturbed?"

"Your opposition to suffrage is not the same as proof that she took her own life. I hardly think any of the reasons you list can be considered proof of insanity."

"It is in my book."

"But Miss Foster Eldridge received a threatening letter. She told a close friend she believed the stage accident to have been no accident at all." Yancey could hear his pulse pounding in his ears like an incoming tide. Yancey reached into his jacket pocket and brought out an envelope containing the photographs he had borrowed from Thomas. He held them each out in front of his boss at eye level.

"What are these?" the chief asked, tapping the photographs with his paper knife.

"They're photographs Thomas Lydale took during the fray yesterday. I was wondering if you saw anything unusual concerning the stage?"

"Why do you want to know?"

"In this one you look like you're talking to Henry Goodwin." Yancey pointed at the photograph showing the boy.

"What of it?"

"That in itself seemed unusual. You are not the sort of man who spends his time socializing with children. And we both know Henry is not a particular fan of the police force."

"Are you implying something I should take offense to, Yancey?"

"No, sir. I just wanted to inquire if you noticed anything amiss with him. Right after he spoke with you he and several other boys began jostling the crowd of marchers and setting off firecrackers. I thought you might have seen something having to do with that."

"No. I can't say that I did. But why would I? If you hadn't shown me this photograph I wouldn't have believed I had spoken to him at all." The chief tapped the second photograph. "And this one?"

"This man is talking to you just before the stage collapsed. I thought maybe one of you might have seen something that would explain how the stage just happened to collapse."

"I was standing right there and you can take from me the entire incident had nothing to do with any of the bystanders. There's no need to go riling people up and starting rumors." Hurley banged his fist down on the desk. "You haven't convinced yourself that there is more to that mess yesterday than a stiff wind and some shoddy workmanship, have you?"

"You don't think it is strange that just as Sophronia announces her intention to expose corruption by some of the people in attendance that the stage supporting her collapses from out beneath her feet? Do you think there is no link between that and her body being found less than twenty-four hours later?"

"I don't think it's strange at all. I think it is proof there is a God and he is paying close attention to this beautiful nation of ours."

"Accident or no accident, can you identify the man standing next to you in the photograph?" Yancey asked as he held it a little closer. Yancey could tell from the way the chief's mustache lifted on one side that he was smiling to himself. Hurley's smiles never made Yancey happy.

"Don't you know who he is?" Hurley asked. "After all, the family resemblance is quite strong."

"So you do know him then, sir?"

"Most people over thirty in the town know him. That's Osmond. George Cheswick's younger brother."

Hurley smiled again. "You can ask all the questions of Osmond or that Goodwin kid that you want but it won't change the fact that this case is closed."

"Sir, you can't close the case without a proper investigation."

"All the investigation that is needed has already been done. I took a look at the scene myself while you were off paying a call at the Belden. There was nothing to suggest she didn't kill herself."

"You must have seen the wound on her head." Yancey silently told his fists to unclench but they refused to listen. "She didn't get that by drowning."

"Good God, man, were you the only one at the march who didn't see the stage collapse? Of course she had a head injury." Hurley leaned his chair on the two back legs. "I told you before, the town fathers will turn us all out of our jobs if anything casts a shadow over the pier opening. Robert Jellison was just here to remind me of their intentions."

"It's funny, isn't it, how often Mr. Jellison's best interests and the intentions of the town fathers line up?" Yancey knew he was pushing the limits of the chief's patience but he couldn't seem to stop himself.

"I'm going to pretend I didn't hear that since I know you have your own reasons to prefer that no case is ever ruled a suicide. But eventually you are going to have to face the fact that some people suffer from weak morals and an imbalance of the mind. The case is closed."

The chief pointed at the door with his paper knife. "Believe me, it's best this way. You don't want to go poking your nose into this any further."

Yancey returned to his desk. When Yancey thought about Lucy's and Ruby's likely reactions to the news about Sophronia's case, he found he had thoroughly lost his temper.

As he sat there he wished he could have been a fly on the wall in the chief's office while Jelly Roll had been in there. It seemed more than a coincidence that as soon as he had visited, the investigation was curtailed. If Jelly Roll were the only one to have paid a call to the station Yancey would have suspected it was a matter of business to shut down the case. After all, a murder was far worse for the tourist trade than a suicide. And Jelly Roll would benefit from the taint on the competition's bathhouse.

But with Frank in on whatever conversation had occurred, too, Yancey had to consider there was more to the story than a business deal that required shoring up. How was Frank connected to Jelly Roll and the chief? Were they covering something up and was it for themselves or the interests of the pier or both?

And a suicide theory did not explain the blow to Sophronia's head. Even an accidental drowning wouldn't explain that. Nothing found in the bathhouse when her body was discovered could have created the wound. He was now sure it was murder, pure and simple. He was going to have to keep investigating without the chief finding out. As much as he didn't want a murder victim branded as a suicide, he wasn't prepared to lose his job.

Yancey was eager to solve Sophronia's case but he was even more invested in solving the murder of Gladys Willard and his own father's death almost twenty years earlier. But to do that he needed to stay close to the center of the action and remain on the force. He needed help, and as much as it pained him to admit it there was only one person who came to mind for the job.

CHAPTER THIRTY-THREE

M ISS PROULX, MIGHT I HAVE A WORD WITH YOU?" I LOOKED
up from my book to see that Officer Yancey stood in the
library threshold turning his hat round and round in his hands. I
found myself happy to have anyone other than Mrs. Doyle calling
my name. Even if that person was a policeman. I tucked a scrap
of ribbon between the pages of *The Memoirs of Sherlock Holmes*
to mark my place and slid the book into the depths of the chair.
I felt suddenly foolish about reading a detective novel in the presence of a real police officer.

"Of course, Officer. Come in." I gestured to the other wingback chair centered in the bookshelf-lined room. As he settled
into the seat beside me I felt the intimacy of the space in a new
way. It felt domestic somehow to be sitting side by side in matching armchairs separated by only a small table.

An unusual shyness overtook me and I found it difficult to
engage in my customary banter. It was vastly easier to manage
Yancey when he raised my ire by being abrasive rather than by
disarming me with good manners. It would never do to let him
know he had left me feeling uncertain. I tucked my reserve down

deep where it usually spent its days and gave him a piercing look. "Have you come to tell me you've already discovered what really happened to Sophronia?"

"I wish I were. Instead, I am here to ask for your help," he said, looking down at his shiny black boots as he spoke. "With the investigation into Miss Foster Eldridge's death."

"I thought you were the only one who was permitted to ask questions." I was quite enjoying myself watching his face suffuse with color and noting the way he shifted his weight in his chair like a small, nervous boy. "I seem to remember that you were very clear only a little while ago that my assistance was not required or desired."

"I should not have said that. I spoke rudely and my only excuse is that I am not in the habit of including those who are not on the police force in investigations."

"I beg to differ. You have routinely asked Mr. Lydale to assist you with your investigations. I believe he has been invaluable," I said.

"But Thomas is not a lady."

"I had noticed that Mr. Lydale seems to be most assuredly a gentleman." If anything, Officer Yancey looked even more uncomfortable than before.

"I only meant that his reputation would not be damaged by association with the police in the same way a lady's would be. After all, there are no women on the force. It is a novel thing to consider working with one."

At least he blamed his remarks on habit rather than personal prejudice. I couldn't resist needling him a bit more despite my overwhelming curiosity.

"Why my help? You don't wish for me to channel Sophronia's spirit in order to ask who killed her, do you?"

"Of course not." Yancey looked like he was suffering from a grievous stomach complaint. "The truth is, the chief has decided to close the case."

"If it's been solved I can't see how you would need my help," I said. "Unless you do not concur with the solution."

"That's it exactly."

"So who is it Chief Hurley believes to be guilty?" I leaned forward eagerly in the chair. "Please tell me you haven't arrested George as Lucy suggested?"

"The chief has been persuaded that Miss Foster Eldridge was an unstable woman who committed suicide." I wished I could say that I couldn't believe my ears but after the way the police had behaved at the march it was clear they didn't value Sophronia's life. Blaming her for her own death was not much of a stretch.

"You aren't planning to stop investigating, are you?" I hoped with fervor that he was not. I hardly wished to think what would happen to the Yancey family if Orazelia and Lucy heard that he had sided with the chief.

"I do not plan to do any such thing," Yancey said. "But the chief has ordered the case closed and all officers on patrol duties for the pier opening. I'm not supposed to continue investigating in any way."

"Which is why you have come to me?"

"Exactly. It occurred to me that those nearest and dearest to the victim would be more inclined to speak with one of their own rather than the police anyway. I was hoping you would be willing to ask questions and share any findings with me, Miss Proulx."

Yancey sounded eager to have my help. I had very much enjoyed our previous joint effort and found myself curiously elated at the prospect of sharing a second collaborative investigation. In fact, the sense of excited anticipation was strong enough to make me also feel rather ashamed of myself. It was not seemly to take pleasure from the death of another.

"How do you propose I should begin to question suspects? If you are not the face of the investigation, what authority do I have to demand that people share their secrets with me?"

"I doubt you'll have any trouble there. I've noticed you have something of a knack for extracting information from others." Officer Yancey actually sounded as though he were complimenting me. "If that doesn't work you could use your unique position as a medium to encourage cooperation."

"I thought you didn't believe in such things."

"I don't but many of the people on my suspect list do. In this case, your perceived authority may well be higher than my own anyway." Yancey gave me a smile that looked more weary than charming. It would be foolish to say no, since I wanted to help. And it looked as though there might not be justice for Sophronia if I didn't lend a hand.

"I am willing to do it but I have a request."

"Which is?"

"You treat me like an equal partner in the investigation. No taking information from me and keeping your information to yourself."

"That's all?"

"That's all. If there is one thing I value, it is respect. The equal sharing of confidences will convey that respect from you."

"I thought you were going to make this much harder on me."

"Why would I do a thing like that?"

"I have behaved quite rudely in the past and have made it clear I was very skeptical of your motives and even your morals. I am not sure if the situation were reversed that I would be as for-giving."

"I didn't say that you were forgiven in the least," I said. Yancey jiggled his leg up and down in place. "I said I would help. I am doing so for Sophronia and for the cause of suffrage."

"How may I make it up to you?" Yancey asked. I found not only was I enjoying the prospect of investigating once more, I was also enjoying Officer Yancey's change of attitude toward me. It almost made me think we could become friends. Almost. I de-cided not to warm up to him too easily. His instincts about my character had been good ones and if the truth about my past surfaced, it was a friendship that wouldn't last.

"You could start by telling me why you left the Belden without questioning the rest of the people here who knew Sophronia," I said, giving him a bright smile and folding my hands in my lap as though I were prepared to wait all day for his confidences to be shared.

"I wanted to question Congressman Plaisted before anyone could forbid me from doing so."

"I understand the urgency. Did you ask him why he assaulted Sophronia in the alley?"

"I thought I would keep that information to myself for a bit. I asked him to confirm the report that he had broken off with Sophronia many years ago and married a friend of hers instead."

"Where did you hear that?"

"From Thomas, of all people. Apparently he used to work for Sophronia at a temperance newspaper she ran with the woman who became Congressman Plaisted's wife."

"That explains the hostility between them but not why he would be angry with her."

"He says she was the one who ended the relationship instead of him," Officer Yancey said. "I hoped maybe you could make some inquiries amongst those who might have known about it."

"Like Theda Rice?"

"Exactly."

"That's something to start with. You've kept yourself well occupied."

"There's more. I stopped in at Thomas's studio for photographs from the march. You were right about Henry Goodwin talking with the chief." He pulled a photograph from his jacket pocket and handed it to me.

"Did you ask your boss why he was talking with Henry?"

"I did." He gripped the chair arms so tightly his knuckles paled. I had hit upon a sore spot.

"What did he say?"

"He denied the conversation had any importance and was not pleased to be asked about it. I am afraid I will lose my job before I have had a chance to complete my investigation." Officer Yancey's knuckles grew even whiter.

"Are you still speaking of the investigation into Sophronia's death?" I asked. "Or something else?" He gave me a long look and then drew in a deep breath. I could see from his expression that he was trying to come to a decision.

"Lucy thinks very highly of you and I am inclined to trust that she is right to put her faith in you." He leaned toward me and lowered his own voice. "I am investigating Chief Hurley himself."

"Because of what happened yesterday?" I asked.

"Because I believe that he is entirely corrupt and has been abusing his position of authority for years." Officer Yancey closed his eyes for a moment. If pressed I would have said he was stalling. "I think it goes back at least as far as my father's case and I think it is still going on today."

"Is there something besides the photo of Chief Hurley and Henry to make you believe that?"

"I am concerned that Robert Jellison may have been involved."

"Robert Jellison? Did he even know Sophronia?"

"Her body was found in a competitor's bathhouse. And he left the chief's office with a smug grin on his face just before Hurley called me in to tell me the investigation was over." Yancey let out a deep breath. "At the very least Jellison is asking for it to be hushed up so as not to put a damper on the pier opening."

"Ask why he suspects his partner." The voice spoke with startling clarity in my left ear.

"There is another person you are worried is involved though, isn't there?" I said. "You are concerned about a role Officer Nichols may have played in the death?" Yancey snapped his head up to look me in the eyes.

"How did you know that?" he asked. "Did his mother-in-law say something?"

"Mrs. Doyle has nothing to do with this." At least I sincerely hoped she did not. That part of the investigation I planned to keep to myself until I had time to mull it over. "As I've already told you, I am not a fraud. I do receive guidance from the world beyond," I said. "So, why do you suspect him?"

Yancey leaned back in his chair and squinted at me in an alarming imitation of Mrs. Doyle. The noises of the room stilled and all I heard were the ticking of the mantel clock and the low rumble of the sea. Something in him seemed to be at war and then I could see the decision flit across his face.

"Frank left the chief's office at the same time as Jellison."

"That isn't so very damning."

"But you remember that a few weeks ago something occurred which put Frank in the chief's debt. I don't believe Frank has a personal motive to have harmed Miss Foster Eldridge but a small part of me wonders if he felt forced to do so at the chief's bidding."

"Albert Fitch?" I asked. Albert Fitch had died in police custody weeks earlier. Frank had given him a beating but swore he hadn't killed him. The chief had turned a blind eye on the incident and even helped to get rid of Albert Fitch's body.

"Exactly. Frank is lucky to still be on the force." Yancey shook his head. "I've been waiting for the chief to start calling in favors ever since it happened."

"If the chief is capable of that he is certainly capable of covering up evidence or hushing witnesses," I said.

"We need to gather more information about what transpired between the chief and Henry," Yancey said. "As soon as possible."

CHAPTER THIRTY-FOUR

A MANDA HOWELL STOOD IN THE DOORWAY OF A SMALL READ-ing room in the spiritual wing of the hotel, saying her good-byes to a group of women who had checked in the week before. I nodded to the ladies and tried to slip past Amanda without engaging her in conversation.

"You must be simply devastated by the loss of Sophronia," she said. A look of total insincerity wreathed her face. If Amanda had not professed her psychic gift to be one of token reading I would have sworn she had an unnatural ability to find a sore spot in anyone's heart and to prick it until it bled. "But, I suppose it was only a matter of time until a woman of such an unbalanced temperament did herself irreversible harm." Amanda smiled at me and drew her finger slowly across her neck.

"Sophronia didn't kill herself."

"Well, you wouldn't think ill of her, now, would you? After all, she made quite a pet of you, didn't she?"

"Just because a woman believes she should have the right to vote does not mean she is out of her mind."

"It should. After all, everyone knows that women who support suffrage will begin to sprout beards." Amanda blinked her dark blue eyes at me slowly. "But I don't only say that because of her outrageous beliefs. It was her nasty temper that convinced me she was unstable. If anyone had truly cared about her in the least they would have shut her away in an asylum before she did such an unforgivable thing to herself." I felt my anger mounting until I gave Amanda's words some thought.

"I never saw the least display of temper from Sophronia. I can't believe you would seek to further damage her reputation."

"I can't imagine how anything could possibly do that. Besides, why shouldn't I say it if it is true? I happened to overhear Sophronia and that gangly friend of hers arguing like a pair of fishwives."

"You were eavesdropping on the guests?" That was the sort of thing that Honoria considered grounds for dismissal. The privacy of all hotel guests mattered but she particularly upheld the secrets of those who often encountered scorn from the outside world on account of their beliefs.

"It isn't eavesdropping if the other party decides to argue in a public space. It can hardly be considered my fault that I entered the dining room and found Sophronia and Miss Rice in the midst of a heated conversation."

"Did they know you were there?"

"Both women acknowledged me with the barest nod of their heads and then they turned back to their own conversation. From their body language it was clear Miss Rice was seething and Sophronia felt she had nothing to apologize for. No one else was in the room besides the three of us but by the time I had helped myself to breakfast they seemed to have completely forgotten I was there." Amanda shrugged. "I did sit as far from them as I was able. It wasn't as though I had any desire to be included in what was clearly an unpleasant conversation."

In my mind's eye I could see Amanda delighting in the show unfolding before her eyes. The trick would be to convince her to tell me what she heard without appearing to want to know. Pretending to disbelieve her seemed the best way to accomplish just that. Fortunately, I rarely believed her so I had had a great deal of practice.

"I can't believe two such dear friends would have been arguing at all, let alone in full view of anyone who happened to wander in."

"For someone who claims to have access to the spirit world you are poorly informed. They were arguing about Sophronia's manuscript and how she planned to use it." A look of triumph passed over Amanda's face. "Miss Rice accused Sophronia of being reckless and hungry for fame and that the mob at the march proved she had finally gone too far. She said something about squandering, too."

"Squandering what?"

"Money, I suppose. What else would you squander?"

"What did Sophronia have to say to Miss Rice's accusations?"

"Nothing at all. She simply slapped her fist down on the table and knocked over a pitcher of milk. Then she stomped out of the room without another word."

"What did Miss Rice do?"

"She just sat there motionless and stared at the table in front of her. It was a good thing the milk was already wasted because the look Sophronia had given her would have curdled it anyway."

"When did the argument take place?" I asked.

"After they returned from the march." Amanda smiled at me again. "You know, if the police were not so sure Sophronia had taken her own life I would have been convinced that Miss Rice had killed her."

CHAPTER THIRTY-FIVE

MISS RICE FINALLY FELT WELL ENOUGH TO HAVE QUITTED her room and now seemed intent on using her renewed sense of health to develop her otherworldly abilities. It is never a surprising thing for those gripped by grief to turn to the spiritual realm. In fact, my father and I had made use of that very proclivity with an impressive degree of success for years. Miss Rice appeared to be one of those same people. Which suited my purposes just fine. After all, if she had still been bedridden and incoherent with grief I would have found it difficult to ask her about her argument with her dearly departed friend. As it was, I felt emboldened to do so.

"Miss Rice, you look like you are on the mend," I said, looking about the room Lucy had taken over as an office when Sophronia had requested her assistance. Miss Rice sat at the table in the center of the room. Pages covered with writing littered the floor and her fingers were stained with ink. Correspondence heaped and tumbled off the desk, too. "What has wrought this remarkable change?"

"Sophronia came to me through automatic writing. Look."

Miss Rice held out a fistful of paper sheets. "While I am loath to do so, she insists I take up her mantle and carry on her work. She insists there is no one else to whom she would entrust such a thing. Look." She thrust the ink-stained pages at me. I looked them over carefully, feeling the weight of her stare upon my face. As far as I could see the message appeared to be a mandate that she take Sophronia's place for the good of the suffrage cause. The pages, as Miss Rice claimed, indicated Sophronia felt no other was up to the task.

"Ask her if the argument was resolved," I heard the voice say clearly in my ear. I took a seat and placed it quite near to Miss Rice's own. I allowed my eyes to close and my head to fall forward as if in a trance. I did not feel good about the deception but if she was already using the spirit world to grant her leave to assume leadership it seemed fair to use something similar to question her. I began to sway slightly forward and back and then stopped suddenly and stiffened. I tipped my ear toward the ceiling and tried to appear as though I were straining to hear something from a distance.

"I am hearing Sophronia's voice and she speaks to me of an argument between the two of you. She says it makes her uneasy to have left this plane without returning to perfect harmony with her dearest friend. Does that make sense to you?"

"There are always things we regret saying. I'm sure it was nothing out of the ordinary."

"She is quite insistent. She is showing me an image of the two of you seated at a table and you both have angry looks upon your faces. She stands and walks away, leaving you there alone. She wishes the two of you had never argued." Miss Rice slumped in her chair, all the puff alarmingly leaking out of her. Perhaps it was a bit soon to give her another shock. Still, the voice never sent me careening in the wrong direction.

"Please let her know I wish things had been different in these last weeks, too. I regret what I said."

"It would give me a better ability to convey your sentiments if I were clearer concerning the source of your regret. I am sensing there was a disagreement about squandered resources."

"That is the crux of the matter. Sophronia had begun to associate with wealthy and influential women, like those involved in the Hay Feverists Society. I questioned her motives in doing so. I regret that now." I paused and cocked my head as if listening to the beyond. "I feared for her safety but she simply laughed it off saying I should know better than to allow it to worry me." Miss Rice reached for a handkerchief and blew her nose loudly.

"Why should you not have felt concern? I felt the same way when I heard about the threatening letter." I felt the familiar tingle along my skin that always occurred when I realized I was on the right track with a reading. I was surprised once more by how much the skills of a confidence artist and those of an investigator overlapped.

"I shouldn't have worried because I knew that Sophronia generally sent such letters to herself."

"Sophronia sent the letter? Why would she do that?"

"To drum up interest in the press. She did it at almost every place we stayed for any length of time." I was stunned. I had not considered how far Sophronia was willing to go to support her cause. If she had been willing to lie about something that produced so much concern in those around her, what else would she be willing to do? Still, if Miss Rice knew that was her habit, why had she still been worried?

"If you knew she did such things, why would you have concerns for her safety? What was unique about this situation?"

"There were two things that bothered me. I told her she was making a mistake when she decided to announce her decision to publish a book about corruption. She wouldn't even let me read it. She said she was the only one who should assume the risk for the secrets it contained." Her voice caught in her throat.

"So you haven't seen her manuscript?" I had to wonder if Sophronia hadn't trusted Miss Rice as much as it had seemed. Or maybe she really didn't want to put her friend at risk. She had shared the secret of her fake hate mails with her, after all.

"Sophronia always kept it secreted away except for when she was working on it. All I know was that she felt it was almost ready to be offered to publishers and that she had the last part all planned," Miss Rice said. "She was overjoyed to be so close to finishing it when we last met."

"Do you know what the last step in her process was?"

"A final revision, from what I understand. The heart of the work was all in place but she wanted to be sure the words were powerful enough to make a compelling case against those she accused of corruption."

"What was the second reason you were so worried for her safety despite what you knew about the note?" I asked.

"It was the arrival of Nelson Plaisted. If I had known he would be in Old Orchard I would have insisted she change her plans to appear here."

Again I felt the crackling of excitement down the back of my neck and along my arms. Nelson Plaisted was my favorite suspect. I would much prefer for him to be guilty than poor George.

"Why would you worry about the congressman?"

"Were you at the rally on the day Sophronia arrived?" Miss Rice asked.

"I was. He was combative and insulting but I took his words to be posturing. I got the impression he is as adept at getting into the newspapers as Sophronia herself," I said. "Was there something more to his behavior than that?"

"There is much more to the story than that." Miss Rice paused and looked at me as if trying to decide whether to share what she knew. Something must have prompted her to do so. "Sophronia's upbringing was not an easy one. Her family was of modest means and her father drank heavily. He made life an utter misery for her mother and all the children. By the time Sophronia's mother had produced the seventh child in nine years her body and spirit were broken. She died giving birth to Sophronia's youngest brother."

"I am very sorry to hear it."

Miss Rice placed her large, square hand over the base of her throat. "After her mother's passing, Sophronia's father's drinking bouts grew more uncontrollable and he was not long after his wife in heading to the grave. In fact, he drowned facedown in a mud puddle one stormy night not fifty feet from his favorite tavern. His pockets had been picked clean and someone had stolen the shoes from his feet." My heart went out to Sophronia as I thought of my own father's drunken rages and how life for me would have been different if I had been raised by my aunt at the Belden instead of by him. "As soon as he no longer controlled Sophronia's actions she joined the temperance movement in Portland."

"I understand that is where Sophronia first encountered Congressman Plaisted."

"It was. She met Nelson Plaisted at a meeting not long after she joined the group. She found they were both passionately committed to the passage of temperance in Maine."

"So they weren't always the enemies they became?"

"The way Sophronia told it was that they were so completely in harmony that even after seeing the drudgery of her mother's life she did not hesitate to accept his proposal of marriage. She did, however, wish to have a long engagement. A little voice kept whispering in her ear that she ought take her time with such a matter."

"And she never did end up marrying him?"

"When temperance laws were folded into the state constitution in 1885, not long after their engagement was announced, Sophronia was overjoyed. But as time went on there seemed to be little difference in the lives of actual women, law or no law. She became convinced that while drunkenness was destructive for families, prohibition was not the cure, women's suffrage was. Nelson did not agree in the least."

"I can see how that would cause a rift even in the strongest of bonds."

"It did. He believed strongly in the cult of womanhood, and Sophronia believed there was more in store for her than making a home a haven for him and the children he wanted her to bear for him."

"Did she break off the engagement or did he?"

"She did. What you witnessed at the rally was the result of that choice. Nelson was humiliated by her decision and he has taken every opportunity to obstruct her and ridicule her in public ever since." Miss Rice stared off toward the horizon, where a sailboat scudded past, its white sails taut in the wind. "He even went so far as to base his political platform on anti-suffrage principles. He refuted all the things she stood for and ended up recruiting many of the powerful businessmen in Maine for his cause."

"Was she afraid of him?" I asked.

"No, Miss Proulx. She was not afraid of him." Miss Rice shook her head. "In fact, she said over and over that, rather, he had reason to be afraid of her but she would never tell me why. She said it was better I didn't know."

I closed my eyes and pretended to listen to Sophronia's spirit again. In my mind's eye I saw Sophronia's face when Congressman Plaisted assaulted her. I wasn't convinced their prior personal relationship explained the anger I had witnessed from him. There had to be more to the story but it didn't seem as though Miss Rice could tell me anything that would explain it.

It was time to leave Miss Rice and to see what I could discover about the Plaisteds. As much as I dreaded questioning the congressman after having witnessed his behavior toward a woman who angered him I knew I must. I spoke once more in the voice I used to deliver messages from the beyond.

"Sophronia says she wishes you would stop feeling guilty and would carry on valiantly working for the cause you shared." I had the familiar sense of grimy triumph that always accompanied my use of people's beliefs to extract information from them. "She says it is the best way to honor her life."

Miss Rice began to sob in earnest and I wondered if I had gone too far. I squeezed her hand and slipped out the door before I made things worse.

Chapter Thirty-Six

Yancey waited until the chief and Frank left the station. It hadn't escaped his notice that they left together. He asked Officer Lewis to track down Henry Goodwin and to bring him back to the station. Yancey ducked into the chief's office and pulled the newspaper from his wastepaper basket. If he were lucky maybe one of the reporters who covered the march would have unearthed something useful.

No such luck. There were editorials on suffrage from both sides of the argument and plenty of speculation as to what might have caused the stage's collapse but nothing that shed any light on Miss Foster Eldridge's life. Nothing new, at least. The newspapers were, however, full of conjecture about the war with the Spanish. Trouble was brewing in Cuba, no doubt about it. The Battle of Manila Bay the month before had ramped things up even further. Every page he turned seemed to contain an article espousing zealous support for the war effort.

Yancey had had more than enough of it when Officer Lewis pushed open the door and entered, jawing about the exact same thing with young Henry Goodwin. That was the worst of it, the thing that really got Yancey's temper to flare—kids like Henry with a gleam in their eyes as they bragged about the way they'd take on an enemy.

"I'd give 'um a wallop. A good one, too," Henry said, slapping his cap against the leg of his knickerbockers to make the point. Still in short pants and full of dreams of battle. It twisted Yancey's guts like nothing else. He fought down the urge to shake Henry until he dislodged the boy's misguided notions.

"Here's Henry to see you like you asked, boss," Officer Lewis said. "He was a little hard to track down but I unearthed him behind the livery, playing with firecrackers. It's a wonder he didn't burn down the town."

"Which are you charging him with? Willful endangerment or public menace?" Yancey asked, giving Lewis a wink on the sly.

"I was thinking it might be best to charge him with both," Lewis said. "That way we have twice as much chance of getting the charge to stick."

"Or he'll face twice as much jail time."

"I promised I wouldn't do it again." Henry stopped slapping his hat. His eyes bugged out of his head and he wrapped his arms across his chest like his lungs were trying to escape.

"If he promised to give us some help with an ongoing investigation, is there any way you could consider forgetting about the incident?" Yancey asked.

"I'm not sure. Fire is serious. You know that."

"We all know that." Fire was serious. It wasn't just patter designed to scare the kid. Fires devastated communities all over the country. With fires used to cook as well as to heat buildings the danger of stray sparks and dirty chimneys was always present. Only two years earlier the Opera House block in the state capital,

Augusta, burnt to the ground. In the devastation a bank, a drug-
gist, and a grocery were lost. Henry was right to be frightened.

"What is it you need?" Henry asked. His voice cracked and
Yancey felt a bit sorry for him. Until he remembered the feeling
of searching the crowd for his mother and sister when the popping noise of the firecrackers began. Or the sickening surprise of
Miss Proulx suddenly disappearing from sight as the stairs she
stood upon went out from under her.

"I want to know about this photograph." Yancey pulled the
picture of Henry and the chief from his jacket pocket once more.
"Why were you talking to the chief? Did he ask you to set off
those firecrackers at the march? Did he tell you to start the jostling?" Yancey kept his eyes fixed on Henry's face as he recognized
himself in the photograph. He definitely had a guilty conscience
but he was surprised by the question.

"No, sir. He did not." Yancey was going to ask what they had
talked about if it hadn't been the subject of mischief when it registered in his mind that the boy had stressed the word *he*.

"Who did, then?" Yancey asked. Henry hung his head and
shifted his weight from foot to foot. When he looked up his expression was one of complete misery.

"The shoving was an accident. We were just excited and them
ladies were packed in like string beans in a pint jar." Henry's
lower lip quivered slightly. "No one was supposed to get hurt.
Honest."

"But someone did ask you to set off the firecrackers?" Yancey
pressed. His money was on Robert Jellison. Oh, how he ached for
it to be Jelly Roll.

"Are you really gonna send me to jail if I don't tell you about
the firecrackers?" Henry's face took on a greenish tinge. Officer

Lewis looked almost like he felt sorry for the kid. He knew better than to say anything though, which spoke well for his future on the force.

"People were hurt, Henry. This is no small thing. But you are a kid and if an adult encouraged you to do something so foolish you ought to say so." Yancey paused to let that thought settle. "If you tell me who it was you can walk out of here a free man so long as you promise never to do such a dangerous thing again."

"You're not just saying that and then you'll stick me in the pokey anyway?" Henry's family history was one that would not encourage confidence in the police department. Yancey knew exactly how he felt, considering his didn't, either. He made it a habit not to lie any more than he could help it.

"No, Henry. I promise not to do that. But I won't be so lenient if you endanger the town like that again. Do you understand?" Henry shuffled his feet and nodded. "Tell me, who was it?"

Henry's voice came out barely above a whisper.

"That lady from the Hotel Belden." Henry met Yancey's eyes. "Mrs. Doyle."

CHAPTER THIRTY-SEVEN

I HAD NO TROUBLE FINDING MR. FREDERICKS ON THE VERANDA sitting in a basket chair in the deep shade. He spent a portion of each day breathing in the sea air just as the articles in the *Hay Feverist Monthly* recommended. Generally Honoria discouraged staff from disturbing the guests but I was certain she would make an exception. I expected to see the gentleman in question consumed by grief but instead, he greeted me with a cheerful expression and a pleasant word.

"Miss Proulx, you look the picture of health today. If I may be so bold as to say so, the roses bloom upon your cheeks most becomingly."

"Unlike poor Sophronia," I said. I watched as his smile faded and he carefully replaced it with a solemn nod of his head.

"Such an unexpected tragedy. It seems unimaginable that someone with as much passion for life as Sophronia had would commit such an act."

"Do you think there is any possibility that she did not?"

"What are you suggesting?" Mr. Fredericks leaned toward me, his watery eyes fairly bursting from his large head.

"I'm simply wondering if her death was not as clear-cut as it appeared to the police," I said. He drew in his breath sharply.

"You can't mean to suggest that someone deliberately harmed her and then made it look like a suicide?" I could almost watch his thoughts parade behind his outsize forehead.

"What do you think?" I said. "Could anyone have borne Sophronia such ill will?"

"Not to my knowledge. She was a controversial figure to be sure but there was nothing to suggest that she had enemies beyond the average public figure." Mr. Fredericks waggled a bony finger in my direction. "In my experience young ladies are often influenced unduly by sensational novels and a thirst for excitement. Could that be the case here?" I regret to say I felt the warm creep of embarrassment moving up the back of my neck and into my face. More often than I cared to recall my father had chided me for my preference for novels instead of weightier works of philosophy or history. Mr. Fredericks's words brought back a flood of unpleasant memories and left me feeling like I needed to justify my taste in reading material.

I asked myself what Sophronia would have thought of allowing a man to belittle her and I felt the flush in my cheeks subside. In fact, as I considered his condescending comments from a suffragist perspective, I felt it was he who should be ashamed of himself. With that thought in mind, I pressed on with my questioning

"She did receive at least one threatening letter while she was here."

"As does anyone who espouses views that run counter to those held by the majority." He shrugged. "If the police here are at all experienced at their jobs I am quite certain they will know what to discount and what to include."

"I should expect the investigation into her death will lead to questions for you before too much longer." Strictly speaking, this was true. If Mr. Fredericks understood that the police were the ones investigating that was his own assumption, not something I actually could be credited with saying. It was a fine point perhaps but one that kept me on the side of the angels.

"Why would you say that?" Mr. Fredericks asked.

"Because you knew her from the Hay Feverists convention. You probably knew her better than anyone else in Old Orchard except Miss Rice," I said, keeping an eye fixed on his expression.

"She knew several people in town besides myself. I am sure they will be questioned as well."

"I don't think the investigation will be much aided by acquaintanceships struck up over the past few days." I cocked my head to the side as if lost in thought. "Do you?"

"There's where you are wrong, young lady. Sophronia and Miss Rice were acquainted with at least three other people here besides myself through our association with the Hay Feverists Society."

"I had no idea hay fever was such a common complaint." I should have been above such a petty dig but Mr. Fredericks's spluttering indignation raised my spirits to a shameful degree.

"Hay fever and all the other sorts of seasonal complaints experienced by sensitive persons such as myself are not in the least bit commonplace." Mr. Fredericks sniffed loudly. "However, it is only natural that those with discernment in their health would be sensitive as to their associations as well. Just because Osmond, Phyllis, and George Cheswick all attended the last Hay Feverists annual convention does not make it a condition which afflicts the masses."

"I'm sure you know far more about such matters than I do." I lowered my eyes to my lap hoping to convince him of my contrition.

"Don't fret, my dear. Becoming educated on such matters is as easy as applying oneself to some issues of *Hay Feverist Monthly*. I would be delighted to lend you a few copies from my personal collection in service of your education. They make for far superior reading than novels that put ideas into young ladies' heads." Mr. Fredericks flashed me a patronizing smile. "Perhaps by the time you've availed yourself of a few issues you shan't have any more thoughts of something as sordid as murder."

"I'm sure they will do me a world of good. I would feel even more at ease if I were reassured that there could be some explanation as to why Sophronia, who had so much to live for, would ever harm herself."

While I make it a personal point of pride to never, ever play dumb, especially with men, who I find often need no excuse to believe themselves intellectually superior, I have absolutely no compunction whatsoever against using feminine charms. Nothing vulgar, mind you, but I have come to realize that one can get further by being decorative as well as useful. I batted my eyelashes until I felt a breeze on my cheek.

"Perhaps hers was not as happy a life as you imagine." He shook his head. "It is easy to idolize those people we admire, but in truth they are no less plagued by doubts and burdens than the rest of us."

"Are you implying she may have had reason to be overcome by melancholia?"

"I would not be surprised if that were the case. You must have been aware of the threat she made concerning her manuscript. That farcical stunt simply reeked of desperation."

"You sound as though you doubt the existence of such a manuscript." I was intrigued. So far, I had not heard anyone else offering up the idea the manuscript might have been more fable than fact. "What makes you believe that she would have lied about it?"

"As an author myself I can say without reservation that I do not believe Sophronia had the temperament to sit alone quietly for hours at a time as the production of such a work necessitates. She was a person who thrived in the glow of attention whether supportive or derisive."

"And you think that making false claims about a manuscript may have led her to take her own life?"

"Imagine the shame of it. She made threats that she could not carry out and she did so in the full view of not only the assembled masses but also the press."

"You suggest her embarrassment was so utterly overwhelming that she felt she couldn't go on?"

"The police must have searched her room very thoroughly. Did they find a manuscript or any note left for anyone alerting them to where it might be? If she really were worried for her life she would surely have made arrangements for the release of information she claimed would so greatly aid the cause of suffrage."

"To my knowledge no such manuscript has been found," I said. Mr. Fredericks made some excellent points and ones that had been rattling around at the far edge of my thoughts since I learned of Sophronia's death. There are certain things none of us wish to believe of those we esteem. The perpetuation of this sort of fraud would surely be something Miss Rice would not want to face about her dearest friend.

"She told me just the other day about her clarity of vision for the future. She sounded very hopeful and assured that her cause would prevail and life for women would be entirely different one day. That doesn't sound like someone who was contemplating ending her life to me," I said.

"Perhaps by telling you this she was trying to convince herself. Even those who appear supremely confident have their doubts." Mr. Fredericks unfolded from his chair and reached for my hand, then raised it to his dry lips. I felt my favorite pair of lace gloves snag as he deposited a desiccated kiss on the back of my hand. "I shall fetch those magazines straightaway lest I forget."

Chapter Thirty-Eight

Someone needed to ask questions of Congressman Plaisted, and since Officer Yancey had been told not to investigate, that job would fall to me. I was not in the least eager to do so. Despite my enthusiasm for detective work and my personal interest in finding the truth of Sophronia's death I would be lying if I said I was not just a bit frightened of Plaisted after seeing the way he had manhandled Sophronia. How much less likely would I be to stir his ire if I asked about his ungentlemanly behavior toward a lady?

Ben flagged me down as I hurried along the hallway. He slid his slim white hand into a pigeonhole of the wall-mounted message center and pulled out an envelope. I tried to take it from him but his hand did not let go of the other side. His blue eyes looked into mine as though he wished for me to understand the gravity of what the envelope contained. As I was hoping for an excuse to delay my conversation with the congressman I was happy to pause and discover what he might be trying to communicate.

"Do you want me to be aware of something special about this

message, Ben?" I asked. He nodded slowly, his gaze never leaving my own.

"Is it important?" He nodded but did not let go of the envelope.

"Is it a secret?" He nodded again with a little more vigor.

"Did the sender tell you this?" I asked. He shook his head even more enthusiastically.

"You just know this about the message in the same way Amanda knows about people by touching their belongings or Mrs. Doyle reads auras?" I asked. Ben gave a noncommittal shrug and released the envelope from his grasp. "I'll keep what you said in mind," I said. I took the message to a chair a few feet away and, using a long hairpin from the collection keeping my heavy curls atop my head, slit the envelope neatly open.

I drew out the single sheet of paper it contained and read over the message from Officer Yancey three times before I felt Ben's gaze bearing down on me. I looked over, wishing he could tell me what to do.

"*Speak to her yourself,*" the voice said. I blinked but Ben hadn't said a thing. He turned his attention back to the appointment book on the desk in front of him. As much as I dreaded heading next door to the Sea Spray to confront the congressman, I was even less eager to head into the kitchen right here at the Belden.

MRS. DOYLE, IT COULD BE SAID, DID NOT LOOK LIKE HERSELF in the least. I did not need to possess her skill at reading auras to be certain something was very wrong with her. The message in my hand from Officer Yancey seemed to me to be a likely explanation for her unsettling change of demeanor. She sat in the rocker at the far end of the kitchen in just the same spot she had occupied the night before the march. She even held her darning egg in her hand with another holey sock slipped over the end.

She lacked, however, a threaded needle in the other hand. She also seemed not to have noticed its absence. She didn't even look up when I entered, let alone run her critical, squinty expression over me from head to toe. I was surprised to find it was an unpleasant feeling to be rid of her intense scrutiny.

I pulled a chair from the worktable to sit next to her rocking chair, and took the darning egg from her hand. She looked up and finally spoke.

"I don't know what's wrong with me today. I burnt the breakfast. I broke our best platter and I can't even find my spool of thread to fix this sock. I'm no good to anyone."

"I expect your aura's gone all funny after yesterday," I said. Mrs. Doyle let out a long sigh. Her shoulders drooped and she suddenly seemed like a tired old woman with a terrible secret. I was startled to realize I preferred her frightening dragon persona.

"You know about Henry, I suppose," she said.

"I know I saw Henry running around at the rally lighting firecrackers. I told Officer Yancey about it and he brought Henry to the station to ask him some questions. It is remarkable what a boy will say if he thinks it will keep him out of jail."

"He told the police I gave him the firecrackers?"

"He said you did and that you asked him to wait until Sophronia was on the stage with the crowd all assembled to set them off."

"It shouldn't have come down to that. If only that woman hadn't had the constitution of an ox," Mrs. Doyle said. "She should have taken to her bed and stayed there for at least a couple of days, maybe more."

"What exactly were you planning?" I asked.

"I told you she was not going to get away with tainting what we do here at the Belden. Not as long as I could possibly help it. I dosed her food with a bit of this and a bit of that. It wouldn't have caused any lasting damage but she should have found it difficult to venture far from a bathroom." I remembered all the peppermint wrappers and digestive powder packets littering Sophronia's bedside table when Officer Yancey and I had searched her room. That explained them.

"But it didn't work?"

"No. It didn't. I had promised you there was no chance you would find yourself on the platform for a reading and I was becoming quite desperate. Miss Foster Eldridge had already begun marching down Grand Avenue when I thought of firecrackers. I just meant for her to be scared off the stage. I never meant for anyone to be injured. Or to cause the stage to collapse."

Mrs. Doyle's dejected demeanor encouraged me to choose my words carefully. "I don't think you were responsible for the stage toppling over. And as far as I know, no one was actually hurt from the firecrackers. Yes, they were startling but it was the rocks and the bottles and the running and the grabbing by the protesters that was responsible for any harm that came to the marchers."

"Are you certain that is so?" Mrs. Doyle sat up a little straighter and squinted at me ever so slightly. I was relieved that I was not trying to pass off a falsehood as the truth. Even in her demoralized state I was sure she would have detected any lies and felt all the worse for it.

"Officer Yancey said so himself. He isn't interested in investigating the firecracker incident any further. But one problem remains."

"Which is?" She scowled harder.

"Officer Yancey is not going to believe you simply took a notion to disrupt the march. If he asks, we will have to provide him with a convincing reason and I shouldn't think it would be in our best interest to give him any more reasons to question the authenticity of the services we offer. I don't need to confess to him that you were saving me from committing public fraud," I said. Mrs. Doyle slumped back in her chair once more.

"How shall we explain it to him? What possible excuse can we give?"

"We won't unless we are directly asked to do so. Why borrow trouble?"

"And should he raise questions about it?"

"We'll stick to the truth as closely as we can. After all, he is a detective and is likely almost as experienced at separating lies from the truth as you are yourself," I said. "I'll just have to tell Officer Yancey that you weren't trying to hurt anyone but rather that you had a terrible feeling something bad was going to happen if I took the stage. I'll say you tried to convince me not to participate after the commotion at the rally the other day but like all young women I wouldn't listen to sense. You became even more concerned after Honoria dreamt of danger coming to the Belden and decided you had to frighten me enough to make me back down."

Mrs. Doyle slid forward in the rocker and planted both feet firmly on the floor in front of her. I was relieved to see her skin-blistering scowl reappear on her face. She looked me over this way and that before speaking.

"That entirely convincing excuse just occurred to you on the spur of the moment?" she asked.

"Yes, I suppose it did." Every time I turned around, evidence of my former life on the medicine show emerged. No matter how hard I tried to leave the past behind me it kept catching up to me anyhow.

"You really are a very accomplished liar. I am still not quite sure what to make of you."

"Aren't you the one who told me about white lies?" I asked.

"I am indeed. I suppose one more won't do any harm."

Chapter Thirty-Nine

I NEVER LIKED ENTERING THE SEA SPRAY HOTEL. IT WAS MUCH grander than our own establishment and the owner, Robert Jellison, had done his best to force Honoria out of business in order to acquire her property on the cheap and so expand his own. The Sea Spray boasted a ballroom, accommodations for 150 guests, and a grand bathhouse.

Mr. Jellison made mention of its many features in all his advertisements, going so far as to claim it was vastly superior to its undersize neighbors in every conceivable way. But I told myself, needs must. I mounted the wide wooden steps and walked through the oversize lobby doors.

If luck were with me I would find the congressman within and would have more answers than I had arrived in possession of. Even though I was investigating at Yancey's behest, I didn't have the backing of the police. I couldn't barge in and start asking questions. There were social niceties to be observed and I couldn't think of a better way to strike up a conversation than at the tea tray.

I followed enamel and brass placards in the direction of the dining room. Chandeliers the size of carriages dangled from the ceiling, and a plush floral carpet muffled the sounds in the room. A young man dressed all in burgundy approached and showed me the way to tables set for tea at the end of the vast room.

I asked if the congressman was amongst those already seated. He regretted to inform me that Congressman Plaisted was out at present. I was preparing to turn around and go when Phyllis Cheswick signaled to me with a wave of an outsize, ostrich-plume fan. I had no desire to spend time with George's odious sister-in-law but there was no gracious way to refuse to be seated with her. I took a calming breath and approached with what I hoped was a confident stride.

She looked me up and down before motioning for me to sit in the empty seat beside her. Phyllis called over a waiter. "You will join me for tea as there is none to be had at the Hotel Belden." It was not a question. I nodded and she waited for the waiter to hurry away before speaking.

"Although, how your aunt can consider her establishment a hotel at all, considering her guests need to leave the premises to meet their basic needs, is beyond me. I suppose, considering the size of the place, I should be grateful there is dinner available in the dining room."

"I'll be sure to tell her you are not satisfied with your experience. I am certain she will be able to fill your room with someone whose needs are more aligned with what the Belden does offer."

"Perhaps I have spoken in haste. It was very accommodating of your aunt to find a place for us, such as it is, after George created his unfortunate mishap with that candle nonsense."

"I'm sure she was pleased to do so. Honoria is the most hospitable woman I have ever met," I said.

"George has had only complimentary things to say about her over the years," she said. "He has formed quite an attachment to her."

"Honoria is very fond of him, too."

"And a good thing it is, too, that there are people who are happy to help him. Lord only knows he needs rescuing most of the time." Phyllis drained the contents of her cup then tipped it toward me to reveal the leaves. "I suppose you read these?" From the tone of her voice the comment was not meant as a compliment. I had the sense she thought very little of George's psychic pursuits.

"My specialty is mediumship. But I shall be sure to mention your interest in tasseomancy to my aunt. Perhaps she will add a tea leaf reader to the faculty at the Belden." I gave her a smile that I hoped said her sarcasm had gone unnoticed. The waiter returned bearing a large silver teapot and proceeded to pour with an elegant flourish into Phyllis's empty cup. After he had filled mine as well, Phyllis returned to the unfortunate subject of George and her conviction that he was in need of charity.

"It seems to me with so many psychics amongst his acquaintance George should have had someone who could have warned him of the dangers of playing with fire. Instead, as usual, all the responsibility falls on my Osmond."

"I was not aware George had made any demands on his brother." That was the plain truth. Honoria hadn't mentioned anything of the kind and as far as I knew, George had not turned to his brother for help when he found himself without a roof over his head. If Osmond had come to the rescue why was George sleeping on a rusticating cot in the Belden's family parlor?

"Osmond hates to take credit and George would not wish the

world to know how he threw himself once more on his brother's mercy. I hate to speak ill of my husband's family but cannot tell you the number of times George has come to Osmond with his hand outstretched."

Phyllis stretched out her own hand and lifted a plump raisin bun from a tiered serving plate before indicating I should do the same. As I had not eaten in hours I availed myself of the opportunity. I helped myself to a slice of pound cake and took a small bite. Mrs. Doyle would be pleased to hear her offerings at the Belden were vastly superior. I took a sip of tea to wash down the dry crumbs making a nuisance of themselves in my throat.

"I had no idea George had run into such a string of misfortune as to require repeated assistance," I said. "I think of George as a man of stable temperament and measured habits. It surprises me greatly to think he would find himself living beyond his means."

"Vice can be found in the least likely of places. Your aunt must have sensed something of the sort from him. Why else would she have refused his suit all these years?" Phyllis peered at me over the rim of her teacup.

"I believe she has no desire whatsoever to marry. I think it safe to say that George bears no responsibility for her refusal."

"Nonsense. Every woman wishes to marry. George and his profligate ways are to blame for that courtship coming to naught. Osmond remarked that if he had not dissuaded Honoria from marrying him through his irresponsible behavior she would have been the one financing his foolishness rather than us."

"It sounds very generous of you both."

"I should say it was. You cannot imagine the thousands of dollars we have poured into his coffers over the years." Phyllis let out a snort then clattered her cup back down to her saucer. "George hasn't even had the decency to thank me for the gifts."

"Perhaps he has simply been so busy he has forgotten and will be by soon to thank you."

"That would be a first. In all the years we have been supporting him he has never once thanked me. And I ask you, what sort of a man forgets the princely sum of five thousand dollars?"

CHAPTER FORTY

FIVE THOUSAND DOLLARS. MY HEAD SPUN JUST THINKING OF it. All the way home I turned over the idea that gentle, well-mannered George was the sort of man who lived off his brother's generosity and never even bothered to thank him for the kindness. It simply didn't tally with what I had seen of him with my own two eyes or even the comments Honoria had made about George in the weeks I'd known them both. If George had no money why would Honoria have believed that he did? Could she know her friend far less well than she believed she did?

I arrived at the Belden before I drew any conclusions and went looking for the one person I could count on to tell me the unvarnished truth. Mrs. Doyle's apron front was white with flour, and the rhythmic thump of her rolling pin filled the kitchen with the promise of pie with dinner. A heaping bowl of late strawberries shone in a sunbeam slanting through the window. It seemed she was back to her usual self.

"What brings you back into my domain looking so muddy?" Mrs. Doyle squinted at me as she always did when assessing my aura. It was a habit she couldn't seem to break no matter how often she saw me. Muddy auras worried her more than almost any other kind.

"I've just heard something that I don't understand," I said. Mrs. Doyle plucked a gleaming strawberry from the bowl and handed it to me. "I thought you might be able to clear things up." She picked up her rolling pin and attacked the pastry once more.

"I do a lot of cleaning and clearing around here as well you know. What's on your mind?"

"Do you know anything about George being in the habit of asking his brother for money?" I asked. Mrs. Doyle banged the rolling pin down on the worktable and jammed her floury hands onto her ample hips.

"Where have you been hearing such ugly lies?" She squinted at me some more and I reminded myself not to let her scowl bother me.

"Mrs. Cheswick said George was forever asking them for money for one thing or another."

"What would you be doing asking questions of Mrs. Cheswick?" I hesitated. Yancey had asked that I not share my part in the investigation with anyone. But Mrs. Doyle wasn't just anyone and I was certain if I lied she would know anyway. Besides, it was in the interest of the hotel for Sophronia's murder to be solved and whatever was in the interest of the Belden was guaranteed to garner Mrs. Doyle's wholehearted support.

"Yancey and I both think Sophronia was not the victim of an accident. Because Chief Hurley has ordered her case closed Yancey asked me to help by quietly asking some questions of the people who might have been involved."

"You're looking for her killer?" Mrs. Doyle clamped her lips into a thin line.

She scowled and squinted some more and I knew my aura

was under scrutiny. It was enough to make me momentarily wish she were still sitting morosely in the corner rocking chair.

"How about we say I am not comfortable answering your question and leave it at that?" I asked. "Besides, you haven't said why you believe Mrs. Cheswick to be lying about George."

"In the first place, George is the responsible one of the Cheswick brothers. If money needed to be given, without a doubt it would flow from George to Osmond, not the other way around."

"But I thought Osmond and his wife were quite wealthy."

"She is. He used to be before he wasted his inheritance on God only knows what." Mrs. Doyle folded the pastry crust and draped it over a waiting pie dish. "When they were both just little things Osmond would pinch candy from the shops and George would go along behind him giving the storekeeper a penny to keep his brother out of trouble."

"That sounds much more like the George I know than the one Phyllis was describing," I said. "She said he never even thanked her for the gifts over the years." I looked over my shoulder to be sure we weren't being overheard. I imagined George would be devastated by such remarks.

"George has come into the kitchen and personally thanked me for every meal he has ever enjoyed in this house. That sounds like so much nonsense to me."

"Do you think Mrs. Cheswick was deliberately lying to me?" I hadn't gotten the sense that she was telling untruths. But none of the people for whom I conducted readings ever seemed to realize when I was embellishing the truth, either.

"Knowing Osmond I'd be more inclined to wonder if she was misinformed." Mrs. Doyle deftly sliced a plump strawberry into a large mixing bowl.

"Why would Osmond lie to his wife about his own brother?" I had little experience of marriage. Since my mother had died when I was such a small infant and my father never married again I had seen no such relationship in close quarters. I knew my father had kept company with some of the more willing women on the medicine shows we worked but none of those encounters were lengthy or legally binding.

Part of me wished Honoria had married George just so I could get a close look at what a marriage might be. From what little I had observed from crowds at the show or from guests at the hotel many, if not most, marriages proved an unhappy alliance.

"I shouldn't like to speculate. I will say George has always said Phyllis kept a close eye on the family finances. And she would, wouldn't she?"

"I don't know. Would she?"

"Well, when a man marries for money either the wife tells herself that he didn't and gives him complete control in order to forget about all that sort of unpleasantness"—Mrs. Doyle shook her head—"or she keeps a close eye on the bottom line and never lets him forget which side his bread is buttered on. You've met Phyllis. Which sort of woman would you say she is?" Mrs. Doyle paused and tapped a juice-stained finger against her lips.

"She seemed quite shrewd to me." I reached for the bowl of berries and began prying hulls from the fruit. "Is it common knowledge that Osmond married her for her money?" I tucked away that nugget of information to share later with Yancey.

"I doubt it. I know because Honoria mentioned it to me. You see, George had been quite worried about Osmond's financial situation before he became engaged to Phyllis. In fact, things between them had become estranged when George refused to

continue to pay off his debts or to front him any more money."
Mrs. Doyle clucked her tongue. "In fact, George was surprised to
be invited to Osmond and Phyllis's wedding."

"They don't seem to be on very good terms now though, either." I wasn't going to embarrass George by carrying tales about
his infatuation with Sophronia if I could help it. But I did want
to know if there was another explanation for the coolness in their
relationship on his part.

"I have wondered about why they continued to be estranged.
But if Phyllis believed George to be a leech on their finances she
would not have encouraged them to be close."

"Why did they pay a visit to him, then?"

"Desperation, I suppose. His wife was absolutely determined
to be part of the opening of the pier. Osmond must not have attempted to make arrangements soon enough to secure rooms,"
Mrs. Doyle said. "He turned to George as a last resort."

"The George I know would not have liked to create a scene by
refusing them."

"Of course he wouldn't," Mrs. Doyle said. "Now run along
with you and leave me in peace. All this talk of such ugly things
is sure to affect the taste of these pies."

CHAPTER FORTY-ONE

YANCEY STUBBED HIS TOE GETTING OUT OF BED. HE PRO-
ceeded to scald his tongue on a cup of coffee at breakfast
then broke a bootlace while trying to dress his feet. Not an auspi-
cious start to what should be the most memorable day in the
history of Old Orchard. At least thus far. He promised Lucy and
his mother that he would keep an eye out for them at the pier
opening and that there would be no danger in their attending.

At least they would be accompanied to the festivities by
Thomas Lydale. He wished he felt certain of his assurances to
his mother and Lucy. While they put on brave faces, both of his
family members had been more rattled by the rioting than they
cared to admit.

Neither had said anything outright but he couldn't help but
notice they left the house far less frequently since the incident.
Lucy was the sort who always loved to run to the store to fetch a
pot of mustard or a cake of soap ever since she was old enough to
be off on her own. Now instead of going to the shops herself, Lucy
had telephoned them and arranged for delivery. She also could not

be convinced to go for a jaunt on her bicycle, not even when reminded of her new cycling costume. He wondered if discovering who had murdered Sophronia would set their minds at ease and return them to the dauntless adventurers he knew them to be.

The crowds had already swelled to an enormous throng even before he reached the base of the pier. Excursion trains had been arranged from as far away as Lewiston and Boston, bringing in thousands. A ferry carrying five hundred from Portland was scheduled to dock at the new landing site. Frank and Officer Lewis were on the earlier shift and Yancey spotted them at the entrance to the pier, where swarming groups of merrymakers stopped off at the pier's twin entrance pavilions to spend ten cents each at the ticket booth or to stow their burdensome belongings in baggage rooms and bicycle stalls.

Despite the rocky start to his day, Yancey felt his mood lift as he found himself buoyed along with the crowd. He passed through the brightly shingled twin-domed entranceway and found himself feeling more optimistic than he had in weeks.

Yancey passed a pair of steel enclosures, one built to hold brightly colored birds and the other for a troupe of cavorting monkeys. He paused for a moment to look at the bizarre sight and wondered what the creatures themselves made of the situation. Yancey doubted any of them felt at home in a cage alongside the North Atlantic. As he drew closer to the ballroom situated at the end of the eighteen-hundred-foot-long pier the crowds grew denser and Yancey's concerns for the safety of those assembled returned. So much, in fact, all his senses snapped to attention when he felt a tug on his jacket sleeve.

"Did I startle you, Officer Yancey?" Miss Proulx stood with

her parasol held aloft. "You are concerned about the possibility of another mob, aren't you?" she asked.

"The thought had crossed my mind," he said. "You aren't here alone, are you?"

"Certainly not. I believe every single person from the hotel is here, including Mrs. Doyle. It is a wonder I was able to slip away from the lot of them long enough to have a private word with you." Miss Proulx inclined her elaborately coiffed head, indicating they should step to the railing together. He used his superior height as well as the influence of his uniform to part the crowd and make for the spot she suggested. "No one shall think a thing of the two of us chatting here. We are hiding in plain sight, I should say," she said, looking around at the clamoring masses.

"Is there a purpose for this meeting?" Yancey asked. "Have you discovered something that you think I should know?"

"Indeed I have. I hardly know where to begin." Miss Proulx gestured excitedly with the hand holding her parasol and attracted an angry glance from a man whose vision she had endangered. "There are two things of especial note. Firstly, Miss Rice and Sophronia had a falling-out just before Sophronia died. Miss Rice reports that she was distressed with the way her friend ignored the danger to herself and others. When I asked if she was worried about the threatening letter she said she was not because Sophronia was in the habit of sending those to herself in every town she held rallies."

"For the publicity?" Yancey asked. Miss Proulx nodded excitedly. "Why should she be worried, then?"

"Because Nelson Plaisted is a powerful man who was willing to accost Sophronia on a public street. Miss Rice feared he was capable of far worse." Miss Proulx's eyes shone and the wind ruffled her hair slightly. "I have not yet had the opportunity to question the congressman and to tell the truth I am not overly eager to do so after witnessing the way he assaulted Sophronia." Yancey was surprised. Miss Proulx always presented herself as the sort of young woman who with no prior experience would fill in for a lion tamer at a traveling circus. The congressman's actions must have reminded her of something particularly distressing from her past. Yancey had disliked the man before. Now he felt as though he would like to be alone in an alley with the man himself.

"There is no need to do so. I have already confronted him about it." The look of relief on Miss Proulx's face was extremely gratifying.

"Does he admit to having abandoned her for another lady with better connections?"

"No. He contends that Miss Foster Eldridge was the one to break off their engagement. He claims she was only interested in his money and when he lost his she was quick to disassociate herself from him."

"Is it possible to prove which story is the truth, I wonder?" Miss Proulx said.

"I very much doubt it. Many years have passed and those sorts of unpleasant situations are generally conducted without an audience. It comes down to a matter of honor and in the case where there is none then a distressing scenario of he said, she said takes place." Yancey looked out over the crowd and saw the Misses Velmont and Dewitt Fredericks heading in their direction. He and Miss Proulx might not have much more time. "What was the second thing you discovered?" He made a small gesture with his hand in the direction of the two elderly sisters, which

Miss Proulx seemed to understand to mean she should go straight to the point.

"According to Phyllis Cheswick, George has been borrowing money from his brother for years. Well, in truth that would mean George was borrowing money from Phyllis since she is the one who controls the purse strings."

"That doesn't sound like the George Cheswick I know. He lives a very modest life and is content to eat plain meals and spend time with the Divination Circle," Yancey said. "Did she say what he needed the money for?"

"She did not but it would have had to have been something far beyond the ordinary sort of expense." Miss Proulx's eyes grew large in her face. "She said Osmond told her George needed five thousand dollars. And what's more, he never even thanked her for it."

Yancey leaned back against the railing for support. The entire structure upon which they stood had cost $38,000. What could George possibly need such an amount for himself for?

"Have you asked him about it?"

"I have not. I first asked Mrs. Doyle if she believed it could be true. She said she felt it far more likely that Osmond was simply blaming his own need for money on George in order to extract it from his wife without implicating himself."

"From what I know of George that sounds more likely. I don't know his brother in the slightest. In fact I had to ask Chief Hurley to identify him in a photograph from the march."

"In my opinion you've missed very little. I should also tell you that I asked George about the incident Lucy mentioned at the Hay Feverists convention. He refused to comment on it and suggested I direct any questions about the matter to Osmond. Encountering him at the Belden has been awkward ever since. As he is staying at the hotel for the time being I think it would be best if you asked him about the money."

"I could do that without it being in an official capacity. I could approach him as a friend concerned about both him and his reputation," Yancey said. "And I can ask him about his brother while I am at it. Maybe he will tell me if it is Osmond who is actually in need of ready cash."

CHAPTER FORTY-TWO

I WATCHED OFFICER YANCEY AS HE SHOULDERED HIS WAY through the throng. I confess, I felt a bit nervous to be in the middle of such a large group of strangers after the violent turn of events at the march. I stood surveying the oppressive crowd pressing in on all sides. I had never felt anything quite like it. Even the very best days at one of my father's popular medicine show performances had never attracted such a number.

If asked to guess I would have said the number milling the pier looking at the exotic birds in cages or listening to the band playing counted in the thousands. I worked my way to the railing on the western side of the pier. Looking back toward the beach gave an entirely different view of it than gazing up or down the beach from the sand.

Hotels along the beach stood cheek by jowl and covered every inch of the shoreline. The Ocean House, the Sea Shore House, and the Fiske, with its distinctive triple roofline, stood out against the blue sky. It struck me afresh how smart Honoria had been to carve out a special niche for herself in such a competitive business and how much was riding on the success of the world-famous pier. Viewed at a distance it was possible to see how much larger most of the other hotels were in comparison.

Just as I spotted the seaside veranda of the Belden I heard the voice.

"Turn around and look."

I surveyed the crowd around me and found nothing of the sort the voice usually would call to my attention. After all, it never seems interested in entertainments or fine swaths of scenery. Then out of the corner of my eye I caught sight of Thomas Lydale. He stood by the enormous exotic birdcage and was arguing with Congressman Plaisted. I felt as though I was experiencing a distorted sort of déjà vu.

Once again the congressman was angry and once again he had his hands raised. This time though, Thomas was not elated as Sophronia had been. Nor was he too small to defend himself. I slipped through the crowd hoping I could draw close enough to hear what all the fuss was about before they came to their senses.

Once again my trusty parasol was the appropriate tool for the job. Not only did it shield my identity from Mr. Lydale, it did an admirable job of encouraging those in my way to remove themselves from my path. I stood on the opposite side of the birdcage and strained to hear their conversation over the squawk of the birds and the roar of the crowd. I was lucky to make out what few words I did.

From what I could hear there was a disagreement about photographs. At first I thought it possible that the congressman had commissioned portraits from Mr. Lydale and had been disappointed with the results. But as the conversation droned on it

seemed too hostile for that. In fact, the congressman had grabbed
the front of Mr. Lydale's lapels and looked as though he were
preparing to cause a scene. After seeing how quickly violent actions spread at the march I easily imagined the congressman's
actions becoming contagious. I had no desire to be a part of another stampeding crowd. It was time to take action of my own. I
stepped around the birdcage and announced my presence. Congressman Plaisted dropped his hands to his sides and wiped his
palms along his trouser legs.

"There you are, Mr. Lydale. I've been looking for you everywhere. I thought you said we should meet at the bandstand but I
must have misunderstood." I gave him a showstopping smile.
When I turned to include the congressman in its beam all I saw
was his retreating form hurrying toward the ballroom at the far
end of the pier. "I expect there is an explanation for why two
civilized gentleman would be about to start brawling in public.
Since the other gentleman had a publicly aired dispute with
Sophronia that also turned violent I would very much like to hear
what it is."

"I'm sure a nice young lady such as yourself would have no
interest in such a sordid story." Mr. Lydale would not meet my
gaze.

"That is exactly the sort of thinking that has kept women from
having the vote. I thought you were a far more broad-thinking
man. I shall have to discuss my disappointment on that subject
with Lucy."

"Lucy is a lovely young woman, whose company I have come
to enjoy immensely, but I am not about to share my secrets to
keep you from telling her that." Mr. Lydale lifted his hat as though
he were about to take his leave of me.

"Would you prefer I mention the congressman's photographs to her instead?" I felt just the slightest bit squeamish at that. It was a bluff but one that managed to create the desired response. His lips parted in surprise, then he bent toward my ear.

"What do you want?"

"I want to find who is responsible for Sophronia's death. The congressman is my favorite suspect and you know things that I believe should be taken into consideration, as I am seeking the truth."

"If I explain things to you will you give me your word that you won't mention any of it to Lucy?"

"I shan't promise until I hear what you have to say. But I can assure you that I have no interest in carrying tales or spreading gossip. I just need to know how this might connect to Sophronia's death." I laid my gloved hand on his jacket sleeve. "Besides, I am a medium. Wouldn't you rather tell me yourself than have me hear about your secrets from someone who has passed on?" Something about my words spurred him to a decision.

"I cannot meet with you today. I have social engagements for the rest of today and client appointments in the morning. I can be available to explain it all tomorrow. Shall we say my studio at noon?" Mr. Lydale glanced down the pier. I followed the direction of his gaze and noticed Lucy making her way toward us. A wide smile spread across her face as she stopped to say hello to the Velmont sisters.

As I watched him watching her I wished fervently that he was not involved in Sophronia's death. I wondered if he were stalling for more time in order to concoct a convincing lie, or worse, to make his escape in the night. Father and I had done the same on many occasions and I knew how easy it was to put a great deal of distance between yourself and your problems over the course of a single night. I wanted to trust him but was unsure whether or not I should do so. But Lucy had left the Velmonts and was almost upon us. Mr. Lydale gave me a pleading look and I hadn't the heart to put him on the spot in front of my friend.

"I'll see you there."

Chapter Forty-three

Miss Proulx was nowhere to be found at the Hotel Belden when Yancey slipped quietly through the midnight blue portieres of the séance room and took a moment to observe George unseen. The older man sat at the center table, his back to the door. His head bent in concentration, and Yancey wondered fleetingly if he had caught George at prayer.

"Damn," George said, and Yancey heard something clatter onto the tabletop. Reassured that he had not interrupted a moment of communion with a deity he announced himself.

"George, might I have a word?" Yancey asked, pulling his small notebook from his breast pocket. George nodded and pointed to a chair beside him at the table. Yancey tried not to stare at George's burnt mustache. He looked like a different man with the dramatically swirling points absent from his face.

"Have you ever tried one of these things?" George asked. On the table between them lay a pair of school slates, a bit of chalk, and three pieces of sturdy string. The surfaces of the slates were flecked with white specks of chalk. As far as Yancey could see there was absolutely nothing special about them. He always had the feeling there was something more to every question he was asked at the Belden.

"I've a passing familiarity with them from my grammar school days. But I can't say I've used any since."

"Then I don't recommend trying. It will drive you to drink." George winked at him and pulled a squat flask from an inside pocket. Yancey shook his head.

"I'll pretend I didn't see that, sir." Maine had been the pioneer in temperance and since the state constitution had been amended to prohibit alcohol thirteen years earlier Yancey hadn't touched a drop. With a bob of his head George uncapped the flask and took a moderate tug. "Are they supposed to be doing something special?"

"They're divination slates. They're supposed to reveal a message from the spirit world. Honoria says you place a piece of chalk between the slates and then tie them together," George said. "If the spirits have message for you it appears written in chalk on the interior sides of the slates."

"It doesn't look like you're having much luck." Yancey picked up a slate and gave it a once-over.

"I never do." George shook his head and toyed with his flask like he was considering another sip.

"I was really very sorry to hear about your house."

"The fire was a terrible shock but I must admit it has been a pleasure to be under the same roof with so many other people for a change." Yancey hadn't given any thought to whether or not George might be lonely. His mother often mentioned she wanted both of her children to marry and settle down so she wouldn't worry about them withering away from too much solitude. He had never given her concerns much credence but Yancey didn't really want to end up in the same sort of condition as George. Still, he had time before he was too old to seriously consider marrying. It would be far better to wait for the right young lady to show interest than it would be to hurry into a marriage. He had seen what had become of the ill-considered match between his parents and he had no desire to find himself in similar misery.

"You look more recovered than I might have imagined you would. Quite well enough for me to ask you some uncomfortable questions." George took another swig from his flask, then pocketed it. Yancey took it as a signal to proceed. If Ruby was right there was good reason to ask uncomfortable questions.

"About the fire?" George asked.

"About your brother."

"Osmond didn't start the fire." George's eyes widened in surprise. "I mean, he's gotten into more than his share of youthful mischief but setting fire to my house would not be the sort of shenanigans he would ever get up to. Besides, the fire was entirely my own fault." George's face reddened. Yancey wasn't sure if it was from shame or indignation. He understood the shame of a family member being accused of a crime all too well. He took no pleasure from putting anyone in the same position but he wouldn't shirk his duty to a victim to spare his feelings or anyone else's.

"Would you think him capable of spreading lies about you to his wife?"

"What sort of lies?"

"Mrs. Cheswick is laboring under the firm belief that you have asked your brother for substantial gifts of money during the entirety of their marriage," Yancey said. He held up a hand as George began to sputter. "And what's more, she reported to Miss

Proulx that you have not even done her the courtesy of thanking her for them." George's shoulders sagged and all the wind seemed to have gone completely from his sails.

"I am outraged to hear such tales have been carried outside the family. He must have been running this game often enough to have her start to resent me. I thought there was an unusual level of coldness in her manner when they arrived in Old Orchard." George dipped his hand back into his pocket and retrieved the flask once more. Again Yancey refused George's offer of a nip. "Osmond has had money troubles for years. It is not much of a secret that Phyllis's main appeal was her wealth." Yancey nodded encouragement.

"You don't seem surprised to hear what Osmond was saying about you."

"I wish I were. Throughout their marriage Phyllis has given him a small allowance. He needs to come to her for any other money he wishes to spend. She is not an ungenerous woman but she could not be expected to finance the sorts of payouts he finds himself obligated to make."

"What sort of payouts are you speaking of, sir?" Yancey felt a ripple of curiosity running through his body as he always did when he was ferreting out pieces of a puzzle.

"Gambling, spirits." George lifted his flask. "Other women."

"Any other women in particular?"

"Osmond never was very particular about the ladies so long as they were discreet and willing." George lowered his eyes as though embarrassed to even say such a thing aloud. "But there was one lady he pursued more enthusiastically than most others."

"Anyone I might know?" Yancey asked. George stared down at his lap as though the answers might be in it. Yancey felt sorry for him but he couldn't just let it drop. After all, Lucy and his mother were still finding it hard to leave the house. "There are other rumors floating around, you know. One that you might not be eager for Honoria to hear." George lifted his gaze to meet Yancey's and appeared to make a decision.

"Osmond was utterly infatuated with Sophronia. He was usually far more careful and discreet but at the Hay Feverists convention he just seemed to go head over heels in his pursuit of her."

"I heard about the gifts and the flowers but I understood responsibility for those was laid at your door," Yancey said. George exhaled slowly and the stubby burnt edges of his mustache fluttered pathetically.

"Osmond placed the orders and charged the bills to my name. He would tease me every so often and tell me I had no idea what a Romeo I truly was."

"So when Miss Foster Eldridge objected to the excess attention you were the one blamed."

"He didn't even have the decency to tell me ahead of time that he had been wooing this woman and it might come down on my head. I have never been so humiliated as I was when the president of the Hay Feverists Society asked me to desist in my attentions to her."

"Do you think it possible that Osmond could have had something to do with Miss Foster Eldridge's death?" Yancey kept his eyes firmly on George's face.

"Osmond and I have had our share of disagreements over the years but I would hardly like to think him capable of such a thing."

"Do you have any idea why he might have needed five thousand dollars?" Yancey watched his words register in George's mind. It was a terrific sum to consider.

"You don't mean to say that is the amount he told Phyllis I required this time?"

"I'm sorry to say that it is. What's more, she isn't being quiet about it. By the end of the week I would expect everyone in your acquaintance to have heard about your profligate ways." Yancey regretted pressing his mother's friend so hard but he reminded himself it wasn't his job to be popular. "I don't believe I would feel obligated to keep my brother's secrets if he had so cavalierly disgraced me."

"Alcohol." George held up his flask once more. "He hinted to me that he was not going to have to keep relying on Phyllis for money much longer. He was planning to buy a portion of an illegal operation. He said it required a large sum of cash to buy in but I never imagined it would be so great an amount."

"He couldn't just ask Phyllis for the money?" Yancey said. In his experience the wealthy were often easier to convince to stray from the straight and narrow than the middle class. After all, most people who had amassed an outrageous fortune did so illegally.

"She wouldn't marry him until he took a temperance pledge. If he had wanted to invest in shady real estate she likely would have given him her blessing. Besides, Osmond wanted money of his own that Phyllis knew nothing about. If he asked for a loan for himself the whole point would be moot."

"Not the sort of marriage one envies, is it?" Yancey asked. "I don't suppose you know if the illegal alcohol operation is set up here in town?" This was exactly the sort of thing that some folks had warned would accompany the addition of the pier.

"He's been very circumspect with the details, so I know very little. From what he has said, Robert Jellison is involved. The two of them were close when we were growing up and they have been almost inseparable during Osmond's visit." George cleared his throat. "I believe it is an ill-kept secret that plenty of spirits are to be had in a back room at the Sea Spray if you know to ask and are willing to pay. I believe Osmond is becoming involved in growing that part of Jellison's hospitality business."

"I'm well aware of the activities at the Sea Spray. It wouldn't surprise me at all if Jellison has gotten tired of shelling out to a middleman and has decided to get involved in the manufacturing end of the business as well as the distribution side. He would stand to make a lot more money if he did."

"It would have to be very profitable. Osmond would have absolute hell to pay with Phyllis if she found out," George said. Yancey thought he detected a note of amusement in George's voice.

"You know, if you set the record straight with your sister-in-law and deprived Osmond of his access to her money it would be doing the town a real service," Yancey said. "Old Orchard has positioned itself to be the Coney Island of New England, not a modern-day Sodom and Gomorrah." Yancey stood to take his leave. From the contemplative look on George's face he felt quite sure Osmond would have a tough time of things with his wife before long.

CHAPTER FORTY-FOUR

MR. LYDALE AGREED TO MEET ME AT HIS PHOTOGRAPHY STU-
dio the next day around noon. I had worried he might
have been trying to put me off, possibly with the idea of running
off in the night. From experience I knew how many miles it was
possible to travel in the dark if a person were desperate enough.
I entered the shop at the appointed time and was pleased to see
he was a man of his word. He looked resigned to taking me into
his confidence and without delay launched into his story.

"Many years ago I knew both Sophronia and Nelson Plaisted.
This was before he had been elected to congress and was a man
of commerce instead." I nodded that he should continue.

"I worked for Sophronia and her friend Caroline, whom you
might know as Mrs. Plaisted, as the sole additional member of
staff on their temperance newspaper. My parents had both died
in a diphtheria outbreak the year before and I was very grateful
to find employment. For reasons that have no bearing on the
disagreement you witnessed between myself and Nelson, I found
myself suddenly out of a job and it could be reasonably argued
the fault rested with him. This, unfortunately, occurred in the

depths of the Long Depression and my financial situation became dire." My heart went out to him. I knew only too well the sleeplessness and despair born of ongoing monetary hardship.

"I understand that people make desperate choices in such circumstances. I can only assume you found yourself presented with unappealing choices." He looked at me with something akin to gratitude and proceeded with his story.

"Even as a lad of seventeen, I was an experienced photographer. Nelson knew of my skills and that I had been forced to sell my equipment in order to feed myself. I had no family to turn to. At my lowest point he approached me with an unsavory proposition." Mr. Lydale fixed his glance on a point somewhere over my shoulder. I wondered if, after he finished his story, he would ever look me in the eyes again.

"The long and the short of it was that Nelson offered to provide me with the necessary equipment as well as a generous compensation to take what he euphemistically described as 'art photographs.'" Mr. Lydale cleared his throat and struggled to continue. I could not in good conscience leave him drowning in his shame.

"I have not been as sheltered as you might imagine. I have a sufficient understanding of the sort of photographs of which you speak. There is no need to go into detail," I said. Mr. Lydale's expression turned to one of surprise then profound relief. "Please go on."

"Nelson had somehow procured a wide variety of models and for the most part they seemed like happy-enough girls who saw the whole experience as a better way to earn good money than the alternatives." He paused for me to nod my understanding, "Or they were the sort of young women who enjoyed engaging in shocking behavior for reasons I didn't quite understand. Either way, there was no shortage of photographs to be taken."

"This seems like the sort of thing a man with political aspirations would prefer to keep quiet about."

"Exactly. Nelson wasn't at risk of exposure since the young women were hired through discreet advertisements and paid in cash at the conclusion of the sessions. The way it was set up, I was the only one they actually met. Everything went along without difficulties until, instead of adhering to the system he had set up, Nelson brought a model to me himself. She was a particularly handsome brunette with a peculiar white streak of hair on the left side of her head." Mr. Lydale cleared his throat. "He wished to have a photograph of the two of them together." It would have taken someone far more naive than I to fail to understand Mr. Lydale's meaning. The medicine shows I had worked often included tents of ill repute and dancing acts where the costumes were designed more to reveal than to conceal. Still, I would confess to being surprised to think such things were as easily found amongst the higher classes of society.

"A photograph that would not have done him any favors with his wife, I assume?" I asked. Mr. Lydale nodded.

"I told him I thought he had behaved rashly but he ignored me. In the end I expect he wished he had not."

"Did Mrs. Plaisted discover what her husband had been up to?"

"Not to my knowledge, although she may've done," Mr. Lydale said. "No, the trouble occurred when the young woman continued to show interest in Nelson after he no longer had any in her. One evening a few weeks later she was waiting for me outside the building where I had taken the photograph. She said Nelson had refused to see her and that she wanted me to pass a message to him.

"Did you do so?" I asked.

"I was hesitant but she said if I did not tell him she wished to see him she would take her request to Mrs. Plaisted. I got in touch with him that very night."

"I can only assume he was not pleased with what you had to tell him."

"In fact he thanked me for alerting him to the problem and said he would take care of it. The next day the papers reported that a young woman had drowned in a nearby pond. She was dressed in a man's coat, its pockets filled with rocks." Mr. Lydale managed to look me in the eye once more. My heartbeat accelerated and I wished Officer Yancey were here to hear the story for himself. "The article went on to say that the young woman's identity was unknown but listed her as having a distinctive white streak in her hair."

"What did you do?"

"I should have gone to the police but I didn't. I cannot excuse my behavior but I will say that I was still very young." Mr. Lydale drew a deep breath. "Nelson came to see me later that same day. He asked if I had seen the papers. When I told him I had, he said if he were in my position he would be worried."

"Did he give a reason?"

"He said the police would be looking for the last person to be seen with the dead woman. He said it would be an easy enough thing to discover my history of taking unsavory photographs and that the police would be unlikely to believe I had nothing to do with what happened to her."

"You must have been very frightened." I thought of my own experience of being threatened with police scrutiny. I did not imagine it had been less harrowing for a young man in Mr. Lydale's position.

"I was, but Nelson offered to pay for me to leave town. In fact, he was the one who suggested I go overseas and see a bit of the world while I waited for the whole matter to be forgotten."

"Did you not find that suspicious?"

"Of course I did but what were my alternatives? I was without a job, influence, or even family. I accepted his offer as the best choice in a bad situation," he said. "But not before I provided myself with a bit of insurance."

"What did you do?"

"I will preface by saying, while I am ashamed to admit it, I secretly made more than one copy of some of the photographs I was commissioned to take. Including the one of Nelson and the dead woman. Because I was unsure if Nelson was trying to help me or trying to blame me for the woman's death, I decided to give the copy of the photograph of the pair of them to one of the few people I trusted, for safekeeping."

"Whom did you leave it with?"

"Sophronia," he said. I gasped. No wonder the congressman had behaved so violently toward Sophronia. He must have been terrified of exposure. Even if he were not connected to the dead woman so many years earlier he certainly had reason to kill Sophronia. Not to mention how a photograph like the one Mr. Lydale described would influence voters. It would be hard to take him seriously as a family man who felt women deserved special protection if his involvement with such things came to the public's attention. It could be assumed that his wife would not be pleased, either.

"Did the congressman know you made copies of your own?"

"I never said that I did and he always took the glass negatives along with the prints I made for him. But he likely suspected that

I did. After all, even if I had not wanted them for myself, the photographs were valuable at a time when I had very few resources."

"What did Sophronia do?"

"She said she would keep the photograph along with the newspaper clipping about the dead woman I also entrusted to her safekeeping. She said that it was one more example of how women would be best protected by gaining the vote."

"Did you collect the photograph from her when you returned to America?"

"I wanted to forget the entire ugly incident. I had not encountered either Sophronia or Nelson again since I returned and had no desire to do so if I could help it."

"Then you must not have been pleased when you discovered they were both in Old Orchard for the pier opening."

"I was happy to see Sophronia still championing her cause but, you are right, I was not eager to meet her. As for the congressman, I confess to actively avoiding him," Mr. Lydale said. "When you saw him speaking to me on the pier he asked me if I had ever spoken to Sophronia about the photographs. And he also wanted to know if I had said anything to his wife."

"Do you think he killed the model all those years ago?"

"I don't know but it can't be a coincidence that Sophronia died in almost exactly the same manner." Mr. Lydale braced himself against the counter. "Are you going to tell Yancey about the photographs?"

"I don't see how I can tell him why he should consider arresting Congressman Plaisted without giving him the whole story," I said. "Are you worried he will think less of you?"

"There's that, certainly. But I had also had the welcome impression that he would support my interest in his sister. That seems unlikely to continue if the truth of this becomes known to him."

I could understand Mr. Lydale's concern and could empathize with it. After all, didn't I have secrets of my own I would rather no one in my life in Old Orchard should discover?

"I cannot promise what will come of any of this. Officer Yancey will have to know about the photographs one way or another."

"Of course you must do what is right. I should expect nothing else from you." Mr. Lydale nodded slowly. It was not only his happiness that might be in jeopardy. Lucy had every right to a romance as well.

"What I can say is that I will tell Officer Yancey I don't believe this sort of incident from the past should taint your reputation in the present. We all have things about our lives we would rather forget. The fact that you were willing to share what you remember about a corrupt and powerful man speaks very well of your character." I rested my hand on his arm briefly then took my leave.

CHAPTER FORTY-FIVE

HIS CONVERSATION WITH GEORGE STILL RANG IN HIS EARS AS Yancey searched Old Orchard for Osmond Cheswick. Not long past noontime he spotted the older man sitting alone on a bench on the boardwalk overlooking the pier. Gulls swooped in close, hoping to snatch a bit of fried fish from the newspaper cone gripped in Osmond's fist. Yancey sat on the other end of the bench. The smell of fried food and vinegar wafted up from the packet of fish and made his mouth water.

"Osmond Cheswick, isn't it?" Yancey asked. "George Cheswick's brother?" Osmond stiffly turned to face him. Yancey had difficulty wrapping his mind around the idea that the man on the other end of the bench and George were brothers. The family resemblance was there, physically at least. But there the likeness ended. Where George was slightly befuddled and affable in the extreme, Osmond sat bolt upright and alert, his sharp eyes boring into Yancey's.

"Do I know you, Officer?"

"We haven't yet been introduced but my mother is great friends with George and when I saw you sitting here I thought I'd introduce myself." Yancey couldn't say for sure but he thought Osmond's posture relaxed slightly. "I understood from George that you and your wife are here because of the pier opening."

"That's right." Osmond lifted his chin toward the pier. "Quite a feat isn't it?"

"Honestly, I'm not sure yet. I'm going to reserve judgment until the whole thing's survived a few nor'easters," Yancey said.

"Come now, the most modern techniques were used. Surely there's nothing to worry about."

"I don't happen to believe that modernity conveys special protections."

"You're not one of those traditionalist young men who think the world would be better off if we had never invented the telephone or the automobile, are you?"

"No, it's not that. It's more my experiences as a police officer. If modernity could be counted on to protect I don't suppose a forward-thinking woman like Miss Foster Eldridge would be dead." Yancey shifted on the bench to look at Osmond rather than the pier.

"I can't see how the stability of the pier and Miss Foster Eldridge's lack of mental stability have anything to do with each other." Osmond took a giant bite of his fish then dabbed at the corner of his mouth with his pocket square.

"Do you think Miss Foster Eldridge was mentally unstable?" Yancey asked.

"She must have been. Anyone who drowned themselves would have to be."

"You must have known her well to be acquainted with her state of mind."

"Not at all. I barely knew the woman. It's just that her ideas and opinions made her sound quite unbalanced." Osmond's tone chilled.

"I thought perhaps you had interacted with her at the Belden. After all, one would need to go out of one's way to avoid other guests at a hotel as small as that one."

"I see. I was, of course, in her company from time to time at the hotel. It would be, as you say, impossible not to encounter her," Osmond said. "But civility in the public spaces of a hotel does not imply any real connection."

"George said it was the second time all of you had been in the same hotel."

"I don't recall." Osmond looked pointedly at his food instead of at Yancey.

"That's strange since George remembered the occasion quite clearly."

"It may have escaped your notice, Officer, but my brother and I are not alike in the least." Osmond Cheswick clearly was not the sort of man accustomed to being asked to explain himself.

"I had most definitely marked the dissimilarities between the two of you. For instance, I doubt very much George would ever relentlessly pursue a woman when he was married to another." The flock of gulls swooped closer and their cries threatened to drown out his words. Yancey leaned closer to Osmond. "I would be at least as surprised to find he hid his unwanted attentions from scrutiny by blaming them on his brother."

"What are you implying, young man?" Osmond asked.

"Nothing at all, sir. I'm just making an observation."

"It sounded to me as though you were suggesting I am a man of poor character." Osmond crumpled the wrapper from his fish and threw it to the ground. The wind buffeted it down the boardwalk and the gulls reeled and fell upon it with zeal. "If you persist in making such insulting allegations I shall be forced to speak to my friend Chief Hurley about your suitability for the position you hold."

"Are you threatening me, Mr. Cheswick?"

"Call it what you like. But if I were you I would stop making such discourteous remarks to me if you value your job with the police force."

"I thought I was being courteous. After all, it would have been much easier for me to question your wife about what George told me regarding your interest in other women, your drinking, and the small matter of the five thousand dollars." Yancey stood. "I'll just head back to the Belden and pay a call on her." Osmond fiddled with his watch chain and looked out over the water.

"Why would my wife believe you instead of me?" Osmond asked. "All you have is my brother's word against mine. My wife has always found my brother to be a particular thorn in her side. Especially after foolishly burning down his own house. I very much doubt I have anything to fear by telling you to suit yourself in this matter." Osmond stood himself and took off at a leisurely pace along the beach in the opposite direction of the Hotel Belden.

Yancey stood looking after him not sure whether to feel anger or grudging respect. Either way, he might as well find a way to ask Mrs. Cheswick about the victim. For all he knew, Mrs. Cheswick was well aware of her husband's behavior and maybe had taken care of Miss Foster Eldridge herself. He headed back to the station hoping Miss Proulx had been faring better with the investigation than he had. She could hardly be doing worse.

Chapter Forty-six

ALL THE WAY BACK TO THE HOTEL I PONDERED THE SITUATION Mr. Lydale would face if his past were to be exposed. I was lost in thought as I entered the Belden and passed along the hallway with the intention of finding a quiet place to think things through. I was so absorbed in the problem that I almost didn't notice Millie as I stepped into the formal parlor for a moment of privacy.

Millie was not the furtive type. Decidedly she was not. Her face, with its honey-colored eyes, pert nose, and smattering of freckles suggested an illustration for a popular brand of dairy foods. It did not lend itself to the keeping of secrets. I thought it likely I had scared a year's worth of life out of her when I entered the room and saw her smoothing a sheet of crumpled paper on a tabletop.

"What have you got there?" I asked. My question did not put her at ease. She looked at me and then down at the paper and then back at me once more.

"Private correspondence." She bit her lower lip until I spotted a dot of blood.

"Why are you so distressed? It looks like it had been discarded."

"It was crumpled up in the wastepaper basket. I often bring home a sheet or two from the hotel to use as spills for my parents' house. Honoria doesn't mind." I understood the practice myself. Father was never in favor of using any extra money for little luxuries like matches when he could spend it on drink instead. I had used spills to light one lamp from another for as long as I was old enough to be trusted with fire. It was a common practice and hardly one to be worried over.

"Then why do you look so distressed?" I asked. "There is nothing wrong with what you've done."

"I was practicing my reading. I joined the Working Women's Educational Institute." Millie looked at the floor and then glanced back up at me.

"That sounds interesting," I said. "Is the institute some sort of a school?"

"It's a new venture by some ladies in Biddeford who have decided to offer classes to women and girls who have not been able to pursue much in the way of schooling," Millie said. "The ladies there say I'm a quick study but I think they're just being kind."

"You seem like an eager student to me," I said, pointing to the paper in her still-trembling hand. "I doubt they would need to give you false encouragement. I always think of you as having a curious mind. That still doesn't explain why you would be worried."

"Mother always tells me curiosity killed the cat." Millie handed me the crinkled sheet. "I'm afraid my curiosity may have gotten me in trouble this time. Please tell me I am not reading it correctly."

I took the paper and began to read. As my eyes made sense of the words on the crumpled page I felt betrayed. The only one who seemed likely to have written it was Sophronia. How could she have done something so terrible? My own experience with a blackmailer in June came back to me in vivid detail. How could I not have seen what sort of person she really could be? Mrs. Doyle had tried to warn me. I swallowed dryly and noticed my own hand trembling as I read the note aloud.

"'You were warned at the march. If you don't wish the public to read about your exploits leave five thousand dollars behind the fireplace screen in the library by five o'clock tomorrow evening.'" I held my breath hoping my disappointment in Sophronia would pass. I exhaled deeply but found I still felt betrayed. I felt small and clammy and foolish. I was surprised to feel tears pricking my eyes. I wasn't sure if they were tears of sadness or those created by the embarrassment of being taken in like a bumpkin at a medicine show. Either way, I was determined not to let them spill over in front of Millie. I forced myself to listen to what she was saying rather than my own thoughts.

"That's what I thought it said. I almost fainted dead away when I read the sum."

"It is an enormous fortune." My voice caught in my throat at the very thought of it.

"What could possibly be worth such an amount?" Millie's eyes were round in her freckled face. With a father and sisters who worked in the woolen mills in Biddeford and a mother who took in washing, it was no wonder Millie did not trust her eyes when she read the note. Her family would likely never see such a sum even if they pooled their lifetime earnings.

"A secret someone is desperate to keep hidden," I said. "From the looks of this I would venture a guess that whatever is in

Sophronia's missing manuscript is worth a great deal to the people whose secrets it divulges."

"Do you know who has something to hide?" Millie gripped the edge of the dresser so tightly it whitened her knuckles.

"The note is in this room for a reason," I said. "It had to have been sent to someone who is a guest or someone accompanying a guest to the hotel." I felt queasy when I thought about the possibility of a murderer calmly sitting down to dinner at the Belden every night. Then I had another thought.

"Did you check the library to see if the money was there?"

"I only just found the note." Millie's face blanched. "Besides, I wouldn't dare."

"I think I'd better go take a look myself, then. Do you mind if I take this with me?" I asked.

"I would feel much better if you did." Millie wiped her hands on her apron and shuddered. "Do you think we are in any danger since we read the note?" Millie looked like she would burst into tears. I stepped closer and put my hand on her shoulder. She was right to be frightened. I was myself. But even more than that I was angry. Angry at Sophronia and at whoever had killed her.

Ever since my arrival, I had thought of the Belden as a sanctuary. Even though people associated with the hotel had died, it had simply not occurred to me that there could be danger associated with the Belden itself. I felt foolish and childlike as a lump rose in my throat and I became aware that something had been stolen from me. Never before had I felt so safe, so much at home. I wasn't about to give it up without a fight.

As soon as I checked for the money I would take the letter to Yancey as further proof that murder, rather than suicide, had claimed Sophronia's life. Maybe it would convince his boss to reopen the investigation and would allow him to continue his inquiries out in the open.

"I think that whoever killed Sophronia is feeling very much at ease now that the police have ruled her death a suicide. But to be on the safe side, please don't mention this to anyone else."

"Not even Mrs. Doyle?" I thought about how much Mrs. Doyle had expressed a dislike for Sophronia and the lengths she had gone to in order to get me out of the platform reading. I answered with a heavy heart.

"No, Millie, not even her."

Chapter Forty-Seven

I REMINDED MYSELF NOT TO BREAK INTO A RUN AS I TRAVERSED the stairs and then the length of the corridor down to the library. My favorite room in the hotel took on an ominous feel as I stepped through the door and headed straight for the fireplace.

It was an ingenious place to hide something at this time of year. The wide, decorative screen needed no maintenance and virtually filled the entire fireplace, making it unlikely anyone would have reason or opportunity to see anything hidden behind it. I made sure I was alone in the room and upon ascertaining that was the case, I bent over the fan and peered behind it. The only things in the cold dark space were a pair of highly polished brass andirons and a single log awaiting a match.

My disappointment was such that I felt weak at the knees and reached for the nearest chair. I wasn't sure if I had hoped to find that the money was still there or that it had gone. It was such a vast sum I would not have had any idea what to do with it had I found it in the fireplace.

I knew the money was not there but I didn't know if it ever had been. There was every possibility that the killer had murdered Sophronia in order to get out of paying in the first place. There was also the possibility that someone else had retrieved the money from behind the fan after the blackmail victim placed it there. I looked around the room. Heavy curtains hung in generous folds at the windows. It was conceivable someone could go unnoticed hiding behind them. It would even be possible for someone to duck behind one of the wingback chairs and remain out of sight for at least a moment or two.

It was also possible that Sophronia had collected the money before she died but I hadn't seen any unexplained amounts of cash in her room when Officer Yancey and I checked it after her body was found. I decided to let myself into Sophronia's room for a second look.

SOPHRONIA'S ROOM WAS SHROUDED IN SHADOWS AND THE AIR smelled musty and close. I considered opening a window to allow some fresh sea air to billow in and clear up the stagnant atmosphere but decided against it. I had no desire for anyone to realize the room was occupied. I locked the door behind me, left the drapes pulled across the long windows, and depressed the wall switch for the overhead light.

I commenced my search for the money with the same degree of thoroughness Officer Yancey and I had exerted when we looked for a suicide note. I opened drawers and the closet. I crouched on the needlepoint rug beside the bed and peered beneath, garnering nothing for my trouble other than the confirmation that Millie had dusted below the bed.

I stood and crossed the room. I searched the pigeonholes of the drop-front desk and even felt around for a secret drawer. I thought of Dewitt Fredericks and how he would likely say I had only thought to look for such a thing because of the sensational novels I so loved to read. Most likely he was right, especially as I witnessed my disappointment in not finding such a drawer.

I pulled out the skirted vanity bench and sat looking at the surface of the table. During my time on the medicine show a large part of my success was dependent on my ability to observe those things others took no notice of and to make accurate assumptions of the person before me based upon them.

I used many of the same skills at the Belden in my tarot readings and my mediumship sessions. The voice played an important role in what I had to say to querents but it could not be relied upon to come through every time I needed to please a client.

On the vanity sat a few scattered items. I picked up and examined a small silk evening bag, a spool of jet-black thread, a plain wooden brush, a pair of embroidery scissors, and a small jewel case. I pressed the catch on the case and looked inside. Only a single pair of earbobs, a slim gold ring set with a small opal, and a pair of ivory hair combs were tucked inside. I pulled apart the bedding and looked in the classic hiding space below the mattress. Nothing.

The vanity drawers held the expected gloves, handkerchiefs, and fans any lady would be expected to have in her possession. I pulled out each of the drawers of the vanity and turned their contents out onto the bed. Again nothing and nothing attached to the bottom of any of the drawers, either. I was ready to give up when I thought of the underside of the seat upon which I sat. I lifted the skirting fabric and peered beneath. There was no sign of the missing manuscript, or the money.

As I bent down to straighten the fabric skirting the bench I noticed two stray bits of thread clinging to it. I reached out and plucked them up. The color of one was an exact match for the jet-black spool of thread sitting on the vanity. The other was a smaller length of black. What were they doing there? Sophronia had not seemed the sort to pursue needlework as a pleasurable pastime as so many women did.

I had difficulty imagining her even taking the time to perform necessary repairs to her clothing. She seemed more the sort to ask a maid or even a seamstress to do such things for her. What could explain the spool of thread? Why two colors? A repair seemed the only answer. I walked to the mirror-fronted wardrobe and opened it once more. Much of Sophronia's clothing was the same dark navy as the smaller piece of thread. I lifted the gowns and bicycling costumes and lay them on the bed one at a time.

I looked for buttons, hooks, hems, or sleeves mended with black thread instead of blue. I turned on the lamp at the side of the bed to assist me as my eyes began to water with the strain of searching for two such similar colors. Still, I found nothing to explain the threads.

I asked myself if there was any way the threads meant nothing. After all, wasn't it possible the last occupant of the room was the one who conducted the repairs and the thread had nothing whatsoever to do with Sophronia? Still, after seeing the cleanliness under the bed it seemed unlikely that Millie would have missed anything between the last occupant and Sophronia.

Besides, I had that buzzing hum moving up and down my spine, reaching the base of my skull and cascading over my shoulders that I always felt when I was on the right track with a client. The feeling that let me know I was closing in on the truth. The thread meant something. I just needed to keep looking. The best thing I knew to do was to ask for help from the voice, as Mrs. Doyle had encouraged me to do. I had never had much success summoning support from the voice until I had come to Old Orchard. I had heard it often enough but it came unbidden and without warning. Any contact between us seemed to originate from the voice rather than from me. I was simply a passive receiver of unsolicited advice.

Since arriving it felt as though the lines of communication between myself and my mysterious counselor had strengthened. Mr. MacPherson, the hotel dowser, believed the hotel sat at a crossroads of what he called a "thin space." He claimed such places were found along lines all across the globe and that the one just below the hotel was amongst the strongest he had ever felt.

According to Mr. MacPherson these places made metaphysical abilities more pronounced in those with a proclivity for them. My own experience had lent credence to his assertions. Over the weeks I had been at the Belden I had heard the voice more often than I had during the rest of my twenty years combined. Maybe it was the place but partly I attributed it to my willingness to believe that I could ask for help.

I closed my eyes and tried to quiet my thoughts to focus only on the matter at hand. I pictured the manuscript and I thought about Sophronia's death. I silently asked if the voice could show me where to look. Immediately I heard a response in my left ear.

"Ask Ben."

Chapter Forty-eight

It was such a simple thing I was disgusted with myself for not having thought of it before. I hurried down the front stairs and arrived in the lobby, where Ben hovered, silent as usual, behind the polished walnut reception desk. His white-blond hair swished across his forehead as he glanced up from a ledger he was updating.

"Ben, did Sophronia give anything into your care to keep safe?" He looked at me with his unreadable expression, then nodded.

"Would it be possible for you to show it to me? I think it may shed some light on what happened to her." Ben laid down the ornate fountain pen used for signing in the guests and motioned for me to follow him into the porter's room behind the desk. The room was supposedly available to all the hotel faculty and staff but everyone, myself included, thought of it as Ben's exclusive domain. I had been there before but only for a moment and then only because I had been looking for Ben.

I looked about the room and thought how at odds it was with its main occupant. Ben's appearance was invariably immaculate: starched, straight, and spotless. The room was anything but tidy.

Wooden bars on brass supports held hangers, some draped with forgotten coats and wraps, others hanging empty and forlorn. Shelves towered from floor to ceiling and threatened to send books, boxes, and wire baskets heaving with odds and ends toppling down upon our heads. Two threadbare velvet chairs whose insides were working their way to their outsides flanked a dainty enameled stove. Stacks of steamer trunks and other assorted pieces of luggage pressed against the back wall.

Ben motioned for me to sit in one of the chairs and I winced as I lowered myself onto a rogue spring.

Ben sorted through the quantity of luggage before finding what he was looking for. He selected a tapestry valise and carried it to me before seating himself in the chair next to mine.

"This was Sophronia's?" I asked. Ben nodded. "I think under the circumstances she would want someone to search it to see if it casts any light on her death." Ben pointed at the handbag in a manner I took to mean he agreed. Or at least that he was not going to stop me. I held my breath as I depressed the clasp on the valise and felt the clasp spring open with a soft pop. I opened it as wide as it would stretch and peered inside.

At first glance the valise seemed empty. My frustration mounted and I felt disappointed in the suggestion of the voice. Perhaps it had been too much to hope that the voice would always provide answers. As I hoisted the bag back off my lap and started to pass it to Ben it occurred to me that the bag seemed too heavy to be empty.

I leaned forward in my chair, trying to better catch the overhead light and ran my finger along the interior seams. Most of the workmanship was high quality. The seams were straight and the stitches fine and lay close together. But as I looked at a single seam along the back of the lining another hand looked to have been at work. The line of stitching wobbled back and forth and the length of the stitches was still short but irregularly spaced.

No one who had so little skill would have been hired to create this bag. As I held the bag under the light I felt my breath catch excitedly in my throat. Black thread had been used in the poorly executed seam rather than blue like the others.

"Do you have any scissors?" I asked. He rose and made straight for a box tucked up high on one of the shelves. Reaching in without even looking into it he pulled out a small pair of brass embroidery scissors. With only a few snips the seam fell away and a long opening in the lining allowed me a peek behind it. I slipped my hand into the gap and poked around with my fingertips until I touched something that felt like paper.

A thick, yellowed envelope lay tucked between the lining and the heavy tapestry of the bag's exterior. I lifted the flap and slid out three photographs wrapped in a newspaper clipping. The less said about the photographs, the better. Suffice it to say they depicted Congressman Plaisted and a young woman wearing little else besides a smile. Her hair appeared dark except for a distinctive pale swath along the left side of her head. Although I think of myself as a woman of the world in many ways, I confess I was not prepared to see such things, especially not in the presence of another person and a man at that.

I returned the photographs to the envelope with trembling fingers and turned my attention determinedly on the newspaper clipping. The paper was brittle and I unfolded it carefully, quite sure of what I would find. It was as Mr. Lydale had said. The article reported that a young woman had been found dead in a local pond wearing a man's coat, the pockets of which had been weighted down with rocks. I lifted the valise once more determined to alert Officer Yancey to what I had found. It might be enough to convince him to arrest Congressman Plaisted.

But as I hoisted the piece of luggage something occurred to me. Surely something that weighed as little as three photographs could not account for the heft of the valise. Upon closer inspection I noticed another row of childish stitches at the bottom of the case. I pricked the seam apart to reveal two stacks of pages wedged in end to end. I widened the seam opening and tugged the pages through, taking care not to disarrange the order of them.

There in front of me was Sophronia's missing manuscript. It was neatly typed with a profusion of corrections and notations covering the pages. And just like that, I knew how and why Sophronia had died.

CHAPTER FORTY-NINE

IF HE WERE COMPLETELY HONEST HE WOULD ADMIT THAT MISS Proulx looked positively radiant. The sun glinted through gaps in the leafy canopy of Fern Park. It bounced off the shiny metal of her bicycle handlebars and the tendrils of her dark glossy hair that had escaped from her hairpins.

When she telephoned the police station the urgent tone of her voice made him abandon his sandwich on his desk, grab his own bicycle from the rack on the side of the building, and pedal as fast as he could to this secluded spot in the woods.

Miss Proulx plucked two paper sacks and a sturdy box from the basket fixed to the front of her cycle. She rattled the bag at him teasingly, then sat on a flat, moss-covered bit of ground to the side of the path. He stood over her, his pulse still racing. Surely she had not lured him to an impromptu picnic by feigning a distress call. She simply wasn't the sort.

"I hurried over here pell-mell because I thought you were in trouble, Miss Proulx," he said. "You can't have called me out here for a meal." Her smile widened and she stifled an unladylike snort of laughter with a small, gloved hand.

"I hardly think this qualifies as a meal. However, I do appreciate your confidence in my commonsense." She pulled off her right glove and dipped her hand into one of the paper sacks. "I took my life in my hands to snitch these for you from Mrs. Doyle's kitchen. The least you could do would be to sit down and eat the evidence while I tell you about the inroads I've made into the investigation."

Yancey wished he had the fortitude to resist the scent of cinnamon wafting toward him from her hand but even if he had had the energy to lie about his hunger, the rumbling of his stomach would have betrayed him.

"Is that a pinwheel biscuit?"

"See for yourself," she said, patting a mounded hump of moss beside her. Miss Proulx waited until he had foolishly filled his mouth with a satisfying bite of fluffy pastry and spiced currants before she spoke again.

"I lured you here to show this to you far away from prying eyes." She lifted the lid on the box. "I called you as soon as I discovered this in the hotel bell room. It was tucked inside a valise left there by Sophronia." Yancey swallowed and lowered himself onto the ground near, but not too near, Miss Proulx.

The box held a sheaf of papers. The top sheet was typewritten.

SPIRITED REVELATIONS:
CORRUPTION, GREED, AND THE QUEST FOR POWER
AS REVEALED THROUGH CHANNELING
by Sophronia Foster Eldridge

"It made for some interesting reading," she said, patting the box. "Sophronia was disheartened by the lack of progress the suffrage movement had made in the last twenty years. She wrote an exposé on the corruption of those in power to show why the system is broken, just as she said she had. There are plenty of people named in here who must be delighted that she is dead." Yancey licked the sugar from his fingers then lifted the stack of papers from the box.

"Any place I should start?" he asked.

"I've listed the pages I believe are most connected to her death on the inside of the box lid," Miss Proulx said. Yancey settled in to read, glad the bulk of the manuscript was typed rather than written in the same hand that marred the pages with comments and suggestions. He turned to the relevant pages and read through them quickly.

The manuscript was clear, unflinching, and easily explained why anyone whose name appeared therein would have been tempted to kill Sophronia rather than to suffer the consequences of their actions. Even as an officer of the law, he found some of the claims quite shocking.

"There are enough accusations made here to cause any number of people to murder her but is there any proof?" Yancey asked. He felt Miss Proulx stiffen beside him.

"There are a few things that concretely support the accusations Sophronia made. I must tell you, some of it is disturbing and distasteful."

"Murder is always both of those things, Miss Proulx." She looked for a moment at the second paper sack placed on the ground beside her. He noticed she kept her eyes on her lap as she handed it to him. He looked inside the bag and removed an envelope. Flicking open the flap he peered inside. It was not the first time he had seen those sorts of photographs but he felt clammy with embarrassment to be seen holding them in front of a lady. Still, something had to be said.

"These could certainly be considered proof." Yancey removed a book and a piece of paper from the bag as well. He opened the book and looked to where Miss Proulx indicated with her finger.

"Now take a look at the paper," she said, pointing at the crumpled sheet. Yancey spread it out and gave it a careful read-through.

"Where did you find this?"

"Millie found it in the formal parlor at the Belden. It was in a wastepaper basket."

"Did you find the money?" Yancey asked.

"I checked behind the fan in the library but there was nothing there," Miss Proulx said. "Between Sophronia's accusations against the congressman, her finger pointing at the illegal alcohol business Mr. Jellison was running, and her allegations that Osmond Cheswick was actually the man relentlessly pursuing her at the Hay Feverists convention, we are spoilt for choice concerning suspects."

"But there is no definitive proof as to who was responsible for her murder. We are no closer to an arrest than we were before you found this. I can't take this to Hurley until I have real proof."

"You can't mean to ignore this," Miss Proulx said. It was not a question but rather a statement. He was surprised at the swelling in his chest at the notion she had confidence that he would do what was right despite the difficulties involved.

"I won't just drop it but I will need to know who to arrest before I tip my hand and let him know that despite his order not to I have been pursuing the investigation. It also won't help the case that the victim claims she wrote the manuscript based on information she received from the dead."

"I would like to remind you that this could be considered in-

formation received from the dead." Miss Proulx gestured to the
manuscript in Yancey's hands.

"It's hardly the same thing, as well you know."

"Would you believe me if I told you I only thought to look in
the hotel bell room because of guidance from a spirit?"

"I would find it easier to believe in your abilities as an intrepid
investigator than as a passive channel through which another en-
tity's wisdom flows." For a moment, Yancey enjoyed watching as
Miss Proulx's lips parted in surprise and for the first time since
he had met her she looked like she could think of nothing whatsoever to say. She turned her full attention to her gloves and set
about deliberately tugging them neatly back onto her small hands.
He decided to take pity on her. "Of course, this has now gone
entirely beyond the abilities of even the most supernaturally
aided amateur investigator. I can see why you would be eager to
turn the entire matter over to the professionals."

"You misunderstand me completely." With a cunning look in
her sparkling brown eyes Miss Proulx gave her left glove a deci-
sive tug. "You said yourself that this evidence does not single out
the perpetrator. Fortunately for you I have an idea as to how we
can force the killer's hand."

"What exactly is it that you propose?" Yancey asked.

"Another crime."

"What did you have in mind?"

"I think it will be an easy thing to get the killer to make an
attempt on my life." Miss Proulx jumped to her feet with a most
unladylike show of athleticism. "That is, if I can persuade Mr.
Lydale to appear with me at dinner at the Belden this evening.
Although I am quite sure he will be more than willing to assist in

whatever way that he is able." Yancey felt a fresh wave of irritation at his friend Thomas.

"You wish to recruit Thomas for the solution to the crime rather than to involve me?" he asked.

"Certainly not instead of you. There is much to do. I am counting on you to help me with a bit of forgery and postal fraud." Miss Proulx flashed him a broad smile.

"Forgery and fraud? How can those help?" Officer Yancey asked.

"I need you to forge a note to the Plaisteds, supposedly from Mr. Fredericks, inviting them to dine at the Belden this evening as his special guests. I think a gentleman's handwriting would be more convincing than my own."

"Why would you want to do that?"

"I'll tell you about it on the way back to town."

CHAPTER FIFTY

E VEN THOUGH THE BELDEN WAS NOT THE LARGEST HOTEL ON
the beach it still required considerable planning on the part
of the staff to keep things running as smoothly as they did. Mrs.
Doyle was ferociously organized and a stickler for routine. Without a doubt she would have a list of Honoria's seating assign-
ments for the entire week at the ready. With only a couple hours
until dinner I knew just where to find her.

The kitchen smelled of roasting meat and potatoes. On the
worktable in the center of the room Mrs. Doyle was spooning a
thick yellow-colored custard over cubes of cake and plump berries already layered into a trifle dish. I felt my stomach squeeze at
the sight. Luncheon had gone on without me and I had not par-
taken of much in the way of breakfast, either. I told myself now
was not the time to think of such things. There would be plenty
of time for eating when the killer was caught even if trifle was
one of my favorite foods in the world.

"You look excited, child." Mrs. Doyle looked up from her work
and fixed me with one of her legendary scowls. I stood still and let
her evaluate my aura, hoping she would determine a predinner

scoop of dessert would fix whatever was wrong with me. "Have an apple." She reached behind her and plucked a small red fruit from a bowl. I polished it on my sleeve and took a bite. It wasn't trifle but it pressed out the pleats in my stomach just as satisfyingly.

"I have good reason to be. I believe by the end of the night I will know what happened to Sophronia," I said. "But I need to seat guests at specific tables at this evening's meal."

"Still playing the detective, are you? Does Honoria know what you're up to?" She squinted at me some more and I knew better than to lie.

"I haven't wanted to trouble her with what I have been doing. You know how distressed she has been on account of her dream."

"So you've been investigating Sophronia's death without Honoria's knowledge?"

"She would have tried to stop me from doing so and I promised Yancey I would help him." I thought I detected a tiny twitch at the corner of Mrs. Doyle's mouth.

"You are keeping secrets from your aunt to honor a commitment to a young man?" She wiped her hands on her apron and came round the table to look more closely at me. "Your mother did much the same thing and look how that turned out."

"I hardly think helping with a police investigation can be compared with an ill-considered elopement." I knew my cheeks were flaming but there was not a thing I could do about it. I was far more uncomfortable with the idea that Mrs. Doyle could see so much information in my aura. It was a frightening thing to be laid so bare.

"Do you not trust your aunt's insight into the future?"

"It isn't that. And it isn't that Yancey has charmed me into assisting him."

"I should think not. Yancey has many fine qualities but enchanting young ladies is not one of them," Mrs. Doyle said. "So why is it that you think I should help you?"

"You encouraged me to listen to the voice, did you not?"

"I did. Does it have something to say on this matter?"

"I know Honoria is concerned about harm befalling me but I know the voice is urging me to pursue this. It has never given me poor counsel before now." Mrs. Doyle looked me up and down once more.

"You'll find a stack of place cards in the linen press next to the dining room. But you'd best hurry. It isn't all that long until dinnertime." With that she turned back to her trifle.

I MET LUCY IN THE HALLWAY AND THE TWO OF US ENTERED THE dining room together. I looked around at the tables and had to remind myself to pretend to look for my own place card as well as Lucy's. I nodded to the MacPhersons as I passed. Mr. and Mrs. Cheswick were already seated when I arrived. They were right where I expected them to be. At the table next to theirs Dewitt Fredericks and the Plaisteds were chatting about friends they had in common. Honoria was on the far side of the room, a place I was betting on being well out of earshot of what I had to say.

George had his eyes firmly fixed on my progress as we made our way toward his end of the room. He raised a hand when he caught my eye and motioned for us to join them. I shook my head and pointed at the adjoining table where Thomas Lydale was already seated but rose to greet us as we arrived. I couldn't help but notice his eyes lingering on Lucy for just a little more time than polite society permitted.

"I am so sorry to be late. I had an important telephone call to place to the journalist who was supposed to have interviewed Sophronia before her death. He only just now returned my call."

"I would be happy to spend all evening waiting for ladies as lovely as yourselves. However did I get so lucky in my table assignment?"

"I understand it helps to be on good terms with the staff," Lucy said.

I leaned toward him and raised my voice just enough to be sure I would be overheard by the adjoining tables.

"We wanted to be sure to secure an interview time early enough to get into tomorrow evening's edition of the paper. Once he heard what we had to say he asked if he could come by before breakfast."

"You must have something newsworthy to contribute if a reporter was that eager," Thomas said, just as we had planned when I had called upon him to ask for his help. His tone and arched eyebrows suggested he was impressed. I only dared look from the corner of my eye but I was certain all the attention from the adjoining tables was on my conversation. Chatter at the other tables had fallen off entirely.

"I was privileged to channel Sophronia's own spirit this afternoon. She wants me to share the news that she did not take her own life."

"The police determined Sophronia's death was a suicide. I doubt very much they will be convinced to change that verdict solely on the word of a medium. Even one as lovely and skilled as yourself," Thomas said.

"I am well aware that the police are usually closed-minded. I have no intention of taking Sophronia's message to them. Which is why I instead contacted the reporter who interviewed Sophronia for the article on the suffrage rally." I took a sip of water from my glass and was pleased to see my hand barely trembled as I lifted it. "Unlike the police, he was delighted to hear there is more to her story."

"Having worked with a fair number of journalists I would agree that they like nothing more than to keep adding to a story for as long as possible. Especially one as sensational as the death of a celebrity." Thomas nodded to the waiter who stopped next to him with a tureen of soup. "You should be aware that whatever they may personally believe about contact with the spirit world, journalists prefer to deal in facts." Thomas dipped his spoon into his soup and took a sip.

"Facts are what I will be offering him. Sophronia led me to a document case she had hidden away from prying eyes." I looked up at the ceiling as if listening to voices from beyond. "I am sure the press will have much to speculate upon when they see what Sophronia had kept hidden there."

"I must admit, Miss Proulx, you have succeeded in piquing my interest. Will you not give me a hint as to what you have discovered?"

"I am afraid I have promised the journalist I shan't breathe a word until he comes by in the morning."

"But if you have actual evidence don't you consider it your duty to take it to the police?" Thomas's eyes widened.

"The police had their chance to do right by Sophronia and in my opinion they failed her utterly. Since they refused to act I shall take the proof of her death to the court of public opinion." I took a warm, fluffy roll from the basket the waiter offered and placed it on my bread plate. "I promised the reporter I wouldn't even mention it to Honoria."

"I shan't be able to sleep a wink tonight. I will toss and turn unceasingly completely consumed by curiosity and speculation." Thomas did look quite miserable. He could not have played his part better if he had been a trained actor.

"I used to have the same trouble shutting my thoughts off at night, but ever since I started taking a preparation of Mrs. Doyle's I sleep like the dead. I'm sure if you stop in at the kitchen before you leave this evening she'd be happy to provide you with some of your own," I said.

"So you are unmovable upon this? Not one hint?"

"My lips are completely, utterly sealed. In fact, let us speak no more of the matter this evening." I turned to Lucy. "Why don't you tell Thomas about the cycling club you hope to start before snow flies?" I leaned back and let my friend take over the conversation. I turned my head slightly to glance at the Cheswicks, the Plaisteds, and Dewitt Fredericks. None of them returned my gaze, but rather fixed their eyes deliberately elsewhere. But while they were lost in thought, I was sure I knew what was on all their minds. The question was: Which of them would not be willing to wait to read the answers in the newspaper?

Chapter Fifty-One

M Y MOTHER'S ROOM HAD BEEN A PLACE OF COMPLETE SANC-
tuary since I had arrived at the Belden. Honoria insisted I
consider it my own and feel comfortable making myself at home.
By and large I had done so. And eagerly, too. But tonight, all the
nooks and crannies, drapes, and pieces of heavy furniture seemed
menacing and custom-built for hiding an enemy.

I tied a piece of fishing line, left over from the last time I had
aided Yancey in an investigation, to the bell pull apparatus mounted
on the wall next to the bed. Then, remaining fully clothed, I
slipped beneath the sheets of the high bed and tied the other end
of the line to the fishing line around my wrist. Every clip-clop of
hooves on the street, every creak of the hotel's elderly joints as it
settled in for the night, made my heart lurch in my chest. I almost wished the sedative I had supposedly taken was not a part
of the ruse.

I was certain I would lie awake, nerves taut, body tense, for
hours. Despite myself and the circumstances, though, I struggled to keep awake. I felt my eyes growing heavy and my breathing slow. No matter what the thinking parts of my brain urged,

the rest of my mind and body worked against it. I could not say
how long I slept, only that the voice was what awakened me and
not with time to spare.

"Remain alert."

In the darkness, through sleepy, slitted eyes, I was jolted fully
awake by the sight of a shape creeping about the room. The figure moved to the desk and quietly opened the drawers, one at a
time. The first two yielded no prize but the third seemed to capture the intruder's attention. In the quiet of the room the rustle
of paper sounded as loud as the roar of the sea. In the low light I
watched as the intruder placed the find on the top of the desk
and slowly crept toward me.

I forced myself to breathe slowly and remain flat on my back
despite every nerve in my body relentlessly urging me to jump up
and flee. I reminded myself of the act Father had devised involving winding snakes about my person. It was supposed to convince
the crowd of the courage-inducing properties of Dr. Pankhurst's
Buck-Uppo Preparation. I told myself that if I could stay still for
snakes, I surely could do so in this circumstance.

The figure stopped at the edge of the bed and reached for a
pillow nestled at the side of my head. In a flash I felt its dense,
prickly weight clamp down over my face. As I bucked and thrashed
against the force of my assailant I felt a rising tide of panic. I
prayed the fishing line on my wrist would do its job before it had
cause to snap. I gave a few strong tugs with my arm and hoped it
would be enough. I would not have believed how quickly it could
feel as though the air in your lungs was utterly used up.

The blood swishing loudly in my ears was the only thing I
could hear. Even the voice was silent. With each passing second I
was losing the strength to struggle. It occurred to me that my as-

sailant might also be tired. After all, the bed was a high one and the amount of strength it would take to keep me down must be taxing. Perhaps if I let my body go slack, the attacker would, too.

I tapered off my resistance a twitch at a time until I lay quite still. I felt a final heavy thrust on the pillow, then a release. The assailant lifted away the pillow and peered down at my face, leaning in so close I felt hot breath on my cheeks. Now was the moment. I planted my hands on my attacker's chest and shoved with all my might.

I heard a thump as I sprang from the bed. I felt the fishing line snap but I no longer cared. Even without help from Yancey I had the upper hand. I leapt onto the attacker just as the door to the bedroom flew open and light poured in from the hallway, throwing Yancey's figure into silhouette.

Honoria bustled in behind him and depressed the light switch, revealing the face I was sure I would see, that of Dewitt Fredericks.

I T WAS HARDLY A DIGNIFIED END TO THE INVESTIGATION AND I was grateful that I had the foresight to remain fully clothed for my nocturnal adventure. I was more grateful for my cycling ensemble than ever before. After all, it was undignified enough to be found straddling a man on your bedroom floor. Trying to live such an incident down if dressed in my nightgown would have been even more of a battle. My forethought seemed all the more fortuitous when Officer Lewis and Mrs. Doyle's son-in-law, Frank, stepped through the door and joined the ever-increasing gathering.

"I told you it would work, didn't I?" I asked, pointing at Dewitt still pinned beneath me.

"I never doubted you," Yancey said. He reached out and helped me to my feet. I confess, I was glad of his strong arm. I found my legs were shaking and showed no inclination to bear my weight. Officer Lewis and Frank hoisted a less grateful Mr. Fredericks between them and each held him by an arm.

"I dreamt you were in distress but I never imagined it was something quite as urgent as this. Whatever has been going on?" Honoria had not had reason to suspect she'd be in the company of visitors during the night and had dressed for bed. Her hair hung down her back in a heavy braid and her eyes were bleary with sleep. As the owner of a hotel she could easily be awakened at any time of the night but she hadn't yet, to my knowledge, been called to the scene of an attempted murder. Especially that of her nearest relation.

"Mr. Fredericks tried to smother me. Officer Yancey and I suspected he was the one who killed Sophronia but we didn't have enough proof to convince Chief Hurley to arrest him, let alone a jury to convict."

"Miss Proulx decided the only way was to threaten to reveal that she found Miss Foster Eldridge's manuscript and intended to offer it to the newspapers on Sophronia's behalf because it is what she would have wanted. She made sure to be overheard discussing what she had discovered with Thomas Lydale last night at dinner."

"Is that why my seating plans were so disarranged?"

"I had to be certain that Mr. Fredericks would overhear me saying I had found the manuscript. I was sure that if he did he would come to my room looking for Sophronia's work and make an attempt on my life. I said I had read the manuscript but hadn't shared what I had read with anyone else."

"I thought the two of you were on good terms." Honoria turned to Mr. Fredericks, her voice raised an octave in disbelief. "What reason could you possibly have had to do these things?"

"It was money, a great deal of it," I said. Mr. Fredericks simply stared at me with his watery blue eyes. "It was ingenious of him, really."

"I don't understand. How would he profit from Sophronia's work or from taking her life?" Honoria asked. She tightened her arms across her chest.

"Sophronia was tired of being vilified in the press. Tired of hearing how women were biologically unfit for positions of power and authority. She decided rallies and marches were not enough to effect change," I said.

"She started investigating corruption and theft perpetrated by men in positions of power and prestige. She hoped by exposing them it would make people more open to questioning the status quo," Yancey said.

"When I found Sophronia's manuscript, it was covered in corrections and suggestions. I recognized Mr. Fredericks's handwriting all over it."

"Miss Foster Eldridge and Mr. Fredericks met at the Hay Feverists convention. He impressed her with his knowledge of publishing. When she decided to publish her manuscript she thought of him and asked him for some advice."

"She asked me for my expert opinion." Despite his confinement by the officers, Mr. Fredericks straightened, looked proud instead of crazed or angry. "She asked me to read it through and offer suggestions for improvements. I was happy to oblige."

"When he read it through he realized he could blackmail the men whose secrets were revealed in the manuscript rather than expose them. All he had to do was kill Sophronia before she shared her story with the world," I said. "He even murdered her in the same manner as the congressman killed his mistress in order to have more blackmail leverage."

"He killed someone over a bit of blackmail money?" Honoria's face flushed. I think she was embarrassed to have had a person of such low character ensconced in her hotel.

"In truth it amounted to a great deal of money," I said. "Five thousand dollars from Osmond Cheswick alone," I said. I heard Honoria gasp. Mr. Fredericks's haughty demeanor collapsed. He visibly sagged against his guards. "Sophronia provided such a wealth of information, with so many specific details, that Mr. Fredericks found the temptation to blackmail irresistible."

"I never would have done it for personal gain. I planned to use the money to purchase a vast tract of land in the White Mountains to preserve it for the Hay Feverists."

"You valued a tract of land more highly than the life of another human being?" Honoria seemed genuinely bewildered. "How could you possibly justify such a position? I thought you and Sophronia were friends."

"She was not what you thought she was in the least. She was ruthless and was willing to use whomever she needed to in order to get what she wanted," Mr. Fredericks said. "As it happened she wasn't even a hay fever sufferer. Sophronia thought garnering the support of women with money and influence was the fastest way to win the vote. The Hay Feverists Society is filled with just such women. More important, women are allowed to vote on matters within the club. Sophronia felt they were exactly the sort of women to convince to support suffrage."

"How did you discover that she had used the Hay Feverists

Society for her own purposes?" I asked. It was the one piece of the puzzle that had not fallen into place.

"I was out on the veranda sitting in a wicker chair breathing in some healthful sea air. The French doors were open and it was easy to hear the comings and goings in the house. Clear as a bell I overheard Sophronia advising her young secretary to join clubs like the Hay Feverists in order to make important connections. Lucy, I think the girl is called, said she didn't have hay fever and wouldn't that keep her from joining?"

"What did Miss Foster Eldridge say to that?" Yancey asked.

"She replied that she was certain a smart girl like Lucy could manage to fake a few sniffles for the greater good." Mr. Fredericks's voice had raised an octave. I was going to be glad to see the last of him. Officer Yancey must have felt the same way because he motioned toward the door. "But I am the one who really is thinking of the greater good. Someday people will be grateful for the impulse to conserve wild and special places. Someday people will think of men such as myself as true visionaries," Mr. Fredericks called over his shoulder as Frank and Lewis muscled him out the door. Yancey gave me a nod and hurried out after them. His night would be a long one, I knew, and I didn't envy him his impending conversation with Chief Hurley.

Chapter Fifty-two

I WATCHED YANCEY LEAVE WITH A SENSE OF DREAD. I SHOULD have told Honoria what I was up to rather than risking her being roused in the night to face something like this, especially with all the strain she had been under lately. It was unconscionable of me and rather than feeling proud of helping to solve the crime I felt quite ashamed of myself.

"I am so sorry to have surprised you like this. It was very thoughtless of me. But I thought if you knew what I was up to you would try to stop me."

"Because of my dream?"

"Yes. You were right about the danger. It was just as you described." I suddenly felt cold and slightly nauseated. "I couldn't breathe and I felt like something was forcing all the air from my lungs. I believe if I also had the experience of prophetic dreams I would not have had the nerve to wait alone in the dark for Mr. Fredericks to come."

"If the real experience was just like what I can recall of my dream it will be a wonderment if you are ever able to be alone in the dark in your bed again." Honoria raised a hand to the base of her throat. "You took such a terrible risk."

"I knew Yancey and the other officers would be nearby listening for my signal if I needed them."

"I can hardly bear to think of it. You must have been more terrified than you have ever been in your entire life." Honoria pulled me to her and wrapped me in a firm embrace. "I know I was when I saw someone on the floor, surrounded by police. I was desperately afraid that my dream had come true and that you had come to harm." I wished with all my heart that I had not worried Honoria. I also wished it were true that Mr. Fredericks's attempt on my life was the most frightening thing that had yet happened to me. But it wasn't. I could only hope that I would never again be as afraid as I was the moment I realized Johnny was dead.

"I am so sorry to have put you through such worry. I just couldn't let Sophronia's death be attributed to a suicide when both Officer Yancey and I were certain she died at someone else's hand."

"I expect you couldn't stand to see a murderer go free, either." Honoria smiled at me and squeezed me even closer to her ample chest. Guilt flooded through me. I hadn't thought I could feel any more miserable than I had when I saw the frightened look on her face when she rushed into the room but, in fact, I could.

When I first met Honoria I wished she would welcome me. And she had, with open arms. When I knew her a little better I wished she would love me like the daughter she never had. She had done that, too. Now, I wished more than anything that I could be worthy of her estimation of me. That I was the sort of person whose moral compass always pointed north. But the truth was that wish wasn't about to come true. I wasn't above letting a murderer go free if it meant saving my own skin. Or saving the skin of those I loved, no matter how little they loved me back. I didn't deserve her faith in me and as long as I kept the truth from her I wouldn't ever merit it.

The desire to make a clean breast of things was almost overwhelming. I opened my mouth to unburden myself. I would tell her about the Invigorizer, about Johnny. I would tell her everything and take whatever consequences came my way. I cleared my throat and then heard the voice more clearly than ever before speaking in my ear.

"Stop."

So often the voice tells me to do things that seem odd or unwarranted. Things that make no sense at the time. It was a rare thing indeed for the voice to tell me to do the very thing I most wanted. So unusual, in fact, that I sent up a silent question as to whether or not it was sure of its counsel.

"Why?" I mutely asked of it.

"Remember her dream." I stopped short. Honoria's dream had warned of my words causing a chasm between us. The voice was right. The burden of my conscience was heavy. The idea of being separated from all I had grown to love in my new life was heavier still. I heeded the voice's advice, kept my confession to myself, and silently returned Honoria's embrace.

Chapter Fifty-three

The next morning Mrs. Doyle had taken one look at my aura and decreed that I was looking peaked and could do with a dose of fresh air and a long rest. She ordered Ben to cancel my sittings for the day, even the one scheduled with the Misses Velmont. Then she tucked me up on a steamer chaise at the far end of the veranda with a shawl and a well-thumbed copy of the popular novel *A Lady of Quality*.

I protested half-heartedly. My face felt bruised from my encounter the night before and I had slept very poorly after all that had happened. In truth, I wondered if I would ever sleep well in my room again. Every time I closed my eyes I imagined the weight of the pillow pressing down on my face. Despite the warmth of the day I felt chilled and drew the shawl tightly around my shoulders before settling in to read. The adventures of Clorinda, the novel's protagonist, absorbed me and I forgot my troubles in hers so completely I did not realize anyone had approached until I heard my name.

"Good afternoon, Miss Proulx." I looked up to find Officer Yancey towering above my chair. "May I join you for a moment?"

"You may. What brings you to the Belden?" I laid the book in my lap and gave him my complete attention. "I should have thought the fracas last night would have kept you busy all day."

"Considering the day started in the middle of the night I felt I could take a bit of a break." Officer Yancey lowered himself in the basket chair next to mine and let out a deep sigh.

"Are you off duty?" I asked.

"I am at the moment. This is a personal call, Miss Proulx." Officer Yancey doffed his uniform cap as if to give weight to his words. It made him look younger somehow.

"I confess, I'm surprised that you would make time to visit me rather than to eat a hot meal or to get some rest," I said.

"I did not feel I could in good conscience do either until I called to ask how you were faring and to express thanks for your assistance with the investigation." Officer Yancey cleared his throat. "If it weren't for you, Dewitt Fredericks would have gotten away with murder."

"Does that mean Chief Hurley has accepted that Sophronia did not commit suicide?" I asked, leaning forward.

"It does. Considering he was caught trying to smother you and then confessed to murder there was really nothing the chief could do but charge Mr. Fredericks with the crime." A small smile twitched the corner of his mouth. "Granted, it did take the colorful testimony of Officers Nichols and Lewis to convince the chief that I was not in cahoots with you to fabricate an outrageous story in order to clear Miss Foster Eldridge's name."

"Why would your chief believe such a preposterous notion?" I asked.

"It's my guess that the chief did not wish to credit a woman with being capable of solving a crime, especially one he had dismissed. It wounded his pride and rattled his belief in the impossibility of female investigators."

"Did he come right out and say that?"

"He said that and a few more things I shouldn't like to repeat in polite company when I told him that you were the one who suggested the means of flushing out Mr. Fredericks." Officer Yancey shook his head. "He refused to believe any of it until Lewis described entering your bedchamber to discover you pinning Mr. Fredericks to the floor without assistance."

"You gave me too much credit, Officer Yancey. It was a joint effort." Still, it was heartwarming to hear he had shared what accolades there were to be had with me when he needn't have done so.

"Perhaps you give me too much credit. If you recall, I was ordered not to pursue the investigation. You could say I revealed your involvement in order not to land myself in difficulties with my superior." Officer Yancey gave a tiny indication of a smile once more.

"To my way of thinking he's in no way your superior," I said. "And no matter what your motivation, I am delighted you asked me to assist you, Officer Yancey. All in all it was a satisfying conclusion to the case."

"I can't help but feel it wasn't entirely concluded, though. After all, there were plenty of crimes alleged in Miss Foster Eldridge's manuscript. At the very least I feel an investigation should be made into the murder of the congressman's mistress."

"Enough time has passed that it might be very difficult to prove anything. Besides, the crime did not take place in your jurisdiction," I said.

"I have a contact on the force up in Portland. He might take a lot of pleasure in needling a sitting congressman."

"If that doesn't work you could always contact the press. Even if Congressman Plaisted were never convicted in a court of law he likely wouldn't survive the court of public opinion. I doubt he would be reelected."

"Not a bad suggestion."

"I am simply bursting with good ideas. If you should need help with any other investigations I would be more than happy to assist," I said.

"I shall be sure to do that. And as an acknowledgment of our association, would you consider calling me Warren instead of Officer Yancey? At least when I am off duty." I felt a lump rise in my throat and my heart soar. Maybe I truly did have a chance of leaving my old life behind me. Despite my skill with the cards I never would have predicted being on terms of familiarity with a policeman.

"Only if you'll call me Ruby," I said. "At least when you're off duty."

HISTORICAL NOTE

One of the very great pleasures of writing historical fiction is the research. This book has been particularly satisfying on that front. Although this novel mostly features people and buildings that are entirely works of fiction, the background circumstances are based on fact.

Politics have long made for strange bedfellows, and the movement for women's suffrage was no exception. At the time of this story women were often seen as fragile vessels in need of protection from the sordid business of the world outside the domestic sphere. It was a view espoused by many people of both genders at the time and, in fact, was the basis of a value system known as the *cult of womanhood*. This worldview emphasized femininity and praised "true women" for their piety, domesticity, purity, and submissiveness. These attributes were praised by popular and influential magazines of the time, particularly those aimed at women themselves, like *Godey's Lady's Book*.

Some women, like the fictional Sophronia Foster Eldridge, used to their advantage the prevailing belief that women were submissive conduits. In the workforce women had the advantage in the new occupations of typists and telegraph operators, as it was understood they served as vessels through which the words of men could dutifully and efficiently flow.

This acceptance of women as conduits extended to the realm of mediumship and channeling. Women had the decided advantage when it came to being believed capable of communicating with disembodied spirits solely due to the perception that they were easily overpowered emotionally as well as physically. Savvy women like Sophronia often found their powerful messages for change more readily accepted if they delivered them under the guise of spirit direction.

Spiritualists were not the only allies the suffragists frequently attracted. The temperance movement had much in common with them as well and often the causes were linked in both membership and public appearances. Maine boasted early dedication to the movement and became the nation's first "dry state." What became known as the Maine Law passed in 1851, in large part as a means to address the detrimental effect alcohol abuse had on women and children. Temperance supporters found natural allies in those people who advocated for the rights of women both inside and outside of the home.

The road to enfranchisement was a long one, with many setbacks as well as small victories along the way. Associations and societies sometimes allowed members of both sexes to vote on issues of interest to their groups long before governmental institutions would do the same. Slowly but surely women were shaping their worlds by speaking their minds and casting ballots in organizations like the Hay Feverists Society.

Self-proclaimed hay fever sufferers were almost exclusively wealthy and educated people. Prominent citizens, like the U.S.

senator from Massachusetts Daniel Webster and Reverend Henry Ward Beecher, counted themselves in their number. These genteel and distinguished sufferers took annual refuge in regions known to provide relief from their symptoms in an era when medicinal remedies were rare and ineffectual. The White Mountain region of New Hampshire provided one such sanctuary. As a result, a fashionable resort community sprang up in Bethlehem, New Hampshire.

Members of the Hay Fever Association believed that air that had passed through conifer forests became purified and thus healthful for them to breathe. Not surprisingly they shared the common cause of forest preservation with the Appalachian Mountain Club and the Society for the Preservation of New Hampshire Forests. Using their wealth and influence, visiting hay feverists applied pressure to local residents to preserve the surrounding forested areas. By 1918 the White Mountain National Forest had been established, in part because of the sustained efforts of such influential people.

Photo copyright © 2013 by Liza Knowlton

Jessica Estevao is the author of the debut novel in the Change of Fortune Mysteries, *Whispers Beyond the Veil*. She loves the beach, mysterious happenings, and all things good-naturedly paranormal. While she lives for most of the year in New Hampshire, with her dark and mysterious husband and exuberant children, she delights in spending her summers on the coast of Maine where she keeps an eye out for sea monsters and mermaids. As Jessie Crockett, she writes the Sugar Grove Mysteries for Berkley Prime Crime. Visit her online at jessicaestevao.com.